"[DEATH IN KENYA] is a small masterpiece in its genre—a mixture of historical novel, romance, gothicism, and suspense. . . . Reading DEATH IN KENYA, you will waver from suspect to suspect, but you're not likely to anticipate the entirely logical and brilliant ending."
—*Hartford Courant*

". . . DEATH IN KENYA offers not only a taut mystery, but a setting that is as lush and exciting as those created in romances like *The Far Pavilions*. . . . M. M. Kaye proves once again that she is a superlative storyteller in whatever genre she chooses to write."
—*The Chattanooga Times*

"DEATH IN KENYA will delight and enthrall M. M. Kaye's hundreds of thousands of fans. It is consummate mystery, written by one of the finest storytellers of our time."
—*Mystery News*

". . . set in a gorgeously beautiful background. . . . M. M. Kaye outdoes Agatha Christie in palming the ace, and the solution of the many crimes is a stunner."
—*The San Diego Union*

"[M. M. Kaye is] adept at concocting entertaining
and suspenseful mystery. . . . DEATH IN KENYA
is a delightfully escapist reading experience
for mystery lovers."
—King Features Syndicate

". . . a pleasantly diverting romantic
mystery . . . the solution to the killings
is well hidden."
—*Chicago Tribune Book World*

"A very readable suspense story. . . .
DEATH IN KENYA has all the ingredients
of a good suspense novel: passion, violence,
sign posts to alert the reader
and unexpected twists
and turns to confuse him."
—*Tulsa World*

"Kaye . . . has been hitting the high spots as a
mystery writer. Mystery, romance, and an exotic
setting, graceful and chilling."
—*Staten Island Advance*

Books by
M. M. KAYE

The Far Pavilions
Shadow of the Moon
Trade Wind
Death in Zanzibar
Death in Kenya

Published by
ST. MARTIN'S PRESS

DEATH IN KENYA

M·M·KAYE

ST. MARTIN'S PRESS
NEW YORK

St. Martin's Press Edition

ISBN: 0-312-90117-6

Cover design by Gene Light
Cover art by Franco Accornero

Printed in the United States of America

First St. Martin's Press Paperback Printing: September, 1984

10 9 8 7 6 5 4 3 2 1

Originally published under the title *Later Than You Think.*

Remembering TINA and JAY—
With Love

Author's Note

Few people nowadays will remember the Mau Mau terrorist rising in Kenya, and millions more will never even have heard of it. But it was an unpleasant business while it lasted. I happened to be in Kenya towards the end of that period, because my husband's regiment had been sent there to deal with 'The Emergency'—which was the white settlers' name for it. And despite some hair-raising moments, I can truthfully say that I enjoyed practically every minute of my stay in that marvellous and exciting country.

The idea for this story came into my mind one evening when I was standing on our verandah in the dusk, and I heard birds calling down in the papyrus swamp that fringed the shores of Lake Naivasha. But the book itself, originally published under the prophetic title *Later Than You Think*, did not take shape until after we had left Kenya. Em's house, *Flamingo*, is an amalgam of several houses built by early settlers in the Rift or on the Kinangop, but I chose to site it on the same spot as the one we ourselves lived in. The opinions voiced by my characters were taken from life and at first hand. For though the Wind of Change was rising fast, very few of the Kenya-born settlers would believe that it could possibly blow strongly enough to uproot them from a country that every single one of them looked upon, and loved, as a '*Land where my fathers died, Land of the pilgrim's pride . . .*'

1

A flock of pelicans, their white wings dyed apricot by the setting sun, sailed low over the acacia trees of the garden with a sound like tearing silk, and the sudden swish of their passing sent Alice's heart into her throat and dried her mouth with panic. The shadows of the stately birds flicked across her and were gone, and she leaned weakly against the gate in the plumbago hedge and fought for control.

It was absurd and childish to allow herself to become so hag-ridden by fear that the mere passing of a flight of birds could set her flinching and cowering. But she could not help herself. She had fought fear for too long, and now at last she had reached the limits of endurance. She would have to leave Kenya: she and Eden. Surely he would see that she could not stand any more. For now, in addition to her fear of the country there was her terror of the house.

Alice had always been afraid of Kenya. It seemed

to her a savage and uncivilized land full of brooding menace, in which only Em's luxurious house had provided a narrow oasis of safety and comfort. But now there was no longer any safety anywhere, for strange things had been happening in the house of late. Inexplicable, malicious, frightening things...

It was the cat, declared Zacharia, the old grey-headed Kikuyu who had served Em for almost forty years, explaining away the first appearance of the invisible vandal who had taken to haunting the house. Who else could have thrown down the K'ang Hsi vase from the top of the cabinet where it had stood for so many years? There had been no wind. As for the bottle of red ink that had rolled, unstoppered, across the carpet upon which the Memsahib set such store, there had been a bird in the room—see, here was a feather! Pusser must have pursued it, and in doing so knocked over both ink bottle and vase.

But Em had not believed it. She had stormed and raged and questioned the African servants, but to no avail. And later, when other things were broken or defaced, Zacharia had made no further mention of Pusser. He and the other house servants had gone about their duties with scared faces and starting, frightened eyes, and Em, too, had said nothing more. She had only become quieter—and looked grim and grey and very old.

Lady Emily DeBrett—Em DeBrett of *Flamingo*—had come to Kenya as a bride in the Colony's early days, and she and her husband, Gerald, had been among the first white settlers in the Rift Valley.

Gerald had never looked upon Kenya as anything more than a Tom Tiddlers Ground. But the seventeen-year-old Emily had taken one look at the great golden valley with its cold craters and savage lava falls, its lily-strewn lakes and its vast herds of game, and had fallen in love with it as some women fall in love with a man.

Gerald had staked out a claim on the shores of Lake Naivasha: acres and acres of virgin land on which he intended to raise sheep and cattle, and grow sisal and maize and lucerne. And on a rising slope of ground, overlooking the lake, he had built a crude mud and wattle hut that had in time given place to a small stone-built house; square, ugly and unpretentious. Em had named the farm '*Flamingo*' because a flight of those fantastic rose-coloured birds had flown across it on that first evening; and *Flamingo* it had remained.

Kendall, Em's son, had been born in the mud and wattle house and christened in the small stone building that had replaced it. There had been no other children, for when Kendall was three years old his father had been killed by a fall from his horse. But *Flamingo* had already begun to justify all Gerald's hopes, and Em had refused to go home. 'This is my home,' she had said, 'and I will never leave it.'

The estate had prospered, and she had pulled down the ugly stone house that Gerald had built, and raised in its stead a huge, sprawling single-storeyed house to her own design. A thatch-roofed house with wide verandahs and spacious rooms panelled in undressed cedar wood, that defied all architectural rules and yet blended with the wild beauty of the Rift Valley as though it had always been a part of it; and Em loved it as she had never loved Gerald or her son Kendall.

She had been a remarkably pretty woman, and she was barely twenty when her husband died; but she did not marry again. Partly because her absorption in the affairs of her estate left her little time for other interests, and partly because hard and unremitting toil soon dispelled that pink-and-white prettiness. She wore, from choice, trousers and shirt and a man's double-terai hat, and as her abundant hair was too much trouble to keep in order, she cropped it short. At thirty she might have been forty-five or fifty, and from forty onwards, though she became increasingly bulky, she was merely an elderly and eccentric woman whose age it would have been impossible to guess.

Kendall was sent home to Eton, and from there to Oxford. And it was from Oxford, on his twenty-second birthday, that he sent a cable telling of his marriage to pretty Clarissa Brook.

Clarissa had proved to be a girl after Em's own heart, and as Mr Rycett, Em's manager, had retired that year, Kendall had stepped into his place, and he and Clarissa had moved into the manager's house; a pleasant stone-built bungalow in the grounds of *Flamingo*, barely six hundred yards from the main house, and hidden from it by a grove of acacias and a plumbago hedge. But Eden DeBrett, Em's first grandson, was born at *Flamingo*.

Em had insisted on that. 'He must be born in this house. It will be his one day.' And looking at the baby she had thought with pride: I have founded a dynasty. A Kenya dynasty! A hundred years from now—two hundred—there will be DeBretts living in this house and farming this land when Kenya is no longer a raw new Colony, but a great and prosperous country...

She was as impatient for grandsons as though *Flamingo* had been a kingdom and the DeBretts a royal house whose succession must be assured.

But there were to be no more grandsons for Em. As there had been no more sons. Kendall and Clarissa had died in a car accident, and there was only Eden. Little Eden DeBrett who was such a beautiful child, and whom his grandmother spoiled and adored and loved only one degree less than she loved the land of her adoption.

After Kendall's death there had been another manager, Gus Abbott, who had lived in the bungalow beyond the plumbago hedge for over twenty years, and died in a Mau Mau raid on *Flamingo* in the first months of the Emergency. His place had been taken by a younger man, Mr Gilbraith Markham, and it was Mr Markham's wife Lisa whom Alice had come in search of on this quiet evening: poor, pretty, discontented Lisa, who loved cities and cinemas and gaiety, and who had been so bored by life at *Flamingo*—until the day when she had had the misfortune to fall in love with Eden DeBrett.

Alice pushed open the gate in the plumbago hedge and walked on down the dusty path that wound between clumps of bamboos and flowering shrubs, thinking of Lisa. Of Lisa and Eden...

It isn't his fault, thought Eden's wife loyally. It's

because he's too good-looking. And just because women throw themselves at his head, and lose their own and make fools of themselves over him, it doesn't mean that he— She stopped suddenly, with a grimace of distaste. But it was a sound, and not her thoughts that had checked her.

The path had come out on the edge of a wide lawn in front of a green and white bungalow flanked by towering acacia trees, and someone inside the bungalow was playing the piano. Gilly, of course.

Gilly Markham was not a conspicuous success as a farm manager, and many people in the Rift Valley had attributed his appointment to his musical rather than his managerial abilities. For it was an unexpected facet of Lady Emily DeBrett's character that she was intensely and passionately musical, and there was probably some truth in the rumour that she had permitted Gilly Markham's musical talent to influence her judgement when Gus Abbott's death necessitated the appointment of a new manager at *Flamingo*.

But it was not Gilly's technique that had checked Alice and produced that grimace of distaste. It was the music itself. The Rift Concerto. As if it wasn't enough to hear Em playing it day after day! And now Gilly too——!

It had been an Italian prisoner-of-war who had written the Rift Valley Concerto. Guido Toroni. He had been sent to work at *Flamingo*, and Em had discovered by chance that he had once been a concert pianist. He had composed the concerto on Em's Bechstein grand, and later, when the war was over, he had gone to America where he had made a name for himself. There he had also made a single long-playing record of the concerto especially for Em, to whom he had sent it as a thank-offering and a memento. Em had been inordinately pleased, and had allowed no one to handle it except herself; but just two weeks previously it had been found smashed into a dozen pieces.

It could not possibly have been an accident. It had been a deliberate and ugly piece of spite that had frightened Alice and infuriated Em. But that had not been the worst of it, for Em had taken to playing the concerto from memory: 'so that I shall not forget it'. She had played it again and again during the last two weeks, until the wild, haunting cadences had plucked at Alice's taut nerves and worn them ragged. And now Gilly too was playing it. Playing it as Em played it, with passion and fury. But with a skill and magic that Em's gnarled, spatulate fingers, for all their love, did not possess.

Alice pushed between the canna lilies and ran across the lawn and up the stone steps that led on to the verandah. The door into the drawing-room stood open, and entering without ceremony she leant across Gilly's shoulder and thrust his hands off the keyboard in an ugly crash of sound.

Gilly spun round on the piano stool and stared at her contorted face.

'God! you startled me! What's up? You look all to pieces.' He rose hurriedly. 'Nothing the matter, is there?'

'No. No, nothing.' Alice groped behind her and

catching at the arm of a chair, sat down rather suddenly. Her breathing steadied, and a little colour crept back into her pale cheeks. 'I'm sorry, Gilly. My nerves are on edge. It was only that tune. Em's been playing it and playing it until I can't endure the sound of it.'

'She has, has she?' said Gilly, mixing a stiff whisky and soda and handing it to Alice.

He poured out a second and larger one for himself, omitting the soda, and gulped it down: 'Then I'm not surprised your nerves are in ribbons. She's a bloody bad pianist. She takes that third movement as though she were an elephant charging an express train.'

He sat down again at the piano as though to illustrate, and Alice said in a taut voice: 'Gilly, if you play that again I shall scream. I mean it!'

Gilly dropped his hands and regarded her with some concern. 'I say, you are in a bad way! Have another drink?'

'I haven't started on this one yet,' said Alice with an attempt at a laugh. 'Oh, it isn't that. It's—well that record being broken. You heard about that, didn't you?'

'You mean the poltergeist? Of course I did.'

'It *isn't* a poltergeist! Don't *say* things like that! It must be someone—a person. But Em swears by all her servants. She's had them for years and they're nearly all second-generation *Flamingo* servants. Or even third! She won't believe it is one of them. But it's worrying her badly. I know it is.'

Gilly poured himself out another three fingers of

whisky, and subsiding on to the sofa, sipped it moodily. He was a thin, untidy-looking man in the middle thirties with a pallid, discontented face and pale blue eyes that had a habit of sliding away from a direct look. His shock of fair hair was perpetually in need of cutting, and he wore a sweat-stained open-necked shirt, grubby khaki trousers and a sagging belt that supported a revolver in a well-worn holster. Altogether an incongruous figure in Lisa's over-decorated drawing-room. As incongruous as Alice DeBrett with her neat dark head, her neat dark expensive linen suit, her impeccable shoes and flawless pearls, and her pale, strained, Madonna face that was innocent of all but the barest trace of make-up.

'Won't do Em any harm to worry,' said Gilly, sipping whisky. 'Told her years ago she should throw out all her Kukes. Everyone's told her! But Em's always fancied she knew better than anyone else. "Treat 'em right and they'll be loyal." *Bah!* There's no such thing as a loyal Kuke. We've all learned that—the hard way!'

Alice said uncertainly: 'But she's fond of her Kikuyu servants, Gilly. And they did stay with her all through the Emergency, and now that it's over——'

'Who said it was over?' demanded Gilly. 'Over, my foot! What about this latest caper—the Kiama Kia Muingi? *A rose by any other name,* that's what! Secret ceremonies, extortion, intimidation—same old filthy familiar ingredients simmering away again and ready to boil over at the drop of a hat. And yet there are scores of little optimists running round in circles saying that it's all over! Don't let 'em fool you!'

He reached behind him, and groping for the bottle of whisky refilled his glass, slopping the liquid on to the rose-patterned chintz of the sofa in the process. 'Who's to say how many Mau Mau are still on the run in the forests, or Nairobi, or the Rift? Why, they haven't even caught "General Africa" yet—and they say it's over! Y'know—' Gilly's words were slurring together—'y'know Hector Brandon? Course you do! Well, Hector's been doin' a lot of interrogation of M.M. old lags, and he says one of 'em told him that there are still a gang of hard-core terrorists hidin' out in the *marula*—the papyrus swamp. Bein' fed by the African labour of the farms along the lake. And Greg Gilbert says he believes General Africa is still employed by a settler. Why, it might be any of Em's Kukes! Who's to tell? Nice quiet house boy or cook or cattleherd by day—Gen'l Africa in a lion skin hat at night. Might even be one of Hector's. In fact, only too likely if you ask me!'

'Oh no, Gilly! Why everyone knows that the Mau Mau swore they'd get Hector because of his intelligence work. Yet they never did, and if General Africa had been one of his own men it would have been too easy.'

'Maybe,' said Gilly sceptically. 'But I'll tell you something that "everyone" doesn't know! And that is that once upon a time Drew Stratton's lot nearly got the "General"—he walked into one of their ambushes with five of his men, and though he managed to get away, he left something behind him: a hunting knife. It had been in a sort of holster at his belt, and by some infernal fluke a bullet chipped it off as clean as a whistle without harming him. But it was the next best thing to getting the man himself, because it had a set of his finger prints on it. The only clue to his identity the Security Forces had ever got their hands on. And what happened to them? Well, I'll tell you. Hector carefully cleaned 'em off! It's always been my belief that he recognized the knife, and that he wasn't taking any chances of one of his darling boys being accused. "Honour of the House", an' all that.'

'Gilly, no!' protested Alice. 'You shouldn't say things like that! It must have been a mistake—an accident.'

'That's what *he* said. Said he thought it belonged to Greg, and merely picked it up off Greg's desk to doodle with. Greg nearly hit the ceiling. It's no use, Alice. You just don't understand what some of these old Kenya hands are capable of; or how their own little patch of land can end by becoming the centre of the universe to them, just because they made it out of nothing by the sweat of their brow, and starved for it and gave up their youth for it, and sacrificed comfort and safety and civilization and a lot of other trivial little things for it. *Brandonmead* is Hector's pride. No—I'm wrong. Ken's his pride. *Brandonmead*'s his life; and he's always sworn by all his African labour. "Loyal to the core" and all that sort of stuff. It would have damned near killed him if it had turned out that one of his precious Kukes was a star Mau Mau thug. I believe he'd have done almost anything to cover it up, and salved his conscience by thinking he could deal with it himself. They're great ones for taking the law into their own hands out here. Haven't you noticed that yet?'

Alice said uncomfortably: 'But Em says——'

'Em!' interrupted Gilly rudely. 'Em's as bad as any of them. Worse! It was silly old bitches like her who caused half the trouble. "My Kukes are loyal. I'll stake my life on it." So they lose— *Bah!* You're not going, are you?'

Alice had put down her half finished glass and stood up. She said coldly: 'I'm afraid I must. I only came over with a message for Lisa, but if she's out perhaps you'd give it to her.'

'She isn't out. She's only gone down to the shamba with the Brandons and Drew Stratton. Here, don't go! Have the other half of that. I didn't mean to get your goat. I know how you feel about Em. You're fond of the old battle-axe. Well, so am I—when she isn't tearing a strip off me! So's all Kenya. Protected Monument—that's Em! Apologize, if I hurt your feelings.'

'That's all right, Gilly,' said Alice hurriedly. 'But I don't think I'll wait, all the same. It's getting late. And if Lisa has guests——'

There was an unexpected trace of embarrassment in her quiet voice, and Gilly's shrewd, pale eyes regarded her with observant interest. He said: 'Ken's not with them, if that's what's worrying you.'

His laugh held a trace of malice as he saw the colour rise in Alice DeBrett's pale cheeks. 'There's no need for you to blush like that, Alice. We all know that you've done your best to snub the poor boy. That is, all except Mabel. But you can't expect Mabel to believe that every woman isn't crazy about her darling son. He's her blind spot. Funny about Ken: I wouldn't have thought you were his type at all.'

'I'm not,' said Alice with a trace of a snap. 'Don't be ridiculous, Gilly. I'm old enough to be his mother!'

'Here! Give yourself a chance! You can't be much more than thirty-five!'

'I'm twenty-seven,' said Alice slowly. 'And Ken isn't twenty yet.'

'Oh well,' said Gilly, dismissing it, and unaware of the blow that he had dealt her. 'Chaps always fall in love with someone older than themselves to start with, and they always fall hard. He'll get over it. Hector ought to send him away. God, I only wish *I* could get the hell out of this Valley! Did you know that Jerry Coles is going to retire soon? You know—the chap who manages the DeBrett property out at Rumuruti. That's the job I'm after. But Em's being damned obstinate. Suit me down to the ground. Nice home, good pay and perks—and no Em looking over my shoulder the entire time, carping and criticizing. Heaven!'

Alice smiled a little wanly and said: 'Wouldn't you find it rather lonely? I shouldn't have thought Lisa would like living so far away.'

Gilly scowled, and his pale eyes were suddenly brooding and sombre. He said: 'That's another reason. It's far away. Over a hundred dusty, uncomfortable, glorious miles away. Far enough, perhaps, to keep her from making an infernal fool of herself over——'

Alice did not let him finish. She walked towards the door, her face white and pinched, and spoke over-loudly, as though to drown out words that she did not wish to hear: 'I really must go. It's getting late and I ought to get back. Will you tell Lisa that——'

Gilly said: 'You can tell her yourself. Here they are now.'

There were footsteps and voices in the verandah, and a moment later Gilly's wife and her guests were in the room. The Brandons, whose property touched the western borders of *Flamingo* and who were such a strangely assorted pair—small, soft-voiced Mabel with her kind, charming face and grey curls, and her choleric husband, Hector, who lived up to his name and was large, loud-voiced and ruddy-featured. Drew Stratton, whose farm lay five miles further along the shores of the lake. And Lisa herself, her bright brown hair bound by a satin ribbon and her wide-skirted dress patterned with roses.

Gilly rose unsteadily and dispensed drinks, and Lisa said: 'Why, hullo, Alice! Nice to see you.'

Her violet eyes slid past Alice with a quick eager look that turned to disappointment, and was neither lost nor misinterpreted by Eden's wife.

Lisa and Eden—! thought Alice. She pushed away the thought as though it had been a tangible thing and said a little stiffly: 'I only came over with a message from Em. She said that you'd asked for a lift next time she went into Nairobi, and to tell you that she'd be going in on Thursday to fetch her niece from the airport.'

'Great-niece, surely?' corrected Lisa.

'No,' said Mrs Brandon in her gentle voice. 'It's her sister's child. Good evening, Alice.' She dropped her knitting bag on the sofa and sat down beside it. 'Lady Helen was Em's half-sister, and a good deal younger than her. She came out to stay with Em during the first world war, and married Jack Caryll who used to own the Lumley place on the Kinangop: Victoria, the daughter, was born out here. I remember her quite well—a thin little girl who used to ride a zebra that Jack tamed for her. He was killed by a rhino while he was out shooting, and his wife took a dislike to the whole country in consequence. She sold the farm to the Lumleys, and went back to England; and now she's died. It's strange to think that she must have been about twenty years younger than Em, and yet Em's still so strong. But I am surprised that Em should have decided to bring Victoria out here. It seems rather an odd thing to do in—in the circumstances.'

For a moment her soft voice held a trace of embarrassment, and Alice's slight figure stiffened. She said coldly: 'Lady Emily feels that it is time she had someone to take over the secretarial work and help with the milk records. She has always done those herself up to now, but she is getting old, and it tires her.'

'But then she has you,' said Mrs Brandon. 'And Eden.'

'I'm afraid I don't type; and Eden has never been fond of paperwork.'

'Eden,' said Hector Brandon roundly, 'is not fond of work in any form! And it's no use your lookin' at me like that, Alice! I've known your husband since he was in short pants, and if you ask me, it's a pity his grandmother didn't dust 'em more often—with a slipper!'

Mrs Brandon frowned reprovingly at her husband and said pacifically: 'You mustn't mind Hector, Alice. He always says what he thinks.'

'And proud of it!' boomed Hector.

Why? thought Alice with a spasm of nervous exasperation. Why should anyone consider it an admirable trait to speak their mind when it hurt other people's feelings?—when it was rude and unkind?

'Rugged individualism,' murmured Mr Stratton absently into his glass.

He caught Alice's eye and grinned at her, and some of her defensive hostility left her. Her taut nerves relaxed a little, and she returned the smile, but with a visible effort.

She liked Drew Stratton. He was one of the very few people with whom she felt entirely at ease. Perhaps because he took people as he found them and did not trouble to interest himself in their private affairs. Drew was tall and fair; as fair as Gilly but, unlike Gilly, very brown from the sun that had bleached his hair and brows. His blue eyes were deceptively bland, and if there was any rugged individualism in his make-up it did not take the form of blunt outspokenness. Nor did he find it necessary, in the manner of Hector, to dress in ill-fitting and sweat-stained clothes in order to emphasize the fact that he worked, and worked hard, in a new and raw land.

Gilly was talking again; his voice slurred and overloud: 'Hear some of your cattle were stolen last night, Hector. Serve you right! Y'ought to keep 'em boma'd. Asking for trouble, leavin' 'em loose. It's men like you who play into the hands of the gangs. If I've heard the D.C. tell you that once, I've heard him tell you a thousand times! Invitation to help themselves—cattle all over the place.'

Hector's large red face showed signs of imminent apoplexy, and Mabel Brandon said hurriedly: 'You know we always kept our cattle close boma'd during the Emergency, Gilly. But now that it's over there didn't seem to be any sense in it. And anyway, Drew has never boma'd his!'

'Drew happens to employ Masai,' retorted Gilly. 'Makes a difference. Makes a hell of a lot of difference! Who owned the Rift before the whites came? The Masai—that's who! And in those days if any Kikuyu had so much as put his nose into it, they'd have speared him! That's why chaps like Drew were left alone in the Emergency. But more than half your labour are Kukes. You're as bad as Em! Won't give them up, and won't hear a word against them.'

'There isn't one of our Kikuyu who I wouldn't trust with my life,' said Mrs Brandon, bristling slightly. 'Why, they've worked for us for twenty years and more. Samuel was with us before Ken was born!'

'Then why do you carry a gun in that knitting bag?' demanded Gilly. 'Tell me that! Think I don't know?'

Mrs Brandon flushed pinkly and looked as dismayed and conscience-stricken as a child who has been discovered in a fault, and Gilly laughed loudly.

'Pipe down, Gil,' requested Drew mildly. 'You're tight.'

'*A hit, a very palpable hit*. Of course I am!' admitted Gilly with unexpected candour. 'Only possible thing to be these days.'

Drew said softly: 'What are you afraid of, Gilly?'

The alcoholic truculence faded from Gilly's pale, puffy face, leaving it drawn and old beyond his years, and he said in a hoarse whisper that was suddenly and unbelievably shocking in that frilled and beruffled room: 'The same thing that Em is afraid of!'

He looked round the circle of still faces, his eyes flickering and darting as uneasily as trapped moths, and his voice rose sharply in the brief uncomfortable silence: 'There's something damned funny going on at *Flamingo*, and I don't like it. I don't like it at all! Know what I think? I think there's something brewing. Some—some funny business.'

'What d'you mean, "funny business"?' demanded Hector Brandon alertly. 'Em been having trouble with her labour? First I've heard of it.'

'No. I could take that. This is something different. Ever watched a thunderstorm coming up against the wind? S'like that! Waiting. I don't like it. Alice doesn't like it. Em don't like it either. She's stubborn as a mule—won't admit that anything could go wrong at her precious *Flamingo*. But she's not been herself of late. It's getting her down.'

'Nonsense, Gilly!' Hector said firmly. 'Saw her myself only this morning. Top of her form! You're imagining things. Only trouble with Em is that she's getting old.' He allowed Lisa to refill his glass and added reflectively: 'Truth of the matter is, Em's never been her old self since Gus Abbott died. She never really got over that. Felt she'd murdered him.'

'So she did,' said Gilly. 'Murder—manslaughter—slip of the gun. What's it matter what you call it? She killed him.'

'Gilly, how *can* you!' protested Mabel indignantly. 'You know quite well that it happened in the middle of that dreadful attack. And it was largely Gus's fault. He saw one of the gang going for her with a panga, and jumped at him just as Em fired. She's never been quite the same since.'

'That's right,' said Hector. 'He'd been her manager since Kendall's day, and it broke her up. You didn't know her before—except by reputation. But we did. It did something to her. Not so much Gus's death, but the fact that she'd killed him. The whole thing must have been a pretty ghastly experience all round. She lost a couple of her servants that night, murdered by the gang, and two of her dogs were panga'd, and half the huts set on fire. But she shot three of the gang and wounded at least two more, and held off the rest until help came. It was a bloody fine show!'

'I grant him bloody—S-Shakespeare!' said Gilly with a bark of laughter. 'An' you're quite right, Hector. I didn't know her before. Mightn't have jumped at the job if I had! She's a difficult woman to work for. Too bloody efficient. That's her trouble. I don't like efficient women.'

He swallowed the contents of his glass at a gulp and Lisa seized the opportunity to return to a topic that was of more interest to her: 'Tell us about this niece of Em's, Alice. What's she like? Is she plain or pretty or middle-aged, or what?'

'I've never met her,' said Alice briefly. 'She must be quite young.'

Her tone did not encourage comment, but Lisa was impervious to tone. She had, moreover, the misfortune to be in love with Alice's husband, and was therefore interested, with an avid, jealous interest, in any other woman who entered his orbit—with the sole exception of his wife, whom she considered to be a colourless and negligible woman, obviously older than her handsome husband and possessing no attractions apart from money. But this new girl—this Victoria Caryll. She would be staying under the same roof as Eden, and be in daily contact with him, and she was young and might be pretty...

'I can't think why, if Em wanted a secretary, she couldn't have got a part-time one from among the local girls,' said Lisa discontentedly. 'Heaven knows there are enough of them, and some of them must be able to type.'

'Secretary, nuts!' said Gilly, weaving unsteadily across to the table that held the drinks, and refilling his glass. 'If you ask me, she's getting this girl out with the idea of handing over half the property to her one day. Dividing it up between her and Eden. After all, they're the only two blood-relations she's got. And there must be plenty to leave. Bags of loot—even if it's split fifty-fifty. Bet you Hector's right! Come to think of it, can't see why else she sh'd suddenly want to bring the girl out in such a hurry. Or why the girl was willing to come! Bet you it's that!'

'Perhaps,' said Mabel Brandon thoughtfully. 'But it's more likely to be what Alice says. Em's getting old, and when you're old there are times when you suddenly feel that the years are running out too quickly, and you begin to count them like a miser and to realize that you can't go on putting things off like you used to do—you must do them now, or you may not do them at all, because soon it may be too late.'

'For goodness sake, Mabel!' said Lisa with a nervous laugh. 'Anyone would think you were an old woman!'

'I'm not a young one,' said Mabel with a rueful smile. 'It's later than you think.'

'Don't!' said Alice with a shiver. The unexpected sharpness of her normally quiet voice evidently surprised her as much as it surprised Mabel Brandon, for she flushed painfully and said with a trace of confusion: 'I'm sorry. It's just that I've always hated that phrase. It was carved on a sundial that we had in the garden at home, and it always frightened me. I don't know why. I—I suppose it was the idea that everything would end sooner than you expected it

to. The day—parties—fun—the years. Life! I used to make excuses not to go near the sundial. Silly, isn't it?'

'No!' said Gilly, harshly and abruptly. 'Do it myself. Make excuses to keep away from *Flamingo*. Same thing. Something that frightens me, but I don't know what. Don't mind a poltergeist that breaks things, but when it begins on creatures, that's different. That's—that's damnable. Working up to something. A sighting shot. Makes you wonder where it will end. What it's got its eye on...'

His voice died out on a whisper and Mabel surveyed him with disapproval and said with unaccustomed severity: 'Really, Gilly, you are talking a great deal of nonsense this evening. And you're upsetting poor Lisa. What are you hinting at? That Mau Mau isn't dead yet and that Em's servants have taken the oath? Well suppose it isn't and they have? There's hardly a Kikuyu in the country who hasn't. But it doesn't mean anything any more. The whole thing has fallen to pieces and the few hard-core terrorists who are still on the run are far too busy just keeping alive to plan any more murders. And if it's the poisoning of that unfortunate ridgeback that's worrying you, I'm sure there's nothing sinister in that. It cannot be wise to keep dogs like Simba who attack strangers on sight, and I am not really surprised that someone took the law into their own hands. I might almost have felt tempted to do it myself, fond as I am of dogs, but——'

'But Simba didn't like Ken; that's it, isn't it?' said Alice, surprised to find herself so angry.

Mabel turned towards her, her gentle voice quivering with sudden emotion: 'That is not kind of you, Alice. We all know that Simba liked you, and of course Em is crazy on the subject of dogs. But considering that he once attacked your own husband——'

'Only because Eden was trying to take a book away from me. We were fooling, but Simba thought he was attacking me. He wouldn't let anyone touch me, and I suppose he thought that Ken——'

She bit the sentence off short, aghast at its implications. But it seemed to remain hanging in the air, its import embarrassingly clear to everyone in the room. As embarrassingly clear as the expression upon Mabel Brandon's stricken face, or Hector's stony tight-mouthed stare.

There was a moment of strained and painful silence which was broken by Drew Stratton, who glanced at his wrist watch and rose. He said in a leisurely voice: 'Afraid I must go, Lisa. It's getting late, and my headlights are not all they should be. Thanks for the drink. Can I drop you off at the house, Mrs DeBrett, or did you drive over?'

Alice threw him a grateful look. 'No, I came over by the short cut across the garden. And I really must walk back, because I promised Em I'd get some of the Mardan roses for the dining-room table.'

Drew said: 'Then I'll see you on your way. Eden shouldn't let you wander about alone of an evening.'

'Oh, it's safe enough now. Good night, Lisa. Shall I tell Em you'll go in with her on Thursday?'

'Yes, do. I want to get my hair done. I'll ring up tomorrow and fix an appointment. Drew, if your headlights aren't working you'd better not be long over seeing Alice back.'

'That's right,' said Gilly. 'Remember Alice's sundial. *"It is later than you think!"*'

He laughed again, and the sound of his laughter followed them out into the silent garden.

2

The sun had dipped behind the purple line of the Mau Escarpment, and the lake reflected a handful of rose-pink clouds and a single star that was as yet no more than a ghostly point of silver.

There had been very little rain during the past month, and the path that led between the canna lily beds and bamboos was thick with dust. Mr Stratton slowed his leisurely stride to Alice De-Brett's shorter step, but he did not talk, and Alice was grateful for his silence. There had been too much talk in the Markhams' drawing-room. Too many things had been said that had better have been left unsaid, and too many things had been uncovered that should have been kept decently in hiding. Things that Alice had never previously suspected, or been too preoccupied with her own problems to notice.

Was it, she wondered, the long strain of the

Emergency, and the present relaxing of tension and alertness, that had brought these more petty and personal things to the surface and exposed them nakedly in Lisa's pink-and-white drawing-room? Had she, Alice, displayed her own fears and her own feelings as clearly as Lisa and Gilly and the Brandons had done? Had the brief coldness of her reply to Lisa's questions on the subject of Victoria Caryll been as illuminating as Lisa's own comments?

'Look out,' said Drew. He caught her arm, jerking her out of her abstraction just in time to prevent her treading full on a brown, moving band, four inches wide, that spanned the dusty track. A river of hurrying ants—the wicked safari ants whose bite is unbelievably painful.

'You ought to look where you're going,' remarked Mr Stratton mildly. 'That might have been a snake. And anyway you don't want a shoe-full of those creatures. They bite like the devil.'

'I know,' said Alice apologetically. 'I'm afraid I wasn't looking where I was going.'

'Dangerous thing to do in this country,' commented Drew. 'What's worrying you?'

Alice would have resented that question from anyone else, and would certainly not have answered it truthfully. But Drew Stratton was notoriously indifferent to gossip and she knew that it was kindness and not curiosity that had prompted the query. She turned to look at his brown, clear-cut profile, sharp against the quiet sky, and knew suddenly that she could talk to Drew. She had not been able to talk to anyone about Victoria. Not to Eden. Not even to Em, who had said so anxiously: 'You won't mind, dear? It's all over, you know—a long time ago. But she shan't come if you mind.' She had not been able to confess to Em that she minded. But, strangely, she could admit it to Drew.

'It's Victoria,' said Alice. 'Victoria Caryll. Eden and she—they've known each other for a long time. They're some sort of cousins. Em's her aunt and his grandmother, and he used to spend most of his holidays at her mother's house when he was home at school—and at Oxford. They—they were engaged to be married. I don't know what went wrong. I asked Eden once, but he—wouldn't talk about it. And—and her mother died a few months ago, so now she's coming out here...'

Alice made a small, helpless gesture with one hand, and Drew reached out and possessed himself of it. He tucked it companionably through his arm, but made no other comment, and once again Alice was conscious of a deep feeling of gratitude and a relief from strain. She could think of no one else who would not have probed and exclaimed, sympathized or uttered bracing platitudes in face of that disclosure. But Drew's silent acceptance of it, and that casual, comforting gesture, had reduced it to its proper proportions. There was really nothing to worry about. It was, in fact, a direct dispensation of Providence that Em's niece should be free to come out to Kenya, for it was going to make it so much easier to break the news to Em that they must leave her. It would have been impossible to leave her alone and old and lonely. But now she would have Victoria. And with luck, and in time, she might even grow to be almost as fond of Victoria as she was of Eden, and if that should happen perhaps she would leave her not only half of the estate, as Hector Brandon had suggested, but *Flamingo*, and the property at Rumuruti, whole and entire, so that she, Alice, would be free of it for ever, and need never come back to Kenya...

A huge horned owl, grey in the green twilight, rose up from the stump of a fallen tree and swooped silently across their path, and Alice caught her breath in an audible gasp and stopped suddenly, her fingers clutching frantically at Drew Stratton's sleeve.

'It's all right. It's only an owl,' said Drew pacifically.

'It was a death owl!' said Alice, shuddering. 'The servants say that if you see one of those it means that someone is going to die. They're terrified of them!'

'That's no reason why you should be,' said Drew reprovingly. 'You aren't a witchcraft-ridden Kikuyu.'

He frowned down at her, perturbed and a little impatient, and putting a hand over the cold fingers that clutched at his arm, held them in a hard and comforting grasp and said abruptly: 'Mrs DeBrett, I know it's none of my business, but don't you think it's time you gave yourself a holiday in England? You can't have had a very easy time during the last five years, but you mustn't let this country get you down. Why don't you get Eden to take you home for a few months? It will do you both good, and this niece of Em's will be company for her while you are away.'

'Yes,' said Alice a little breathlessly. 'I—we had thought...' Her colour was coming back and she breathed more easily. She stilled the nervous shivering of her body with a visible effort and said: 'I'm sorry, Drew. I'm behaving very stupidly. You're quite right; I should go home. I'm turning into a jumpy, hysterical wreck. Do you know what Gilly said to me this evening? He said, "You can't be more than thirty-five." And I'm twenty-seven. Eden's only twenty-nine. I can't look six or seven years older than Eden, can I?'

'Gilly was tight,' observed Drew dispassionately.

He studied her gravely, thinking that Gilly's estimate of Mrs DeBrett's age, though ungallant, was understandable. But Drew had seen nerves and shell-shock and sleeplessness before, and recognized the symptoms. He said: 'You look pretty good to me,' and smiled.

He possessed a slow and extraordinarily pleasant smile, and Alice found herself returning it. 'That's better,' approved Drew. 'You look about seventeen when you smile, not twenty-seven. You should do it more often. Are you and Eden going to this dance at Nakuru on Saturday?'

He talked trivialities until they reached the plumbago hedge that marked the boundary of the Markhams' garden, and Alice dismissed him at the gate:

'I'm not letting you come any further, or you won't get home before it's dark. And I'm perfectly safe, thank you. No one is likely to try and murder me between here and the house! Not now, anyway.'

'Probably not,' said Drew, 'but I imagine that it will be some years yet before half the women out here will feel safe without a gun.'

He watched her walk away across the garden and was conscious of a brief and unexpected flash of sympathy for Eden DeBrett. Not really the type for a settler's wife, thought Drew. She'll never stay the course.

A dry twig cracked in the soft carpet of dust behind him and he turned sharply. But it was only Gilly Markham.

'Came out for a breath of air,' explained Gilly morosely. 'Mabel's gone off to pick a lettuce or a pineapple or something, and Hector says he's going to walk home, so Lisa's locked up the booze. Women are hell.'

He leaned heavily on the gate, his eyes following the noiseless flight of a bat which swooped and flittered along the pale blossoms of the plumbago hedge, and said with sudden violence: 'God, what a country! What wouldn't I give to get out of this god-forsaken, uncivilized, gang-ridden hole! Can't think how you stand it.'

'No reason why you should stand it, Gilly,' observed Drew without heat.

'That's what *you* think!' said Gilly sourly. 'Easy enough for you. But I can't afford to up-sticks and get the hell out of it. D'you suppose I wouldn't if I could?'

Drew said dryly: 'If you're getting the same screw as Gus Abbott got, you can't be doing too badly. By all accounts, Gus left a packet.'

'Gus didn't have a wife!' retorted Gilly bitterly. 'You don't know Lisa. If I were making twenty times what I get, Lisa'd spend it. Thinks I don't know why she's always buying herself new clothes and having her face and hair fixed. Well I may be a fool, but I'm not such a fool as I look! Take my advice and don't ever get married, Drew.'

'I'll bear it in mind,' said Drew solemnly. 'So long, Gilly.'

'No, don't go!' said Gilly urgently. 'Stay around for a bit. Got the purple willies on me this evening and that's a fact. Know why people like talking to you, Drew? Well I'll tell you. It's because you're so bloody detached. You don't give a damn for any of it, do you? But tell anyone else anything, and before you know it it's all round the Colony. Why can't they mind their own business?'

'Why indeed?' said Drew. 'Sorry about it, Gilly, but I've got to go. It's late.'

Gilly ignored the interruption. 'Hector, fr'-instance. Never forgiven Eden for marrying a woman who he doesn't consider is "The right type for Kenya". What's it got to do with him? Anyone would think he'd invented the place! Probably thinks that as soon as Em dies Alice'll persuade Eden to sell out to that syndicate of Afrikaners who offered a fortune for *Flamingo* last year. Wouldn't suit Hector one bit to have that sort of concern on his doorstep! Ruin the market for him. And the next thing you know they'd build a decent road round the lake, and how he'd hate that! Hector and his like may talk a lot of hot air about the Colony, but the one thing they're terrified of is development around their own little bit of it. They like it just as it is. Just exactly as it ruddy well——'

He broke off abruptly and lifted his head, listening intently.

There was no breath of wind that evening. The vast stretch of the lake lay glass-green in the twilight, and even the birds were silent at last. But someone in the big rambling house that lay beyond the pepper trees and jacarandas in Em's garden was playing the piano. The quiet evening lent clarity and a haunting, melancholy beauty to the distant sound, and Drew, who had turned away, paused involuntarily to listen, and said: 'What is she playing?'

'The Rift Valley Concerto,' said Gilly absently.

His thin, nervous, musician's fingers moved on the top bar of the gate as though it was the keyboard of a piano, and then clenched abruptly into fists, and he struck at the gate in a sudden fury of irritation and said savagely:

'Why the hell can't she play that third movement as it's meant to be played, instead of hammering it out as though it were a bloody pop tune? That woman 'ud make Bartok sound like "Two Eyes of Grey" and Debussy like "The British Grenadiers"! It's murder—that's what it is! Plain murder!'

He relapsed into glowering silence, slumping down on a square concrete block that stood among the grasses by the gate. His brief spurt of rage gave place to an alcoholic sullenness, and he took no note of Mr Stratton's departure.

* * *

Alice was half-way back to the house when she remembered the Mardan roses that Em had wanted for the dining-room table, and she turned off the path and walked across the parched grass, and through a sea of delphiniums that grew waist-high and half wild at the foot of a small knoll that was crowned by a tangle of bushes and the trunk of a fallen tree.

From the crest of the knoll, and between a break in the bushes, she could look out over the lush green of the shamba and the wide belt of grey-green vegetation, dark now in the fading light, which was the *marula*—the papyrus swamp that fringed the shores of the lake with a dense, feathery and almost impenetrable jungle, twice the height of a tall man.

A broken branch of the fallen tree supported a cascade of white roses that were not easy to pick even by day, for they were plentifully supplied with thorns. But Em loved them, and during their brief season she liked to arrange them in the Waterford glass bowls that had belonged to her grandmother. Was that why she asked for them now? So that she could fill other bowls with them and pretend that she did not care? For the Waterford glass bowls had gone. They had been found one afternoon almost a week ago, broken in pieces, though the house had been quiet that day, and the dogs had not barked...

'Don't touch them!' Alice had said, looking at Em's drawn, ravaged face. 'There may be finger prints on them. We can find out——'

'And have the police all over the house, trampling all over *Flamingo* and bullying my servants? No!' said Em. And she had gathered up the broken pieces with old, pitiful, shaking hands and given them to Zacharia, telling him to throw them away.

Em had refused from the first to send for the police. She had set a number of traps, but no one had fallen into them. The poltergeist seemed to be able to circumnavigate burglar alarms, trip-wires and similar booby traps, and to avoid by instinct objects smeared with a substance guaranteed to inflict an unpleasant sore on any hand that touched it. But the effects of its depredations had been more demoralizing to the whole household than anything achieved by the Mau Mau during the years of the Emergency. The servants were frankly terrified, Eden was angry and on edge, and Em grim and stubborn.

'If someone thinks that they can frighten me into leaving, they'll find they're wrong,' she said. 'The Mau Mau thought they could frighten us into leaving our farms, but we are still here. I don't know what anyone hopes to gain by destroying things I am fond of, but whatever it is, they won't get it!' And as if to emphasize her defiance she had sat down at the piano and played from memory Toroni's 'Rift Valley Concerto': playing it furiously and loudly and not very accurately.

That had been on the day that the recording of the concerto had been destroyed, and that same evening, looking tired and defeated and very old, she had told them she had sent for Victoria.

Victoria's mother had died that spring and Victoria was at present sharing a small flat in London with two friends, and working as private secretary to the assistant manager of a firm of importers.

'I have asked her to come out here and work for me,' said Em, not looking at Eden: looking at nothing but the candle flames on the dining-room table and, perhaps, the past. 'I am getting too old to deal with half the work I do. I need someone who can be a confidential secretary, and whom I can work hard. And at this time I would rather it were someone who—who belongs. It will also mean that I am doing something for Helen's child. Giving her a home as well as an adequate salary.'

She had looked at Alice for the first time, her eyes blank and unfocused from the dazzle of the candle flames, and said gently: 'You, who are an orphan too, will know what that must mean to her. But she shan't come if you would rather she did not, my dear.'

Perhaps Alice might have found it possible to protest if it had not suddenly seemed to offer a way of escape. She did not want to meet this girl whom Eden had once meant to marry and with whom he must once have been in love. And she did not want Eden to meet her again. But if Em's niece came to live at *Flamingo* perhaps she, Alice, could persuade Eden to leave Kenya: to take her back to England. It would not be as though they were leaving Em alone. She would have Victoria...

Alice looked down at the white roses that filled her hands, and letting them drop to the ground, sat down tiredly on the smooth trunk of the fallen tree and thought with affection and desperation and despair of Lady Emily DeBrett. Of Em and Eden. It was not going to be easy to tell Em that she could endure Kenya no longer. Em had a reputation for impatience, hard-headedness, shrewd business acumen, an iron nerve and a refusal to suffer fools gladly. Yet she had suffered Eden's wife, who according to all her lights must have seemed a fool. She had mothered her, protected her, encouraged her, and stood between her and danger.

Sitting in the dusk on the knoll at *Flamingo*, Alice recalled her first sight of Eden's grandmother, and the shock it had given her. Eden had mentioned casually that his grandmother was inclined to be eccentric in the matter of dress, but he had not prepared her for the grotesque figure that had appeared on the porch steps when the car that had brought them the fifty-odd miles from Nairobi Airport drew up before the big thatch-roofed house on the shores of Lake Naivasha.

The years had thickened Emily's stately figure to more than ample proportions, but had not eradicated her antipathy to skirts. She had never willingly worn feminine attire, but she had a fondness for bright colours and a leaning towards eccentricity. Em's scarlet dungarees and vivid blouses—both of which served to exaggerate her impressive bulk to a distressing extent—and the flamboyant wide-brimmed hats that she habitually wore crammed down upon her short cropped hair, had for more than thirty years been as familiar a sight to half Kenya as the roving zebra herds, the wandering, ochre-smeared Masai warriors, or the snows of Kilimanjaro. But they had done nothing to reassure Alice DeBrett, three weeks a bride and arriving at *Flamingo* dizzy from repeated attacks of air-sickness and dusty and shaken from the last fifteen miles over an unmetalled road—a newcomer to a strange country torn with savagery and violence, where even the women carried guns and all men were afraid of the night, never knowing what darkness might bring.

It was odd, looking back on that day, to think that Em had been the only reassuring thing in all the months that had followed. She had been both mother and grandmother to Alice, who had never known either. It was Eden who had failed her. But then it could not be easy to be Eden, thought Eden's wife. To be so fatally good-looking that women looked once and fell desperately in love—as she herself had done. She had been married to Eden for almost five years now, and she still could not look at him without a contraction of the heart.

She loved him so much, and if he had loved *Flamingo* as Em loved it she would have forced herself to staying there for ever: to fighting her terror, her hatred of the land, and the ill health that constant fear, the height and the climate had inflicted upon her. But she did not believe that Eden's roots were too deep in the Kenya soil, or that the land meant to him what it meant to Em. And lately she had persuaded herself that he would be just as happy in England with an estate of his own. Happier! for it had always been a sore point with him that Em had not made him manager instead of Gilly. 'But *Flamingo* will be yours one day,' Em had said. 'You'll need a manager then, and it's better to have one who knows the ropes. Gilly's not much use at present, but managers are hard to get these days, and he'll learn. Besides, he needs the job.'

'I didn't know we were running a philanthropical society!' Eden had said crossly. 'You're losing your grip, Gran darling.'

'That's where you're wrong. You've got a hold over a man who needs a job. None over one who doesn't. And I like things done my way.'

Eden had laughed and kissed her. 'You do hate to have anyone accuse you of having a soft spot, don't you, darling? You gave Gilly the job because he was broke, and you know it—and because he knows the difference between Bach and Brahms!'

Em had made a face at him, but she had not denied it.

It was on Em's account more than Eden's that Alice had tried to reconcile herself to spending the rest of her days in Kenya, for although she had come to believe that she might be able to make up to Eden for the loss of *Flamingo*, she knew that she could never compensate Em for the loss of Eden. But now at last she had reached the breaking point. It had not been Victoria who had proved to be the last straw, but the things that had happened in the house during the last weeks: a situation that Eden had once referred to as 'this silly business'.

'It isn't silly,' Alice had said, and for the first time there had been hysteria in her gentle voice. 'It's horrible! Don't you see—everything that has been broken or spoiled has been something special and irreplaceable. It's as if someone who knew everything about Em, and wanted to hurt her specially, knew just the things to choose. Someone—someone *evil*.'

Eden had said sharply: 'That's nonsense! You

mustn't be hysterical about this, Alice. Believe me, darling, it'll turn out to be some silly Kuke who fancies he has a grievance, or thinks he's had a spell put on him. You mustn't lose your sense of proportion. After all, even if the things are irreplaceable, they're still only things.'

But two days later it had not been a thing. It had been Simba.

Alice had not thought Em capable of tears, and the sight of her red and swollen eyes had been almost as shocking as the discovery of Simba's stiff, contorted body lying among the crushed geraniums below the verandah. She had been frightened before, but it had never been like this. The wanton destruction of Em's most cherished possessions had been horrible enough, but the poisoning of her favourite dog betrayed a cold-blooded malice that went deeper than mere spite.

Gilly was right, thought Alice, cold with foreboding. The 'things' were only a beginning. Simba was another step. Supposing—it is *someone* next? Someone Em loves. *Eden——!* We must get away. We must! While there is still time...

It had been a particularly trying day for Alice. Eden had gone to Nairobi and would not be back until late, and Em had been noticeably jumpy and on edge all day. She had apparently had a minor squabble with Mabel Brandon in the course of the morning, and had not been pleased when Ken Brandon had presented himself at the house in the afternoon and had to be asked to tea.

Alice had not been pleased either. She found young Ken Brandon's adolescent and unsnubbable infatuation for her more than a little trying, and had read him a stern lecture on the subject only the day before, which he had not taken well. He had ended by threatening to shoot himself—not for the first time—and Alice had lost all patience with him, and observed tartly that it would be no loss. She had hoped that this would put an end to his adoration, but Ken had turned up that afternoon asking to see her, and evidently intending to apologize for the dramatics of the previous day. Em had saved her from another scene by plying the boy with tea and arbitrarily taking Alice out shooting with her immediately afterwards.

Alice never went out shooting if she could help it, but on this occasion she had accepted gratefully, and they had taken Kamau, one of the boys, and driven out in the Land-Rover to shoot a buck for the dogs. Em had shot a kongoni out on the ranges, and helped Kamau to degut it and hoist the limp ungainly body into the back of the Land-Rover, where it lolled in a sticky pool of blood that smeared the seats, stained Em's hands and clothing with ugly dark splotches and filled Alice with shuddering revulsion. It was one of the many things about Kenya that she could never get used to. The casual attitude of most women towards firearms and the sight and smell of blood.

I haven't any courage, thought Alice drearily, staring into the green dusk. Perhaps I had some once, but it's gone. If only I can get away... If only I need not go back into that horrible house...

Em was still playing Toroni's concerto, and the too familiar cadences, muted by distance, plucked at Alice's taut nerves, demanding her attention and forcing her to listen.

She had never been able to understand Em's and Gilly's admiration for the concerto. It had seemed to her a tuneless noise, alternating from the discordant to the intolerably dreary. But tonight she seemed to be hearing it for the first time, and it was as if the Valley itself were speaking. The enormous golden Valley and the great yawning craters of extinct volcanoes—Longonot and Suswa and Menengai. The impassable falls of dead lava: the frowning gorge of Hell's Gate: the vast, shallow, flamingo-haunted lakes, and the long twin ramparts of the Mau and the Kinangop that were the walls of the Great Rift.

Em had told her that Toroni had loved the Valley. But Em was wrong, thought Alice, listening to the music. Toroni had not loved the Rift. He had been afraid of it. As she herself was afraid of it. She shivered convulsively, clutching her hands tightly together in her lap; and as she listened a little breath of wind whispered through the bushes and swayed the hanging trails of roses, and somewhere near her a twig cracked sharply.

Quite suddenly, with that sound, the garden was no longer a friendly place, but as full of menace as the house, and Alice stood up quickly and stooped to gather up the fallen flowers, aware that her heart was thumping painfully against her ribs. She had not realized that it had grown so dark.

Below the knoll and beyond the shamba, from the shadowy belt of the papyrus swamp, birds began to call; their clear piping cries mingling with the sweet clear notes of the distant piano. But the day had almost gone and the sky was already shimmering with pale stars, and there was as yet no moon. There should be no birds calling at this hour. Had something, or someone, startled them?

She remembered then what Gilly had said less than an hour ago. Something about General Africa—still at large despite the heavy price that the Government had set on his head, and suspected of being in the employment of one of the settlers in the Naivasha district. Something about a gang under his command who were rumoured to be still in hiding somewhere in the papyrus swamp, being fed by the African labour of the farms that bordered the Lake.

She had not paid much attention to it at the time, but now she remembered it with alarm, and remembered, too, Em's instructions that she should not stay out after sunset. But the sun had set long ago, and now it was almost dark, and the evening breeze had arisen and was stirring the leaves about her and filling the green dusk with soft, stealthy rustlings.

A twig cracked again immediately behind her, and turning quickly she caught a flicker of movement that was not caused by the wind. Her hands tightened about the roses, driving the thorns into her flesh, but caught in a sudden spider's web of panic she was almost unaware of the pain. Her brain told her to run for the house, but her muscles would not obey her. She could not even scream; and she knew that if she did so no one in the house would hear her, for the music of the piano would drown any sound from outside. But there was someone watching her from among the bushes; she was sure of it——

Alice stood quite still, as helpless and as paralysed with terror as the victim of a nightmare. And then, just as she thought that her heart must stop beating, a familiar figure materialized out of the dusk at the foot of the knoll, and the blood seemed to flow again through her numbed veins.

She dropped the roses, and with a choking sob of relief began to run, tripping and stumbling over the rough grass in the uncertain light. She was within a yard of that dimly seen figure when something checked her. A sound...

There was something wrong. Something crazily and impossibly wrong. She stopped suddenly, staring. Her eyes widened in her white face and her mouth opened in a soundless scream. For it was someone else. Someone suddenly and horribly unfamiliar.

3

'And as I was saying, what with Income Tax and strikes and the weather, well it's no wonder that so many people decide to live abroad. In fact, as I told Oswin—that's my present husband—I can't understand why more of them don't do it. Don't you agree?'

There was no answer, and Mrs Brocas-Gill, observing with annoyance that her neighbour had fallen asleep, turned her attention instead to the desolate green and brown expanse of Africa that lay far below her, across which the big B.O.A.C. Constellation trailed a tiny blue shadow no bigger than a toy aeroplane.

Miss Caryll, however, was not asleep. Only an exceptionally strong-minded woman, or one in need of a hearing-aid, could have slept in the company of that human long-playing record, Mrs Brocas-Gill. Victoria was neither; but she had endured Mrs

Brocas-Gill's indefatigable monologue with barely a break since the aircraft had left London Airport, and as they had been delayed for twenty-four hours at Rome with engine trouble this meant that she had been compelled to listen to it for the best part of two days. Even the nights had not silenced Mrs Brocas-Gill, who had slept with her mouth open, and snored. And Victoria wanted to think.

She had not allowed herself much time for thought during the last three weeks. Once she had made her decision and cabled her acceptance of Aunt Emily's offer, there was little point in stopping to think; and little time in which to do so, for there had been a hundred things to see to. But there would be the flight to Kenya; twenty-four hours of sitting quietly in an aeroplane with nothing to do. There would be time then to think, and to sort out the turmoil in her mind and face the past—and the future. But she had not calculated on Mrs Brocas-Gill, and now they were flying over Africa, and the Dark Continent lay spread out below them with Nairobi Airport only half an hour ahead.

Half an hour! thought Victoria in a panic. Half an hour in which to sort out her thoughts and prepare herself for meeting Eden. To face all those things that she had cravenly refused to face during the past three weeks, and that she had forced herself not to think of for more than five years. Half an hour...

It was difficult to remember a time when she had not loved Eden DeBrett. She had been five on the day when she had tried to make Falda, the little zebra which her father had caught and tamed for her, jump the cattle gate by one of the waterholes. Falda had not taken kindly to the idea, and Victoria had pitched head-first into the sloshy churned-up mud by the drinking troughs where, in addition to winding herself badly, she ruined the clean cotton dress in which she was supposed to appear at a luncheon party.

It was Eden, nine years old and spending the weekend with his great-Aunt Helen, who had saved the situation. He had retrieved Victoria from the mud, dried her tears on a grubby pocket-handkerchief and suggested the immediate removal of clothes, shoes and socks, and their immersion—and Victoria's—in the clean water of the cattle troughs.

His suggestion had been followed, with such excellent results that when the gong had sounded she had been able to walk demurely up to the house in a crumpled but undoubtedly clean dress, and no one had noticed that her long brown plaits owed some of their sleekness to the fact that they were damp. Eden's superior male intelligence had saved her from disaster and from that day he was Victoria's hero.

She had been a plain little girl, with a tendency to stammer slightly when shy or upset; thin and leggy and very brown. Brown sunburnt skin, brown eyes and long, lank brown hair. But although her own lack of good looks had not interested her, she had been deeply impressed by Eden's beauty.

Even as a child Eden DeBrett was beautiful, and he did not outgrow that beauty as so many children do. It seemed, in fact, to increase as he grew older, and it had its effect on everyone he met, so that there were few people, if any, who were ever to know what he was really like, or to be quite fair to him: their judgement being invariably swung out of true by his amazing good looks.

He was ten when Em hardened her heart and sent him home to a famous preparatory school in England, and the six-year-old Victoria had wept bitterly and uncontrollably, and greatly to Eden's disgust and her own mortification, on the platform of Nairobi railway station where she had gone with her parents to see him off.

Her gay and charming father had died two months later, and the tragedy of his death, the sale of the farm and the misery of leaving Kenya—even the parting with her ponies and dear fat friendly Falda—had been mitigated by the thought that she would be seeing Eden again. For it had been arranged between Em and Helen that Eden should spend the Christmas and Easter holidays with the Carylls, and return to Kenya once a year to spend the two months of the summer holidays at *Flamingo*.

In actual fact he had spent all his holidays for the next six or seven years with them, and had seen nothing of Em and *Flamingo;* for tragedy on a Homeric scale had taken over the stage, and the war put an end to countless plans, as it was to put an end to countless lives.

Eden had missed active service, but he had done his National Service with the Occupation Forces in Germany, and followed it by three years at Oxford, during which time he had seen little or nothing of the Carylls, for he spent his vacations with Em in Kenya, flying between London and Nairobi. Victoria had not seen him for over a year when Em suddenly announced her intention of paying a visit to England and staying with her half-sister. She had not seen either for years, and she and Eden would spend July and August at Helen's instead of at *Flamingo*.

Victoria's Aunt Emily, who was Eden's grandmother, was exactly as Victoria remembered her, save for the fact that in deference to the post-war nerves of the Islanders she had refrained from wearing her favourite Kenya garb of scarlet dungarees, and was soberly and somewhat disappointingly clad in a brown coat-frock that whispered of moth balls and the Gay Twenties.

Eden had arrived two days later, and he had looked at Victoria as though he were seeing her for the first time: as though she were someone whom he had never seen before.

She had been picking roses and her arms were full of the lovely lavish honey-pinks of Betty Uprichards; but that had been an unrehearsed and entirely fortuitous circumstance, as Eden had not been expected for another two hours. She had blushed under Eden's startled gaze, and Eden had said foolishly: '*Vicky—!* What have you been doing to yourself? You've—you've grown up.'

And at that they had both laughed, and he had leaned forward and kissed her above the roses and they had fallen in love.

No, that was not true, thought Victoria. At least, it was not true of herself, for she had fallen in love with Eden years and years ago, when he had picked her up out of the mud by the cattle troughs and dried her tears with a handkerchief that smelt of Stockholm tar and chewing gum. And she had never stopped loving him.

It was Eden who had fallen in love that day. Or had he? Had it only been affection for someone he had known all his life? Sentiment and a summer evening, and a pretty girl in a yellow dress with her arms full of roses? *Any* pretty girl? No! thought Victoria. No. It isn't true. He did love me. He did! I couldn't have been mistaken.

It had been an enchanted summer. They had danced together, and dined together, and walked and talked and planned their lives together. Em had been pleased; but Victoria's mother had not approved of the cousins marrying, and she had been against it from the first.

'I might agree, if they were first cousins,' Em had said, 'but they are not.'

'Eden has Beaumartin blood in him,' said Helen unhappily.

'And Carteret and Brook and DeBrett blood too! It will be a great success.'

But Helen had counselled delay. Eden was only twenty-three, and Victoria four years younger. They could afford to wait. Eden was to do a year's course at an agricultural college so as to fit him for taking over *Flamingo*—as his years at Oxford would fit him, so his grandmother hoped, to hold political office one day in the country of his birth and her adoption.

'He is a second-generation Kenya-ite,' said Em, 'and there are not so many of them. The Colony needs men who love the country to run its affairs.'

By Helen's wish there had been no formal engagement, and no announcement to friends. Em had gone back to Kenya when the summer was over and Victoria had gone on with her secretarial course, because, she told Eden, it would be a help in the running of *Flamingo*.

They were to be married when Eden was twenty-four, and he had actually married when he was within a week of his twenty-fourth birthday. But it had not been to Victoria. It had been to Alice Laxton. Five years ago... Yet even now, to think of it brought back some of the suffocating, agonizing pain of those days.

It had happened suddenly and without warning. Eden had arrived one afternoon to see her mother, and left again without waiting to see Victoria, who was out. Helen had looked pale and upset but had said nothing more than that Eden had been unable to stay as he had to spend the weekend with friends in Sussex, but that he would be writing.

The letter had come three days later, and Victoria could still remember every line of it as though it had burned itself into her brain. They had made a mistake, wrote Eden, and confused cousinly affection and friendship for something deeper. Nothing could alter that fondness and friendship, and he knew her too well not to know that if she did not agree with him now, she would one day. One day she would fall in love with someone else, as he himself had done, and then her affection for him would fall into its proper place. And as they had never really been engaged, neither of them need suffer any public embarrassment.

As he himself had done... In the face of that statement there was nothing for Victoria to do but write an unhysterical letter accepting the inevitable and agreeing that his decision was the right one. She had saved her pride, and probably salved Eden's conscience, by doing so; if either of those things were worth doing.

Helen had been relieved and had not attempted to disguise the fact. 'I never think that marriages between cousins are a good idea,' she said. 'Inbreeding never did anyone any good.'

Em had written from Kenya. She had quite obviously accepted Eden's view that the break was mutual, and the letter had been charming and deeply regretful, and had ended with the hope that they might both think better of it. But on the same morning as its arrival *The Times* and the *Telegraph* had published the announcement of Eden's engagement to Alice Laxton, and less than a month later they had been married.

Oh, the agony of those days! The tearing, wrenching pain of loss. The shock of casually opening an illustrated paper at the hairdressers and being confronted with a full page photograph of Eden and his bride leaving St George's, Hanover Square. Eden, grave and unsmiling, and as heart-breakingly handsome as every woman's dream of Prince Charming. And Alice, an anonymous figure in white satin whose bridal veil had blown across her face and partially obscured it.

'Better looking than Robert Taylor or any of those,' said the hairdresser's assistant, peering over her shoulder. 'Ought to be on the films, he ought. It's a waste. Don't think much of her, do you? Can't think how she got him. Money, I expect. The papers say she's got any amount of it. Wish I had! What about just a touch of brilliantine, Miss Caryll?'

Any amount of money . . . Had that been why Eden had married her? No, he *could* not be so despicable! Not Eden. But *Flamingo*, she knew, had been losing money of late, and Eden had expensive tastes. Em had spoilt him. It would be nice to be able to think that he only married Alice Laxton for her money, for then she could despise him and be sorry for his wife, and apply salve to her own hurt pride. But what did hurt pride matter in comparison to the pain in her heart? I won't think of him any more, decided Victoria. I won't let myself think of any of this again.

It had not been easy to keep that vow, but hard work had helped, and at last there came a time when memory did not rise and mock her whenever she was tired or off-guard. She had not thought of the past, or of Eden, for months before Helen died, and afterwards she had been able to read his letter of condolence, and reply to it, as though he had meant no more to her than the writers of a dozen other such letters. She had sold the house and taken a secretarial post in London. And then that unexpected letter had arrived from Kenya.

It was not the sort of letter that Em had ever written before, and there was an odd and disturbing suggestion of urgency about it. The same urgency that Helen had sometimes betrayed when she had wanted to do something, or to see someone, and had been afraid that she would not have time to do it before she died. A fear that was both harrowing and pitiful. But there was something else there too. Something that Victoria could not quite put her finger on, and which disturbed her even more.

The letter had contained only one reference to the past: 'You know that I would never have suggested your coming if I had not been quite sure that you and Eden could meet as friends. And I know that you will like his wife. Alice is such a dear girl, but we are neither of us strong, and I fear that I am getting old. I need help.'

Em had provisionally booked a passage for her on an air liner leaving for Nairobi on the twenty-third of the month. Which meant that she would have to decide at once, as the company would not keep the reservation for long. Was that why Em had done it? So that she would be forced to make up her mind quickly, and could not waver and hesitate? Was Em, too, afraid of dying too soon, and aware, as Helen had been, that it was later than she had thought?

England had been enduring an exceptionally cold and wet spell that year, and Victoria, clinging to a strap in a crowded bus on her way to work, the letter in her pocket, had looked out over the damp, bedraggled hat of a stout woman in a wet mackintosh, to the damp, bedraggled London streets that streamed past the rain-spotted windows, and thought of the Rift Valley——

The enormous sun-drenched spaces where the

cattle grazed and the herds of zebra and gazelle roamed at will under the blue cloud shadows that drifted by as idly as sailing ships on a summer sea. It would be wonderful to see it again. It would be like going home. And *Flamingo* would be a home to her. Aunt Emily had said so. Aunt Emily needed her, and it was so comforting to be needed again. As for Eden, he was happily married, and Alice was 'such a dear girl'. The past was over and done with. She need not think of it.

The stewardess of the air liner said: 'Fasten your safety belts please,' and Mrs Brocas-Gill said: 'Wake up, dear. We're going down to land. Are you feeling all right? You're looking very pale.'

'No,' said Victoria a trifle breathlessly. 'No. I'm all right thank you. It's just that——'

The plane tilted on one shining wing and the ground rushed up to meet it. And then they were skimming low over roof-tops and trees and grass and bumping down a long runway, and Victoria was thinking frantically and desperately and futilely: I shouldn't have come! I shouldn't have come! What shall I do when I see Eden? It isn't all over—it won't ever be all over! I shouldn't have come...

4

The sun was blindingly bright on the white walls of the Airport, and there seemed to be a great many people meeting the plane. But there was no sign of Lady Emily. Or of Eden.

A small stout man with a red face and bald head, wearing a singularly crumpled suit and, somewhat surprisingly, a revolver in an enormous leather holster, waved a white panama enthusiastically from beyond the barrier and yelled a welcome to someone called 'Pet'.

'There's Oswin,' said Mrs Brocas-Gill.

'You're late!' shouted Mr Brocas-Gill, stating the obvious. 'Expected you yesterday.'

He embraced his wife and was introduced to Victoria. 'Bless my soul!' said Mr Brocas-Gill. 'Jack Caryll's girl. I remember your father when—— Why, dammit, I remember *you!* Skinny little thing in plaits. Used to ride a zebra. Glad to see you back.'

He relieved his wife of a dressing-case and an overnight bag and trotted beside them into the comparative coolness of the Airport building:

'Who are you stayin' with? Oh, Em. Hmm. Isn't here, is she? Can't understand it! Bad business. Just shows that it doesn't do to get too complacent. Who's meetin' you?'

'I don't know,' confessed Victoria uncertainly.

'Oh well, they're sure to send someone. We'll keep an eye on you for the moment. Hi! Pet——!' He plunged off in pursuit of his wife who had departed to greet a friend.

Left alone Victoria looked about her a little desperately, searching for a familiar face, until her attention was arrested by a man who had just entered the hall and was standing scanning the newly arrived passengers as though he were looking for someone.

He was a tall, slim, sunburnt man in the early thirties, who carried his inches with a peculiar lounging grace that somehow suggested the popular conception of a cowboy. An effect that was heightened by the fact that he, like Oswin Brocas-Gill, wore a belt that supported a revolver. But there the cowboy resemblance ended, for the cut of the carelessly careful coat, in contrast to Oswin's crumpled attire, spoke almost offensively of Savile Row, while his shoes were undoubtedly handmade—though not in Kenya.

It was not, however, his personal appearance that had caught Victoria's attention, but the fact that he was now observing her with interest and a distinct suggestion of distaste. Men were apt to look at Victoria with interest. They had been doing so in increasing numbers since somewhere around her sixteenth birthday, so there was nothing new in that. What was new was the distaste. No man had ever previously regarded her with the coldly critical lack of approval that was in the blue gaze of the gentleman by the doorway, and Victoria involuntarily glanced down to assure herself that she was not showing six inches of petticoat or wearing odd stockings. She was engaged in this apprehensive survey when he crossed the hall and spoke to her:

'Are you Miss Caryll?'

It was an agreeable voice—or would have been agreeable if it had not been for her conviction that for some reason its owner disapproved of her.

'Y-yes,' said Victoria, disconcerted by that disapproval and annoyed to find herself stammering.

The man reached out and calmly possessed himself of the small suitcase she held. 'My name's Stratton. Lady Emily asked me to meet you. You'd better give me your passport and entry permit and all the rest of it, and I'll get someone to deal with it. Got any money on you?'

'A little,' said Victoria.

'You'll have to get it changed into local currency.'

He held out his hand and Victoria found herself meekly surrendering her bag.

'Stay here. You'd better sit on that sofa,' said Mr Stratton, and left her.

Victoria took his advice and sat staring after his retreating back with a mixture of indignation and relief. She could not imagine why Aunt Emily should have sent this disapproving stranger to meet her, but at least it was not Eden.

She had not realized that she could feel like this. So shaken and unsure of herself and so afraid of being hurt. Well, it was entirely her own fault. She had refused to face facts while there was still time, and now it was too late. She leaned back on the sofa and rested her head against the wall behind it, unaware that she was looking exceedingly pale and shaken.

A stout figure bore down upon her, exuding an overpowering wave of expensive scent, and Mrs Brocas-Gill was with her once more, breathing heavily as though she had been running.

'Ah, I see you've heard,' said Mrs Brocas-Gill, panting a little. 'What an appalling reception for you. *Too* dreadful!'

Victoria struggled to her feet, endeavoring to collect her scattered thoughts, and said: 'Aunt Emily's sent someone to meet me. A Mr Stratton.'

'Oh, Drew,' said Mrs Brocas-Gill. 'I wonder she didn't send Gilly Markham. He's her manager, you know. I was telling you about him. I should have thought he was the obvious person to—but then I don't suppose any of the *Flamingo* people could get away today. Too ghastly for you, my dear. Oh, there you are, Oswin. Isn't it *too* dreadful?'

'Yes, yes, yes!' said Mr Brocas-Gill, thrusting passports and permits into his wife's hands. 'Don't let's go over all that again. Hullo, Drew. What are you doing here? Oh, you're collecting Jack's girl, are you? Splendid. Splendid! Was going to keep an eye on her myself until someone turned up. Knew Em wouldn't be here, of course. You'll be all right with Drew, m'dear. We shall be seeing you. Come *on*, Pet! Damned if I'm going to hang around here all day!'

He seized his wife's arm and hurried her away, and Mr Stratton piloted Victoria into the customs shed and said: 'Here's the rest of the your luggage. Have you got the keys? You may have to open them.'

Five minutes later she was out in the bright sunlight again and being driven away from the Airport through an area of ugly slums and unattractive bazaars.

There was nothing in these mean, crowded streets that was in any way familiar to Victoria, or that struck any chord of memory. And as they left the town behind, and eucalyptus trees and vivid masses of bougainvillaea replaced the squalid huts and shop fronts, she caught glimpses between the green trees of neat, white, red-roofed houses—primly British and more suggestive of Welwyn Garden City than Darkest Africa—that could not have been here when she had last driven through Nairobi over sixteen years ago.

Mr Stratton spoke at last, breaking a silence that had lasted since they left the Airport:

'I take it that you didn't get your Aunt's cable? She was afraid you might not. That's why she asked me to call in at the Airport, in case you were on the plane.'

'In *case* I was? I don't understand. What cable?'

'I gather she sent one care of your bank, as she thought you might be spending the last few days with friends.'

'I was,' admitted Victoria, bewildered. 'But why did she cable? Didn't she want me to come?'

'Well, hardly, at a time like this. After all, it's a fairly nasty mess to land you into.'

'What mess?' demanded Victoria. 'Is Aunt Em ill?'

Mr Stratton's head came round with a jerk and the car swerved on the road as though his hands had twitched at the wheel. He said incredulously: 'Do you mean to say you don't know? But surely the Brocas-Gills—— Look, wasn't it in the home papers?'

'Wasn't what in the home papers?' Victoria's eyes were wide with apprehension. 'Aunt Em... *Eden!* He isn't——'

'No,' said Mr Stratton shortly. 'He's all right. It's his wife. She was murdered three days ago. I'm sorry. I thought you'd know. It was on the B.B.C., and it must have been in the home papers.'

'No,' said Victoria unsteadily. 'I mean—I didn't listen to the news. There was so much to do. And I—I missed the papers. How did it happen? Tell me about it, please. I'd rather hear now. Before I meet... Aunt Emily.'

She had hesitated for a moment before speaking her aunt's name, as though she might have intended to use another one, and Mr Stratton, who was at no time unobservant, did not miss it. He turned his head and looked at her, and there was once again, and unmistakably, dislike in the hard line of his mouth and the cold glance of his normally bland blue eyes.

He looked away again and said curtly: 'Alice—Mrs DeBrett—was murdered in the garden of your aunt's house. Someone killed her with a panga—a heavy knife that the Africans use for chopping wood and cutting grass. Your aunt found her. It can't have been a pleasant sight, and though she's bearing up pretty well she was in no state to drive over a hundred miles into Nairobi and back in order to meet you. And neither was Eden. What with the shock, and the police and press swarming all over the place, they've both had a pretty bad time of it. And in any case the funeral's this morning.'

Victoria did not speak, and presently he glanced at her again and suffered a momentary pang of compunction at the sight of her white face. She looked a good deal younger than he had expected her to be, yet she must be at least twenty-four if she had been engaged to Eden DeBrett before he had married Alice. Quite old enough to appreciate the feelings of his wife, who could hardly be expected to welcome the idea of her husband's ex-fiancée as a permanent fixture in the home.

Drew had liked Alice, and he had been sorry for her. And remembering her haggard, defenceless face and haunted eyes, he took a poor view of Miss Caryll, whose arrival seemed to him vulgar and tactless, if not intentionally cruel.

Victoria spoke at last, and in a voice that was barely audible above the hum of the engine:

'I thought it was all over. The Emergency, I mean. Mrs Brocas-Gill said it was. But if the Mau Mau are still murdering people——'

'I see no reason to suppose that it was a Mau Mau killing,' said Drew shortly. 'It merely makes a better headline in the press that way.'

'Then who——?'

'God knows! A maniac. Or someone with a fancied grievance. You never can tell what goes on in an African's head. And there have apparently been a lot of odd and unpleasant happenings at *Flamingo* lately.'

'I knew there was something wrong,' said Victoria in a whisper, and once again Drew's head turned sharply.

'Why do you say that?'

'It—it was Aunt Em's letter. She wrote and asked me if I would come out. She said she was getting too old to do without someone to help her, and that Eden wasn't—and she would rather have someone who belonged, than a stranger. My mother was her only sister you see, and they were fond of each other. But there was something in the way she wrote. As if she had something on her mind that was— Oh, I don't know— But it was an odd letter. A rather frightening one.'

'Frightening in what way?'

'Well—perhaps not frightening. Uncomfortable. She sounded as though she really did need me. Badly. And she'd always been very good to me. My father didn't leave much money, and I know Aunt Em helped with the school bills. So I came.'

'Was that your only reason?'

'No,' said Victoria. She looked up at the blue sky and the blaze of sunlight, and thought of the London rain and fog, and of her longing to live once more under that hot sun and that wide sky. Her lovely mouth curved in the ghost of a smile, and she said softly: 'No. There were other reasons.'

'So I inferred,' said Mr Stratton unpleasantly.

Victoria turned to look at him in surprise, puzzled by his evident hostility, and after a moment or two she said a little diffidently: 'What did you mean about odd and unpleasant things happening at *Flamingo*? What sort of things?'

'Some person or persons unknown has been smashing up your aunt's possessions in a manner usually associated with poltergeists—or ham-handed housemaids.'

'A p-poltergeist! You can't believe that!'

'I don't. I'll start believing in evil spirits only when someone has eliminated all possibility of the evil human element; and not before! Your aunt must have been mad not to send for the police at once, but she's been fighting a rear-guard action with the authorities over her Kikuyu servants for the last five years, and I suppose she wasn't going to give Greg or the D.C. a chance of having them all up and grilling them again, and jailing a handful under suspicion. Trouble is, she's an obstinate old lady, and once she decides on a course of action she sticks to it. She says now that she realized it must be the work of one of her house servants, but that whoever it was must be acting under orders—or threats.'

'But why? Why should anyone do that?'

Mr Stratton shrugged. 'A Mau Mau gang attacked *Flamingo* during the Emergency, and your aunt stood them off and killed several. One of the dead men was rumored to be a relative of the man who calls himself "General Africa" and who is still at large; so it's just on the cards that this is a private vendetta on the part of the "General". He was always one of the more cunning of the Mau Mau leaders, and there has been a story in circulation for several years that he was and still is employed on one of the farms in the Naivasha area.'

'You mean—you *can't* mean that someone, a settler, is deliberately hiding him?' said Victoria incredulously.

'Good lord, no! If it's true, you may be quite sure that his employer hasn't a clue as to his identity, and that he is using that as a cover. Playing the part of a faithful and probably dull-witted retainer by day, and organizing prison breaks and thefts of cattle, and planning bloody murder by night.'

'Surely that isn't possible!'

'Why not? There is no photograph of him in existence and he wears a mask. A square of red silk with holes burned in it for eyes, nose and mouth. None of the men who have turned informer have ever seen his face, so that it's quite possible that he might be going about openly and quite unsuspected. It's also possible that he may have planned this poltergeist business at *Flamingo* as a prelude to murder, and intimidated someone into carrying it out. From all accounts he is intelligent enough to work out a really subtle revenge.'

Victoria shivered despite the hot sunlight, and said: 'I don't see anything subtle about murdering someone with a panga!'

'It isn't the method,' said Drew impatiently. 'It's the murder itself, coming as the climax of a series of petty outrages. If Mrs DeBrett had been murdered out of a blue sky, so to speak, it would have been ghastly enough. But it wouldn't have had half the impact that this has had. Especially on a woman of Lady Emily's temperament. Em can take a straight left to the jaw and survive it, but there's a kind of creeping, cumulative beastliness about this business that makes it all the more frightening for her. A sort of softening-up process. Starting in a small way and getting progressively crueller. She thought it was only an attempt to scare her into selling up and getting out, but when her dog was poisoned she ought to have been warned. That was what Gilly Markham called a "sighting shot". It seems to have scared *him* all right! He's manager at *Flamingo*.'

They were passing through the Kikuyu Reserve, and the scenery was at last vaguely familiar to Victoria: terraced hillsides and clusters of neat round beehive huts; fields of maize and small white patches of pyrethrum; the spiky foliage of pineapples and the vivid green of vegetables and banana palms. Mile upon mile of native shambas, bright against the red-ochre clay, and interspersed with plantations of eucalyptus. But Victoria had no eyes for the scenery. Even the sunlight had ceased to feel warm and gay, and she felt cold and a little sick. '*A sighting shot . . .*'

She turned sharply to look at her companion, and

spoke a little breathlessly: 'Is it the end? Or——'

She found that she could not finish the sentence, but Mr Stratton appeared to have no difficulty in translating her confused utterance. He said:

'I imagine it's that thought that is getting Em down. Ever since it started it's been a case of "What next?" Now I should say it's "Who's next?"'

'*Eden!*' said Victoria in a whisper, unaware that she had spoken aloud.

Drew gave her a cold glance and said curtly: 'Why do you think that?'

'Who else would it be? Unless—unless it were Aunt Em herself.'

'Oh, I don't know,' said Drew with deliberate brutality. 'Anyone she liked—or who was useful to her. Or to *Flamingo*.'

'I don't believe it!' said Victoria suddenly and flatly. 'Things like that don't really happen. Not to real people.'

'They've happened this time,' said Drew dryly.

'Oh, I don't mean that Eden's wife hasn't been killed. That must be true. But the other things. There must be some quite ordinary explanation. After all, things get broken in everyone's houses. And the dog might have picked up poison that was meant for rats—or, something.'

'Have it your own way,' said Drew.

'But don't you think it could have been that?'

'No, I don't. I think someone was getting at your aunt. And very successfully, at that! This isn't merely a question of getting rid of a settler. Even the Mau Mau dupes didn't take long to drive up to the fact that if they killed one white settler another one—

and not his Kikuyu servants!—would take over. If Em died tomorrow, and Eden the day after, another white settler would take over *Flamingo*.'

'I should,' said Victoria.

Drew's blond eyebrows twitched together in a sudden startled frown and he said slowly: 'Yes, I suppose so. I'd forgotten that you'd be the next-of-kin. Well, there you are, you see. That's why I don't believe that this poltergeist business was aimed at frightening a large landowner into doing a scuttle. In any case, anyone who knew the least thing about Em would know it wouldn't work; and whoever is at the back of this knows a great deal about her, and just how to hit her where it hurts most. Which is what makes me interested in this "General Africa" theory. The average African gets no pleasure out of just shooting an enemy. He prefers to kill him slowly, and watch him suffer.'

It can't be true! thought Victoria. And yet worse things had happened in this country; far worse things. And he was carrying a gun. He didn't look the sort of person who would carry a gun without a good reason for doing so. She said abruptly: 'What about the police? Surely they'll be able to find out who did it?'

'Smashed Em's bric-à-brac?' enquired Drew.

'No. Who killed Mrs DeBrett. People don't get away with murder!'

'You'd be surprised what they get away with in this country!' said Drew cynically.

'But didn't anyone hear anything? Surely she would have screamed?'

'I expect she did, poor girl. But as luck would

have it your aunt was playing the piano, and so no one in the house would have heard her. I should never have left her.'

'You?' said Victoria. 'Were you there?'

'Yes,' said Drew bitterly. 'In fact I was the last person, bar the murderer, who saw her alive. I knew she never carried a gun, and it was getting dark; but it was only a short distance to the house and it seemed safe enough. I could even hear that damned piano! Oh well—what the hell's the use of making excuses for oneself now? It's done.'

He wrenched savagely at the wheel as they swerved to avoid a stray goat, and accelerated as though speed afforded him escape from his thoughts.

'But there must have been *some* clues,' persisted Victoria. 'Footmarks—tracks—bloodstains. *Something!*'

'You've been reading detective stories,' remarked Drew satirically. 'Possibly in books the body is not moved and no one mucks up the ground, but it's apt to happen differently in real life. Your aunt wasn't thinking of clues when she found her grandson's wife dead in the garden. All she could think of was that she might possibly be alive, and she tried to carry her to the house. She almost managed it, too! But she had to fetch one of the house boys in the end, and by the time the D.C. and the doctor and Greg Gilbert and various other people arrived, the "scene of the crime" had been pretty well messed up.'

Victoria said: 'Didn't they find anything, then?'

'Yes. They found a blood-stained cushion, belonging to one of the verandah chairs, in the long grass about twenty feet or so from where Mrs DeBrett's body was found. It looked as though it had been thrown there. And they found some marks amoung the bushes that seemed to suggest that someone had been standing there for quite a time, presumably watching her. There's a track that runs through the bushes and that links up at least three of the lakeside estates. It's an unofficial short cut that the labour use, and that the Mau Mau undoubtedly used during the Emergency.'

'So it was a gang murder after all!' said Victoria with a catch of the breath.

'Perhaps,' said Drew. 'But not on that evidence. Whoever had been watching from the bushes had never left them. The ground just there is pretty dusty, and it was obvious that he had merely turned and gone back the way he came.'

5

The car had been singing down a long straight stretch of road when it brought up suddenly with a screech of tortured tyres, and an abruptness that jerked Victoria forward and narrowly missed bringing her head into violent contact with the windscreen.

'Sorry,' said Mr Stratton, 'but I believe that was a friend of mine.'

He put the gear lever into reverse and backed some fifty yards through a dust cloud of his own making, to draw up alongside a stationary car that stood jacked up on the grassy verge where an African driver wrestled with a recalcitrant tyre.

A tall European in shirtsleeves and wearing a green pork-pie hat jammed on the back of his head appeared from the other side of it, wiping dust and sweat off his face with a handkerchief, and came to lean his elbows on the window of Mr Stratton's car:

'I might have known it,' he remarked bitterly. 'My God, Drew, the next time you do that I'll have you up for dangerous driving and get you sixty days without the option if it's the last thing I do! Didn't you see me flagging you?'

'No,' admitted Mr Stratton, unabashed. 'My mind was on other things. Greg, you won't have met Miss Caryll. Miss Caryll, this is Mr Gilbert, our local S.P.—Superintendent of Police, Naivasha.'

Mr Gilbert reached across him and shook hands with Victoria. He was a long, lean man who except for the fact that his hair was streaked with grey at the temples did not appear to be much older than Mr Stratton. His square, pleasant face was less deeply sunburnt than Drew's, and he possessed a pair of sleepy grey eyes that were anything but a true guide to his character and capabilities.

'You must be Lady Emily's niece,' said Mr Gilbert. 'She told me you were coming out, but I understood that she'd sent a cable to stop you.'

'Yes, I know. I didn't get it. I——'

'Do you want a lift, Greg?' cut in Mr Stratton, brusquely interrupting the sentence.

The S.P. threw him a quick look of surprise. 'Are you in a hurry?' he enquired.

'Not particularly, but Miss Caryll could probably do with something to eat. Her plane was late. Where do you want to be dropped?'

'Same place as Miss Caryll. *Flamingo*.'

'Oh. Anything new cropped up?'

'Not much,' admitted the S.P. climbing into the back of the car. He called out a few instructions to his driver and sat back, urging Mr Stratton to abstain from doing more than fifty: 'My nerves are shot to pieces. I thought we'd finished with this sort of thing for the time being, and I find it pretty exhausting when it crops up again. Old James has gone straight in off the deep end. I've never known him to be in such a bad temper. He bit my head off this morning for making some innocuous remark about the weather.'

'Where was this?' asked Drew, re-starting the car.

'Up at the Lab. They'd been doing a test on that ruddy verandah cushion.'

'Any results?'

'Oh, Alice's of course. Or same blood group, anyway. It was unlikely to be anyone else's. But it was just as well to make sure. Odd, though.'

He tilted his hat over his nose, and closed his eyes. Victoria twisted round in her seat to face him, and as though he were aware of the movement he opened them again and said: 'I must apologize for talking shop, but I'm afraid you're in for a lot of this. In fact you couldn't have chosen a worse time to arrive, and I wish I could suggest that you turn right round and go back again; though I can see that it is hardly practicable.'

'I wouldn't go if it was,' said Victoria with decision.

'Why not?' enquired Drew shortly.

Victoria turned her head to look at him, aware for the first time that his antagonism was personal and not a mere matter of irritation or bad temper. She said coldly: 'I should have thought it was obvious. If my aunt needed someone to help her before, she must need it even more now.'

She met his gaze with a hostility that equalled his own, and then deliberately turned her shoulder to him and gave her attention to the view.

The road wound and dipped through hot sunlight and chequered shadows, and swinging to the right came out abruptly on to the crest of a huge escarpment. And there below them, spread out at their feet like a map drawn upon yellowed parchment, lay the Great Rift. A vast golden valley of sun-bleached grass, speckled by scrub and flat-topped thorn trees, and seamed with dry gullies; hemmed in to left and right by the two great barriers of the Kinangop and the Mau, and dominated by the rolling lava falls and cold, gaping crater of Longonot, standing sentinel at its gate.

Nothing has changed! thought Victoria. But she knew that was not true. The passing of a handful of years might have made little difference, superficially, to the Rift, but everything else had changed. And looking out over that stupendous view she was dismayed to find that her eyes were full of tears.

At the foot of the escarpment the road ceased to wind and twist. The forests of cedar and wild olive fell away, and the car touched ninety miles an hour and held it on the long straight ribbon of tarmac that the Italian prisoners-of-war had built in the war years, until at last they could see the shining levels of Lake Naivasha.

'Might I suggest,' said Mr Gilbert gently, breaking a silence that had lasted for some considerable time, 'that you slow down to sixty before you take the turn? I have no wish to provide Naivasha with two funerals within twenty-four hours, and neither am I in any hurry to meet the mourners.'

Drew removed his foot from the accelerator, and as the car slowed down and swung left-handed into an unmade side road that branched off the tarmac of the main Nairobi road to circle the lake, Victoria said huskily: 'When is it—the funeral?'

'Eleven o'clock. Didn't Drew tell you? That's why none of them could meet you. But they'll have got back by now. How long is it since you last saw your aunt?'

'Six years,' said Victoria.

'Then I'm afraid you'll notice quite a change in her. This business has hit her pretty badly. She always seemed to me like a bit of the Kenya landscape—eternal and indestructible. But now she's suddenly an old lady. It's like seeing a landmark crumble. Poor old Em!'

'I can't see why you have to bother her, today of all days,' said Mr Stratton disagreeably. 'You might at least spare them a further grilling on the day of the funeral. It's going to be bad enough for them to have to— Oh, well. It's none of my business.'

'None,' agreed Mr Gilbert equably. 'For which you can be devoutly grateful. Asking personal questions on this sort of occasion, and of people who are your friends, is not exactly a pleasant task, I assure you. But the fact that we now know for certain whose blood was on the cushion opens up a new field of enquiry. It's an odd facet of the case, that cushion. What was it doing there, and why?'

Drew said: 'No one heard Alice screaming, and she must have screamed. I know that was probably because Em was playing the piano, but there might be another explanation.'

'You mean the cushion might have been used to smother her? I don't believe it. It would have been damned difficult to hold a cushion over the face of a struggling woman while hacking at her with a panga. Unless there were two people in it. But— No, somehow I don't think that it was that. I can't get it out of my head that that cushion ought to tell me something if I weren't too stupid to see it. It doesn't fit.'

'With what?' demanded Mr Stratton, swerving to avoid a pothole of unusually outrageous dimensions that added to the hazards of the dusty, unmetalled road.

'With any of the obvious theories. That cushion was removed from the verandah and carried to the spot where Alice was killed, and then thrown away into the long grass. Yet no one will admit to having touched it that day.'

Drew said: 'I suppose it hasn't occurred to you that Mrs DeBrett might have taken it down herself to sit on, and was merely carrying it back? Or is that a too simple solution for you and your sleuths to contemplate?'

'You should know the answer to that one,' said Mr Gilbert amiably. 'You were the last person to admit to seeing her alive. Was she carrying a brightly coloured cushion?'

'No,' said Drew, 'but——'

'But you think that despite the fact that the sun

had set, and that it is apt to get a bit chilly around dusk, she went all the way back to the house in order to fetch one off the verandah? I doubt it! Yet someone took it out there, and I'd like to know why. If I did, I imagine we'd be a lot further on. But as it is, I don't know what to think, and all the things I do think of are decidedly unpleasant. I don't like anything about this case, and I wish to God I could wash my hands of it!'

'Why not hand it over to the C.I.D. squad from Nakuru?'

'I've tried that one, but this time it won't work. They happen to have rather a lot on their plate just now, what with the Hansford case and that Goldfarb business, and James says I can dam' well handle it myself—even though half my personal friends are involved.'

'You mean *because* half your personal friends are involved,' said Mr Stratton dryly. 'You know us all very well. Too well!'

The S.P. made no reply; which might have meant anything—or nothing.

The cold shadow of a cloud drifted across the sunlit scene, draining the colour from the grass and the flat-topped thorn trees and lending the landscape a fleeting suggestion of aloofness and hostility, and Victoria shivered again and was suddenly afraid: afraid of the valley and of Africa, and of arriving at *Flamingo*, the house that was Eden's home and where Eden's wife had died a horrible death.

What have I let myself in for? thought Victoria in a panic. What does he mean? That someone in the house is a murderer? Eden's wife— She's dead now. He's free. I should never have come...

The car ran out of the belt of shadow and past two tall Masai warriors, each carrying a serviceable spear; the red-gold of their lean, ochre-smeared bodies and elaborately plaited hair, and the clean-cut lines of their haughty aquiline features, reminiscent of ancient Egypt. Recognizing the car, they saluted gravely: a courteous salute tinged with gracious condescension, such as might have been accorded by the delegates of a powerful state to a member of a small and friendly nation.

'They don't change much either,' commented Mr Gilbert, following up a private train of thought. 'The Masai are the only ones who have looked at the things of the West and decided that they prefer their own ways, and have stuck to them. Who can say they are not right? The modern African youth with his European clothes and his inferiority complexes is not impressive, but it has never so much as crossed the minds of the Masai that they might be inferior to anyone.'

'Boot's on the other foot!' said Drew laconically, and Greg Gilbert laughed.

Victoria said: 'Father used to employ Mkamba. I can still remember most of them by name. They used to carry bows and arrows in those days—poisoned arrows, too!'

'They still do,' said Mr Gilbert with a grin. 'And that despite the fact that it is strictly against the law! I should say that at a conservative estimate several tons of arrow poison are manufactured yearly in this country. Talk about the "Secret Arrow Poison of the South American Indians!"—this has it licked into a cocked hat, for the simple reason that it's no secret. All you need is a saucepan, a box of matches and grandmother's recipe. The ingredients are growing all over the landscape, and——'

He broke off and hurriedly wound up the car windows as a black and grey sedan raced towards them and shot past, enveloping them in a choking cloud of dust.

'Ken Brandon,' said Drew briefly.

'Oh. How's he taken it?'

'On the chin,' said Drew.

'He's a spoilt brat. These conceited, mannerless young egoists bore me to distraction. Hector is pretty hot on the subject of motes in his neighbour's eye, but young Ken is the outstanding beam in his own.'

'You mean in Mabel's,' corrected Drew dryly. 'Ken is Mabel's sun, moon and stars, and always will be. She is devoted to Hector, but she'd probably have walked out on him if he'd laid a finger on her darling boy. She may be half Hector's size, and a dear, but she's quite capable of standing up to him.'

'I still don't think that excuses him,' grunted Mr Gilbert. 'Or his son! What Alice must have gone through with that boy is nobody's business!'

'It isn't ours, at any rate,' said Drew shortly.

'There,' corrected the S.P., 'you are wrong. It happens to be mine. Anyone or anything that had to do with Alice DeBrett is, at the moment, my business. And that,' he added gently, 'includes you.'

'Um,' said Mr Stratton thoughtfully, and refrained from further comment.

Five miles and eight minutes later a square, weather-beaten notice board bearing the single word '*Flamingo*' came in sight, and the car turned off the lake road on to a rough track that crossed a stretch of barren, rock-strewn ground bordered at the far side by a thick belt of trees and a glint of water. The wheels bumped in and out of deep dust-filled ruts and over and around boulders, roots and hummocks of parched grass, and leaving the hard sunlight, ran under the freckled shadows of pepper trees and giant acacias, to emerge on to a wide smooth sweep of ground before a long, rambling, thatch-roofed house whose bow windows and deep verandahs looked out on the glittering expanse of Lake Naivasha, blue and beautiful in the full blaze of the noonday.

What appeared at first sight to be half a dozen dogs of assorted shapes and sizes rushed out to greet them, barking vociferously, followed by two African houseboys wearing green robes and scarlet tarbooshes, who hurried out to remove suitcases and assist the travellers to alight. A door at the far end of the verandah opened, and an arresting figure walked towards them and stood waiting at the top of a shallow flight of stone steps. The Lady Emily DeBrett of *Flamingo*.

Em had worn a dark coat and skirt for the funeral, but she had discarded them immediately upon her return, and had changed back into the scarlet dungarees and vivid blouse that were her favoured wear.

Her white closely cropped hair was adorned with a wide-brimmed hat of multi-coloured straw of the type that tourists buy in such places as Ceylon and Zanzibar, and there were diamonds in her ears and on her gnarled and capable hands and imposing bosom. She should have presented a grotesque appearance, but somehow she did not. She might, instead, have been the Queen of some barbaric kingdom. Hatshepsut of Egypt. Old Tzu-hsi, the Dowager Empress of China. Or Elizabeth the First, old and raddled and dying, but still indomitable: still royal.

Em had at no time been demonstrative, but she greeted Victoria with an unusual display of affection which contained, despite herself, a strong suggestion of relief.

'It's so good to see you, dear,' said Em, embracing her. 'And so good of you to come. I am sorry not to have been able to meet you at the Airport; but then Drew will have explained everything. We need not talk of that just now. How well you look. And how like your mother! You might be Helen all over again. Come along into the house. Drew will——'

She stopped as her gaze fell upon Greg Gilbert, and Victoria felt her stiffen. 'Greg! I didn't know you were here. Did you want to see me?'

'I'm afraid so,' said Mr Gilbert, leisurely mounting the verandah steps. 'I'm sorry about this, Em, but needs must. One or two things have cropped up. I won't keep you long. Eden here?'

'You are not,' announced Em with deliberation, 'going to worry Eden with any more questions today. And that is that! I like you, Greg, but there are some things I will not put up with, even from my friends. If you must worry the servants again, I suppose I can't stop you. But you can leave Eden alone. He can't tell you any more than he has already told you. None of us can!'

'I'm sorry, Em,' repeated Mr Gilbert quietly. 'I'm not doing this for choice.'

Lady Emily's bosom swelled alarmingly until the seams of her scarlet blouse appeared to be in imminent danger of parting. And then all at one she appeared to deflate, both physically and mentally. She stretched out a hand to him and spoke in a voice that was no longer measured and autocratic, but pleading:

'Greg, you can't! Not now. Not today. Surely it can wait?'

Mr Gilbert did not reply, and after a moment her hand dropped and she turned away and spoke to Victoria:

'Come dear, you will want to see your room. Drew, you will find drinks in the drawing-room. Help yourself. Greg had better stay to luncheon as he's here. He can ask his questions afterwards.'

The invitation could hardly have been less pressing, but Mr Gilbert said placidly: 'Thanks, I will," and followed them into the house.

The room that was to be Victoria's was large and comfortable, with windows that looked out on to a wide strip of lawn, a blaze of bougainvillaea and a view of the lake. Em sat down on the edge of the big old-fashioned bed as though she were very tired, and said: 'I hope you will be comfortable here, dear. And happy.'

Victoria said warmly: 'Of course I shall be, Aunt Em! It's so lovely to be back in Kenya. I can't tell you how grateful I am to you for all your kindness.'

'I have not been kind,' said Em heavily. 'I have been selfish. But I needed someone to help me, and I didn't want a stranger—some secretary who would spread gossip about *Flamingo* to half the Colony. I thought if I could only keep it to the family...' Her voice trailed away, and she shivered.

Victoria came quickly across the room and put her arms about her aunt's sagging shoulders and hugged her. 'It wasn't selfish of you, darling. It was wonderful of you to want me. If only you knew how nice it is to feel wanted again!'

Em patted her hand absently and was silent for a moment or two, and then her fingers tightened suddenly about Victoria's wrist and she looked up into her niece's face with eyes that were bright and intent and full of anxiety. She said harshly, and as though she were forcing herself to speak: 'You must choose for yourself, Victoria. I did not—I was not honest with you when I wrote. I did not tell you everything. Perhaps I was afraid that you might not come. But you are Helen's child, and you must have your chance to decide whether you will go or stay. No!—don't interrupt! Let me say what I want, and then it will be your turn——

'I shall not blame you if you decide not to stay. Remember that. I sent you a cable to try and stop you, but it must have missed you. I do not know how much Drew Stratton will have told you, but I suppose you know that Eden's wife was murdered. There is rumour that the remnant of a Mau Mau gang are hiding out somewhere near here, but the police cannot be certain that it is they who are responsible, because—because there have been strange things happening in this house for some weeks past. Not very serious things, but—but worrying, of course. It has meant that all my servants are under suspicion, which is not very pleasant. So if you would prefer not to stay, I shall quite understand.'

Victoria said: 'But of course I'm going to stay, Aunt Em. If you'll let me. Or even if you won't. Just try to get rid of me!'

Em's fingers relaxed their hold, and she said approvingly: 'Good girl.' The emotion and the strain vanished from her face and she stood up briskly and said: 'Luncheon will be ready as soon as you are. You will find us in the drawing-room.'

The door closed behind her, and Victoria turned to stare thoughtfully at her own reflection in the looking glass: a slim, remarkably pretty girl in a leaf-green frock.

'Yes of course I'm going to stay!' said Victoria, speaking aloud in the silence. 'I belong in Kenya. And as for Eden, that's all over and done with—so don't let's have any more nonsense about it!'

She nodded severely at her reflected face, and went off to the bathroom to remove the dust of the lake road.

6

There were four people waiting in the large, casual, beautiful drawing-room: Em, Greg Gilbert, Drew Stratton and Eden.

Eden had been standing by the window talking to Drew when Victoria entered, and he had turned when he heard the door open, and stopped in the middle of a sentence, looking at her.

There was a brief moment of silence, and it was Eden who spoke first; his voice an echo from a day six years ago when he had spoken to a girl in a yellow dress who held an armful of roses. *'Vicky——!'*

Victoria closed the door behind her and said lightly: 'Hullo, Eden. I hope I haven't kept you waiting, Aunt Em?'

Luncheon was an uncomfortable meal, full of odd, abrupt silences and patches of forced conversation.

No mention was made of the funeral or any of the happenings of the last three days, and it was not until coffee had been drunk in the drawing-room and Zacharia had removed the empty cups, that Mr Gilbert at last referred to the errand that had brought him to *Flamingo*.

'I'm sorry about this,' apologized Greg, 'but owing to one thing and another I'm afraid I shall have to ask a few more questions.'

'I thought every African on the estate had already been questioned *ad nauseam*,' said Eden bitterly. 'What more do you think you'll get out of them?'

'Not much,' admitted Greg equably. 'But then I'm not really interested in them at the moment. I merely want to know a few more things about last Tuesday. Your movements, for instance.'

'My *what?*' Eden's handsome face was suddenly white with anger and he said furiously: 'Are you by any chance suggesting that I might have murdered my own wife? Because if you are——'

'Don't be ridiculous, Eden!' Em's voice was sharp and commanding. 'Of course he doesn't mean any such thing! We all know how you feel, but I presume that Greg has got to ask this sort of question, so at least let us get it over quickly, and without losing our tempers.'

Greg said pacifically: 'No one is accusing you of anything. But if we can tie up everyone's movements on that day it will at least help to fill in the background. So let's start with yours.'

The colour came back to Eden's face and he thrust his hands into his pockets and turned away to stare blindly out of the window at the sunlit garden. He said: 'You already know exactly where I was and what I was doing that day. You've heard it all before.'

'Roughly, yes. "Exactly"—no.' Gilbert broke off and looked at Drew Stratton. 'Thinking of going anywhere, Drew?'

'Yes,' said Mr Stratton, preparing to leave. 'I can't see that I am serving any useful purpose by staying. See you later, Em, and thanks for the luncheon.'

Mr Gilbert said: 'Just sit down again, will you? I was coming to see you later, but if I can get what I want now it will save me a ten mile drive. You too, Miss Caryll.'

Em said haughtily: 'There is no question that you need ask my niece. She was not even here, and she knows nothing about this.'

'There is one question at least that I think she can answer,' said Greg quietly, 'and I would like her to stay.'

He turned back to Eden before Em could speak, and said: 'You went to Nairobi on Tuesday, didn't you?'

'Yes. To see Jimmy Druce about a Land-Rover he wants to sell. We had luncheon at Muthaiga. You can check up with him if you like.'

'We have. And you left here about ten o'clock. Can you by any chance remember if all the verandah cushions were present and correct when you left?'

'Of course I can't! I don't even know how many there are.'

'Four, I believe,' said Greg. 'And they are fairly striking.'

'I still wouldn't have noticed if there were three or six or a dozen! It's not the sort of thing that anyone would notice.'

'Except Zacharia,' said Mr Gilbert thoughtfully. 'He should have known, but he insists that he can't remember.'

'He's getting old,' said Em in extenuation.

'Ye—s. All the same, you'd think he'd notice a thing like that. It's part of his job. And anything in Harlequin checks and primary colours is apt to be eye-catching. Which makes it look as though they were all there. He would probably have noticed if there was one short.'

Em said: 'So you think that someone removed it off the verandah sometime during the day, and you don't think it's likely to have been done by a stray terrorist from some hide-out in the *marula*.'

'Do you?' enquired Mr Gilbert.

'No,' said Em bleakly. 'No.'

She had been sitting regally erect in a large wing-back chair by the piano, but now she seemed to shrink and crumble and change before their eyes from a vigorous and commanding figure into a tired and anxious old woman. 'You are right, of course. It would have had to be someone from this house.'

'Or someone who could come openly to this house,' amended Mr Gilbert. 'And there is always, of course, the possibility that it was taken out for some entirely unimportant and trivial reason. So trivial that whoever did it has forgotten about it.

Which is why, if we can work out where everyone was at every moment of that day, it may jolt someone's memory. What did you do after luncheon, Eden?'

Eden started slightly at the abruptness of the question, and said: 'Shopped in the town. Fetched a suit from the cleaners, collected a clock that had been taken in to be mended, bought a couple of shirts and took in a film to be developed. I think that was all.'

Mr Gilbert consulted a small notebook that he had removed from his coat pocket, and nodded as if satisfied. It was obvious that he had been doing quite a bit of checking on his own, and he made no attempt to conceal the fact. He said: 'Where did you have tea, and when?'

'I didn't. I skipped it.'

'When did you start back?'

'Oh—er—around about seven, I suppose. I'm not sure.'

Mr Gilbert said thoughtfully: 'The shops shut at five, and according to Jimmy Druce you left the Club just after two. Were you really shopping for three hours?'

Eden flushed angrily and said: 'No, of course I wasn't. As a matter of fact, I drove out to the Game Park.'

'When was that?'

'About four, I suppose. Might have been a little earlier. But you won't be able to check that, because I didn't get there. I remembered that the Park is infernally crowded these days, so I pulled up by the side of the road instead, and just sat there.'

'Why?'

'I had a few things I wanted to think about,' said Eden shortly. 'And none of them, Greg, if I may say so, are any of your dam' business!'

Mr Gilbert shrugged and consulted his notebook again. He said: 'Any idea as to how long you sat there? And did anyone you know pass you?'

'No. I wasn't paying attention to passing people, and I only pushed off at last because it was getting late. I'd told Alice I probably wouldn't be back until nine or ten, and I'd meant to dine in Nairobi or somewhere on the road. But I decided that I'd get back for a late meal here after all. I got back here about nine o'clock, and found——'

He did not finish the sentence, but turned once more to stare out of the window.

Mr Gilbert said briskly: 'Thanks very much. Now what about you, Em? First of all, have you remembered anything about that cushion? Moving it, or noticing that it was missing—or not missing?'

'No,' said Em doubtfully. 'I—I may have moved it. But I must admit that I don't remember doing so, and I don't think that there is anything I would have wanted it for. Perhaps Alice did.'

'When?' demanded Greg. 'Her day has been pretty well accounted for. She spent the morning shopping in Naivasha, the afternoon in her room, had tea with you on the verandah, and went out shooting with you immediately afterwards—in order to avoid, I gather, what looked like being an embarrassing *tête-à-tête* with young Ken Brandon. And as it was just after you got back that she went across to the Markhams with a message for Lisa, there doesn't seem to be any point during the day when she could have carried a cushion out to the knoll. Now, can you remember what you yourself did on Tuesday, Em? In detail?'

'I think so,' said Em, frowning. 'Let me see—I had breakfast in bed and didn't get up until just before Eden left. I asked him to fetch the clock and to ring up the Airport and check the time that Victoria would be arriving, and we discussed the purchase of Jimmy's Land-Rover. After Eden had gone I saw the cook and told Kamau what I wanted in the way of vegetables, and then Alice and I made out a list of things we wanted from the stores in Naivasha. As soon as she had gone I started on the milk records, and then Lisa came over to see Eden, but Zacharia told her he'd left. She said she wouldn't disturb me, and left a note asking if we'd give her a lift next time either of us went into Nairobi. I heard the dogs barking and went to see who it was, but she was already half-way across the garden by then, so I didn't stop her.'

Greg said: 'Do the dogs always bark when anyone comes to the house?'

'If they're around. But they stop at once if it's anyone they know.'

'What time was it when Lisa came over?'

'About twenty to eleven I should say: Alice had just left. Then at eleven Gilly came over on business and stayed for half an hour, and he'd only just gone when the Brandons dropped in. We had coffee, and Hector went off to see Kamau about some fodder we're selling him, while Mabel and I talked.'

'What about?'

The question was asked so casually that Em had started to answer it before she realized where it would lead her. 'She'd seen Alice's car in Naivasha and knew she wouldn't be here, and she wanted to see me alone because she was worried about——'

She stopped abruptly, her face flushing in the unbecoming and mottled manner of the old, while her lips folded into a tight hard line.

Eden gave a short and mirthless laugh, and finished the sentence for her. 'About Ken. You needn't worry, Gran darling. It's no secret. What did she want you to do? Ship Alice home, or slip some arsenic in her soup?'

'Eden!' Once again Em's voice was sharp and commanding, and this time it was edged with anger.

'I'm sorry,' said Eden impatiently. 'I quite see that under the present circumstances that was a bloody silly remark to make. But you must admit that Mabel's been making a complete cake of herself over her precious Ken. It wasn't Alice's fault that her kid had a hopeless crush on her. Heaven knows she did everything she could to choke him off! But it wasn't at all easy for her, what with Ken threatening suicide and generally behaving like an amateur actor getting his teeth into Hamlet. She ought to have let me deal with him.'

'She was quite right not to,' said Em tartly. 'She took the very sensible view that it was really only like measles or teething—something that everyone gets when young, though some children get it worse than others. He'd have got over it soon enough. But if you'd taken a hand and lectured him, we'd have had a first class Brandon-DeBrett feud on our hands, and we neither of us wanted that. Hector and Mabel are good friends of mine, and good neighbors; but Ken is their Achilles heel.'

'Ken,' said Eden morosely, echoing sentiments recently expressed by Mr Gilbert, 'is a spoilt, egotistical pup who fancies himself as a cross between Byron and an Angry Young Man. For God's sake, what's he got to be crazy or mixed up about? He's only had to ask for something, to be given it!'

'Perhaps that's why,' said Em with a sigh. 'He's just finding out that now he is grown up there are a good many things he can't have for the asking, and he feels that someone is to blame for it. He'll grow out of it.'

'Returning to Mabel,' said Mr Gilbert firmly. 'How long did she stay on Tuesday morning, and could she have removed that cushion?'

'No, of course she didn't!' said Em with a snap. 'Why on earth should she?'

'That's not the point. The question was "could she?" Or was she with you the entire time?'

'Well, no,' said Em reluctantly. 'I— Well it was all rather stupid really. I suppose I wasn't very sympathetic, and Mabel was hurt. She said she'd wait in the garden until Hector was ready to leave, and I went back to the office. But if you think that Mabel had anything to do with Alice's murder, you must be going out of your mind! She was a bit upset about this infatuation of Ken's, but that was all. And of course she had nothing to do with that cushion. Unless——'

She paused, frowning, and Greg said: 'Unless what?'

'Well, I suppose she might have taken it up to the knoll and sat there to wait for Hector. I never thought of that. There you are—I expect that's all there is to it. A perfectly simple explanation.'

'Perfectly,' said Greg. 'But if so, why didn't she admit to it? We asked everyone about it the next day.'

'I expect she forgot,' said Em flatly.

'Perhaps. We can always try and jog her memory. What did you do for the rest of the day?'

'Nothing special. Alice got back around one, and after luncheon I rested, and as you already know we had tea on the verandah at half-past four. Ken arrived in the middle of it, so we had to offer him some. He said he wanted to discuss something with Alice, but I said he would have to postpone it as she was coming out in the Land-Rover with me. I was rather afraid that he'd still be there when we got back, but he wasn't.'

'What time did you get back?'

'About a quarter to six. It was only then that I remembered Lisa's note, and Alice said she'd walk over and tell her that I'd be going into Nairobi on the Thursday to meet Victoria, and she could come in then. I shouldn't have let her go. But—how was I to know?'

Em's voice cracked and Eden crossed the space between them in two strides and put an arm about his grandmother's shoulders. 'Don't, Gran! It wasn't your fault. You've nothing to blame yourself for.'

Em said almost inaudibly: 'Yes I have. If I hadn't sent her over— Or if I had only——'

Eden released her and said harshly: 'If!—if, if,

if! Why worry yourself over ifs?— If I hadn't married Alice she wouldn't have come to Kenya. And if she hadn't come to Kenya she wouldn't have been murdered. But does that mean that I am responsible for her death?'

He flung away and dropped into another chair, his legs stretched out before him and his hands deep in his pockets, and Mr Gilbert regarded him thoughtfully for a moment or two, and then turned his attention to Drew Stratton.

'Now about you, Drew. I'd like an account—a detailed account, please—of your last meeting with Mrs DeBrett.'

'I'll try,' said Drew, and embarked on a reasonably accurate account of that evening. 'She was,' he ended deliberately, 'very much upset at the prospect of Miss Caryll's arrival.'

Victoria shrank back in her chair as though he had struck her, while Eden flushed a dull red and Em said indignantly: 'That is not true! You are imagining things. I told her that if she would rather Victoria did not come she had only to say so.'

Drew said: 'Lady Emily, I did not know your granddaughter-in-law very well. But I knew her well enough to know that she would not allow her own feelings in the matter to stand in the way of your wishes; and I cannot imagine any normal woman feeling much enthusiasm for having an ex-fiancée of her husband's installed as a permanent fixture in the home.'

'Is that true?' demanded Mr Gilbert of Victoria. 'Were you two engaged?'

'I——' began Victoria, but got no further. Eden

was on his feet again, his handsome face ugly with anger.

'No it is not! There was at one time what I believe is termed an "understanding" between us, but it was a purely private matter, and still is. So you needn't think that you're going to wash a lot of dirty linen in public and drag Victoria into this beastly business. You can keep her out of it!'

'My dear Eden, no one is trying to drag Miss Caryll into anything,' said Greg pacifically. 'But, unfortunately, the personal relationships of people who are involved, however inadvertently, in a murder case, are always a matter of interest.'

'Victoria is not "involved" in any of this!'

'Only indirectly.'

Em straightened herself in the wing-back chair, and once again it was an autocrat who sat there, imperious, regal and accustomed to being obeyed. She said: 'I think we had better get this quite straight, Greg. I am not a fool, and I dislike beating about the bush. It wastes time. What you are attempting to discover is whether Eden, or possibly myself, murdered Alice—*be quiet, Eden!* That is it, isn't it?'

'As a matter of fact,' said Mr Gilbert, 'and speaking solely for myself— No. But that is because you are both personal friends of mine and I know you fairly well. Speaking officially, however, it is not outside the bounds of possibility, and therefore it is just as well to consider that angle so that it can be abandoned. Helps clear the decks, if you know what I mean.'

'I know exactly what you mean,' said Em tartly.

'And you will allow me to tell you that I consider the suggestion an impertinence.'

'Impertinence my foot!' blazed Eden. 'It's a damned insult!'

Em said wearily: 'Oh, *do* be quiet, Eden. To term it an insult is to take it seriously. I suppose that such a thing might just be possible, but it is in the highest degree improbable.'

Drew gave her an odd sideways look and said reprovingly: 'You ought to count up to ten before you make statements like that, Em. It was, I think, the late lamented Sherlock Holmes who announced that in any problem, if the impossible was eliminated, what remained, however improbable, was bound to be the answer. Or words to that effect.'

'If that is so, Greg had better arrest me at once!' retorted Em with spirit. 'Of course I *could* have done it! I was here, wasn't I? In fact I was the only person who *was* here. Eden was in Nairobi, and as far as I know no one else called at *Flamingo* that evening. However, I assure you that I did not do it. And now perhaps we can terminate this unpleasant interview. Unless of course there are any more questions that Greg wishes to ask?'

'A few,' said Greg placidly. 'These queer incidents in the house—the breakages. Can you remember exactly when they started?'

Em wrinkled her brow in thought and after a moment or two said slowly: 'Let me see—the first thing was the K'ang Hsi vase. We found it on the floor in bits when we came back from a luncheon party. And there was red ink all over the carpet.'

'The Langleys' party,' said Eden. 'Eleventh of last month.'

Greg jotted down the date and said: 'When was the next time?'

'Only a few days later,' said Em. 'It must have been a Saturday, because that's the day I give out the *posho*, and I'd just finished doing it when Zacharia came to say that something else had been broken. Mother's Rockingham plates.'

'Fourteenth,' said Greg, who had been checking the dates in a pocket diary. 'I gather you had a good many incidents of this kind. Any sort of pattern?'

'No. After that it was almost every day. Then nothing for several days, and we thought it had stopped, and then it started again. It—it began to get on my nerves.'

Greg said: 'You ought to have reported it to the police at once.'

'I know that—now. But at the time I— Well, you know quite well why I didn't, Greg! I won't have my servants taken away and held for questioning or jailed on suspicion. They couldn't all have been in it, and why should the rest suffer because one man had got some queer, twisted African idea into his head, and imagined himself to be paying off a grudge? I thought it would work itself out. If I'd realized——'

Em's voice failed, and Greg said: 'When did you decide to send for Miss Caryll? Before all this started? Or afterwards?'

'Afterwards. I think—I think on the day the record of the concerto was broken. That—upset me.

I found that I couldn't concentrate any more on the things I usually did myself. And Alice was frightened. I felt I must have someone to help me, and I thought of Victoria.'

Greg turned an enquiring look on Victoria and she answered the unspoken question. 'Aunt Em's letter arrived about three weeks ago. It gave me just time to have all the inoculations and things done, and that was all.'

Mr Gilbert nodded absently and turned back to Lady Emily. 'Just one more question. After your dog was poisoned, were there any more acts of vandalism in the house?'

'No.' Em's voice was a hoarse whisper, and Eden spoke harshly, his back still to the room: 'Gilly was right: that was one step further and we ought to have realized it. It started with something quite trivial, and finished with—Alice.'

'If it has finished,' said Greg soberly.

Eden spun round. 'Why do you say that?'

Greg shrugged his shoulders and said: 'It has been fairly conclusively proved that someone who kills once, and gets away with it, will kill again. Either to cover the first killing, or because the snuffing out of a human life is like taking to drugs. Terrifying, but stimulating. That's why the initiation rites of any secret society of the Mau Mau description include a murder. Because it's only the first killing that is difficult. After that it becomes progressively easier and breeds a callousness towards human life and a frightening megalomania. There's no reason to suppose that your wife's death will put a stop to whatever ugly business has been going on here, and that is why we have got to find the murderer if we have to screen every African—and every European!—in the Rift. Which reminds me, Em, did the Brandons bring a driver with them when they came over here on Tuesday morning?'

'Yes. But Samuel has been with them for over twenty years. He would never——'

She was not allowed to finish. 'Why is it,' demanded Mr Gilbert bitterly, 'that none of you, in spite of all you have been through, can be brought to believe that a faithful servant can also be someone who has taken a binding oath to rid the country of all whites?'

He slammed his notebook shut, returned it to his pocket, and rose with a sigh. 'Well I think that's about all for the moment, though I'm afraid we're going to have to interview all your servants and the labour again tomorrow, Em. But Bill Hennessy will be dealing with that. Be gentle with him, won't you? He tells me that ever since you took a stick to him when you caught him playing toreadors in the bull paddock at the ripe age of ten, he's been scared stiff of you.'

'I wish I could believe that,' said Em bleakly. 'But I don't suppose that there is any more truth in it than in your inference that we ourselves shall not be called upon to endure any more of these inquisitions.'

There was the faintest possible suggestion of appeal in her voice, but Mr Gilbert disregarded it. He said: 'Until we find out who killed Mrs DeBrett,

I'm afraid we shall have to go on asking questions. And I cannot believe that any of you would have it otherwise.'

He collected his hat, nodded amiably at them, and left.

7

Em leaned forward in her chair listening to the sound of his retreating footsteps, and a minute later, hearing a car start up and purr away down the dusty drive, she sighed gustily and relaxed.

'Thank heaven for that! I was afraid his driver would not have arrived and that he would fill in the next half-hour upsetting the servants. I am too old for this sort of thing.'

She turned to look at the French ormolu clock that stood on a lacquer cabinet at the far side of the room, and said: 'Four o'clock already! I suppose we had luncheon very late. Will you take tea with us, Drew?'

Mr Stratton declined the invitation, saying that he must get back, and Em heaved herself up out of her chair and accompanied him to the verandah, Victoria and Eden following.

There was someone on the path beyond the jacaranda trees, walking at a pace that suggested urgency, and Eden shaded his eyes with his hand and after a brief inspection announced with a trace of annoyance: 'It's Lisa. What do you suppose she wants?'

'You, I imagine,' said Em with some acerbity. 'Go and head her off, Eden. I don't want to see anyone else today. All I want is tea and peace!'

She turned to Drew with some query relating to a rumoured outbreak of swine fever on a neighbouring estate, and Eden went quickly down the verandah steps, and along the narrow path that led across the garden in the direction of the plumbago hedge and the manager's bungalow.

Victoria saw the woman break into a little run as he approached her, and reaching him, clutch at his coat sleeve. They were too far away for their voices to be audible above Em's plangent strictures on the inefficiency of quarantine precautions, but even from this distance it was possible to see from the woman's gestures and the very movement of her head that she was either excited or upset.

Victoria saw Eden throw a quick look over his shoulder in the direction of the house, and it seemed to her that his face was oddly colorless against the tree shadows. The woman tugged at his sleeve as though she were urging him to walk away with her, and Victoria caught the high-pitched urgency of her voice, pleading or arguing. Then suddenly Eden grasped her arm, and turning about came quickly back to the house, dragging her with him.

Em, immersed in farming shop, was not aware of them until they reached the foot of the verandah steps, and hearing the click of high heels on stone and the jingle of Mrs Markham's charm bracelets, she turned with a look of undisguised impatience.

'Well, Lisa? What is it?'

But it was Eden, and not Mrs Markham who replied. There was a white shade about his mouth and his voice was not quite steady:

'Lisa's got something to say that I think you should hear at once. She——'

Em threw up a hand in an imperious gesture and checked him. Her shrewd old eyes went from one face to the other, and then to the silent figures of Zacharia and a house-boy who were laying afternoon tea in a corner of the verandah. She said coldly: 'If it is important—and I take it that it is?—then we had better go back into the drawing-room. Goodbye Drew. Thank you for collecting my niece. It was kind of you. I'll send Eden over tomorrow to look at those calves.'

She nodded at him and turned away, and Victoria said a little stiffly: 'Goodbye, Mr Stratton. Thank you for all your trouble.'

'It wasn't any trouble,' Drew said shortly. 'I happened to be in Nairobi and this was on my way back.'

He went away down the steps to his car, leaving Victoria, who possessed a healthy temper of her own, with an itching palm and an unmaidenly desire to box his ears.

Em was speaking peremptorily to her grandson:

'My dear Eden, if this is something that concerns us, it must also concern Victoria, since she is now one of the household. By the way, Lisa, you will not have met my niece, Miss Caryll. Victoria, this is Mrs Markham——'

Victoria shook hands and found herself looking into a pair of large violet eyes, expertly enhanced with pencil and mascara and as unmistakably hostile as Drew Stratton's had been. And then Em said: 'Lend me your arm, dear,' and led the way to the drawing-room with a firm step. But her weight pressed heavily upon Victoria's arm as though she really needed that support, and her bulky body was trembling with fatigue.

She lowered herself into the wing-chair once more, and Eden said: 'Look, Gran, Lisa didn't want to worry you with this, but it seems to me that it's something you should know. She says——'

His grandmother turned a quelling eye upon him and said firmly: 'Let her speak for herself, please. Well, Lisa?'

Lisa flumped down sulkily on to the window seat and rubbed resentfully at the marks that Eden's ungentle grip had left on her bare arm. 'I only thought that Eden ought to know, and then he could decide what to do about it. I wasn't going to tell anyone else. Not even Gilly! Though of course everyone's bound to know sooner or later, as Wambui's sure to tell someone else, and once the servants know it—well, you know how they can never keep anything to themselves.'

Em gave a short bark of laughter. 'How little you know this country, Lisa. They may not be able to keep a secret from their own people, but they can always keep it from us. Make no mistake about that! What is it that you have to tell me? If it is just some servant's gossip, you may be fairly sure that it is unimportant.'

'It wasn't gossip,' said Lisa angrily. 'It was serious.' There was a sudden flash of spite in her violet eyes: '*Very* serious! That's why I thought I ought to discuss it with Eden first. But if he prefers it this way, it's his own look out. It was Wambui, if you want to know. My *ndito*. She's been behaving very oddly the last day or two. Dropping things and forgetting things, and jumping as if she's been stung if anyone made a sudden noise. So this afternoon I tackled her about it, and it all came out. She's in a state about Kamau.'

'You mean *my* Kamau?' demanded Em.

'Yes. It seems he's been courting her, and they've been meeting every night in the bushes on the far side of the knoll.'

Em stiffened where she sat, and her expression was no longer one of bored patience. She said sharply and a little breathlessly: 'You mean they saw something? Is that it? They know who did it?'

Lisa shook her head. 'I don't know. You see Wambui couldn't get away on Tuesday evening, but it seems that Kamau waited for her for quite a time, and now he's hinting to her that he knows something about—Alice's murder.'

There was a sudden silence in the room, and in it Victoria heard a soft sound that was something like the click of a latch and seemed to come from the direction of the door that led out of the drawing-room into the hall. But the next moment her attention was distracted, for Em was speaking again:

'But the police questioned all the servants!' said

Em. 'They've seen them half a dozen times already. Surely they would have told us if they'd got any information out of them? Why, Greg Gilbert has been here half the afternoon.'

'Wambui says Kamau told the police that he didn't know anything.'

Em made an angry, impatient gesture. 'Then I don't suppose he does. He's probably only showing off for Wambui's benefit.'

'But we know there was someone in the bushes that night,' insisted Eden. 'Why couldn't it have been Kamau? In fact why couldn't Kamau have been the poltergeist?—and the murderer, for that matter!'

'Don't talk nonsense, Eden,' said Em crossly. 'Kamau's father was one of your grandfather's first servants, and Zacharia is his uncle. He would no more harm me than—than Zacharia would! And you seem to forget that he was the one who killed Gitahi. If *that* isn't proof of loyalty, I'd like to know what is!'

'Oh, all right—all right. I know it's useless to try and persuade you that any of your darling Kukes might be anything but a hundred per cent loyal. But what about the man in the bushes? It squares with that, you know. *Someone* was there!'

'If it was Kamau, it is proof that he was not Alice's murderer,' said Em stiff with anger. 'Whoever was there had not approached the body. You know that quite well.'

'Of course I do. But he could have seen something, couldn't he? He could be telling the truth there.'

'If you think that,' snapped Em, 'I suggest you ring up Greg Gilbert immediately and tell him exactly what Lisa has told us. Then the police can deal with it—and with Wambui!'

'But you can't do that,' gasped Lisa leaping to her feet, her eyes wide with dismay. 'They'd take her away and hold her for questioning. You know what they're like. She might not be back for days, and I simply can't manage without her. Oh, I wish I hadn't said anything! I wish I hadn't.'

Her eyes filled with tears and she sat down abruptly and began to search blindly and without success in the inadequate pockets of her linen suit.

'Here,' said Eden, handing over a handkerchief. He patted her shoulder awkwardly and said: 'Don't cry, Lee.' Lisa dabbed at her tears, and groping for his hand, clung to it, looking up at him with eyes that were openly and helplessly adoring.

Eden withdrew his hand with more speed than gallantry, and Em said dryly: 'You would have done better to come straight to me, would you not, Lisa. Although I am aware that as a confidante I am likely to prove less sympathetic than my grandson! However, you are right in one thing. Unless they resort to violence the police will get nothing out of Kamau. And I will not have my servants intimidated. I will talk to him myself. He can do the rounds with me this evening after dinner. That will be the best way. I often take one of the boys with me, so it will arouse no suspicion; and he will talk better in the dark. They always do. And now let us have some tea.'

Lisa could not stay, but Eden did not offer to see

her home, and after lingering for a few moments she turned from him with a petulant toss of the head and walked away down the long garden path, and he came back to his chair, and subsiding into it, stared moodily into space while his tea grew cold. He made no attempt at conversation, and Victoria sat silent, covertly studying him.

The passing of the years had not detracted from his spectacular good looks, and although he looked older and thinner, and there were frown lines on his forehead and fine lines at the corners of his eyes that had come from screwing them up against strong sunlight, there was no denying the fact that in appearance at least he was, if anything, more attractive now than he had been six years ago.

It's not fair! thought Victoria resentfully. How can anyone tell what he is really like when they can't get beyond what he looks like? What do I know about Eden? What did I ever know? Am I still in love with him . . . ?

Em too had been disinclined to talk, and now she pushed away her almost untasted cup and came to her feet with sudden decision, announcing that she for one did not intend to sit about all evening doing nothing, and that as they needed dog meat again she proposed to take out the Land-Rover and shoot a buck. Victoria and Eden had better come with her.

Eden said: 'You'll only tire yourself out, racketing round in the Land-Rover, Gran. Why don't you stay here and put your feet up for a change? I'll go. Victoria can come with me if she'd like to.'

Em shot a quick anxious look at her niece and

said obstinately: 'I don't wish to put my feet up, thank you. I wish to get out of this house and into the fresh air.'

'What you mean,' said Eden, 'is that you're feeling upset. And whenever that happens you work it off by going out and driving round the countryside far too fast. Shooting for dog meat is just an excuse, and you know it.'

'It's nothing of the sort,' snapped Em. 'You know quite well that they get through a buck in about four days—what is left of it after the servants have had the best cuts. And fresh meat doesn't keep in this weather.'

She stumped off down the verandah and Eden turned to Victoria with a rueful grin. 'You'll have to make allowance for us, Vicky. We're all rather badly shaken up by this. It's a pity you had to arrive just now and get involved in it all. I wish I could have kept you out of it.'

Victoria said soberly: 'Eden, I haven't had time to tell you before how sorry I am about—your wife. But——'

'That's all right,' said Eden hastily. 'You don't have to say anything. Listen, Vicky——' He hesitated, flushed, and then said abruptly: 'I suppose this is quite the wrong time to mention it, but I know you must think I behaved pretty brutally to you in the past. I did, of course. There were reasons why— Oh well, there's no point in going into them now. But what I wanted to say is that I'm damned glad that you're here. I had no right to expect that you'd come, but we need a bit of sanity in this place. And you're right about Gran needing you. She's cracking up, and if we don't watch out she'll end up by having a stroke or running off the rails. Try to see if you can't get her to ease up a bit—on the work, if nothing else.'

Victoria said: 'I'll do what I can. You know that.'

'Yes, of course. But it isn't going to be easy. As you can see, you've landed right into the middle of a really nasty situation. Gran *will* have it that everything is over now, and I wish I could believe it. But I didn't like what Greg said about "only the first killing being difficult". Supposing he was right, and that Alice wasn't the end, but the beginning? Look here, Vicky, if you feel that you'd rather not stay, you—you don't have to, you know. I could always arrange a return passage for you.'

Victoria said: 'Aunt Em said that too. Are you trying to frighten me, Eden? Or merely get rid of me?'

'Good Lord, no! From what I know of you, you don't frighten easily, and thank God for it! Believe me, it's going to be a nice change to have someone about the house who doesn't jump every time a door opens or a leaf drops! But I don't want you to feel that you have to stay. That's all.'

He put out a hand and touched the tip of her nose lightly with one finger. It was a familiar, caressing gesture that he had used so often in the past, and which had been peculiarly their own, and Victoria stepped back as swiftly as though it had been a blow, and turning from him went quickly away.

Em and Eden were both waiting for her in the Land-Rover when she reappeared ten minutes later, and they had driven out on to the ranges, where Em had shot a kongoni and a Thomson's gazelle.

It had been dark by the time they returned, and Em had pronounced herself too tired to change for dinner that night, so they had dined as they were, in the candle-lit dining-room where portraits of dead and gone DeBretts and Beaumartins looked down from the walls. But afterwards, as Zacharia was leaving the drawing-room carrying the coffee tray, Em spoke briefly to him in Swahili.

Victoria did not understand what she said, but Eden turned sharply: 'Kamau? You aren't *really* going to see him tonight? You're far too done up! For goodness sake, Gran, leave it for the morning! He won't run away.'

'How do I know that?' enquired Em morosely, moving towards the door. 'Of course I'm going to see him. Besides, Zach says he told him after tea that he was to go round with me tonight, so he will be waiting. I said he was to bring a lamp and meet me at the gate into the shamba, as I wanted to make sure that the hippos haven't broken the wire again. It is too good an opportunity to miss: I have been told things after dark that I would never have heard by day, and I know these people better than you do—even though I'm not Kenya born!'

'For Pete's sake, Gran!' said Eden, exasperated. 'You're surely not going to do the rounds tonight?'

'Why not? I've never missed it yet.'

'But you're tired out! And anyway, it's not necessary any longer. Oh, you needn't remind me about what happened to Alice! Do you think I need reminding? But even Greg doesn't think that was anything more than an isolated attack, and if the Emergency is over—and we keep being told that it is—then what's the point of going round the place every night to see that the labour are all in and the place is properly locked up, and all the rest of this Commando nonsense? We can't keep it up for ever. Look here, I'll go instead. And what's more, I'll talk to Kamau for you.'

'No, dear,' said Em gently but quite definitely. 'He wouldn't talk to you as he will to me.'

'Then I'm going with you. You know I've never liked you wandering around alone after dark, but you would do it. It's quite time it was stopped. Victoria——'

He turned towards her as though for support, and Em said crisply: 'Victoria has nothing to do with this, and it's quite time she went to bed. Don't be silly, Eden. You've never tried to stop me doing it before, and I can't imagine why you are doing it now.'

'I did try, but——'

'But your wife wouldn't let you go instead of me, and she wouldn't allow you to go with me because she was afraid of being alone in the house. I know, dear. But you must see that this is no time to relax our precautions. If you really want to take over doing the rounds we'll discuss the matter tomorrow, but if we want to get anything out of Kamau it's important that I see him alone. So don't let's have any more argument about it. Victoria dear, go to bed. You must be tired out. And you too, Eden! There's no need for you to wait up for me. Good night, dear.'

The door closed behind her with decision, and Eden took a hasty step forward as though he would have followed her, and then looked at Victoria and shrugged his shoulders.

'Now you see what I meant when I said you wouldn't find it an easy job—helping Gran! You'd better do what she told you and get off to bed. I expect you could do with a bit of sleep. Good night.'

He turned and went out by the verandah door, leaving Victoria alone in the silent drawing-room.

8

Despite the anxieties and disturbances of the previous day—or perhaps because of them—Victoria slept soundly and dreamlessly, and awakened feeling refreshed and invigorated and capable of coping with any and every one of the problems that life at *Flamingo* might offer.

Breakfast had been laid on the verandah, and Eden, wearing riding breeches and a thin tweed coat, was sitting on the verandah rail and drinking black coffee. He was looking tired and heavy-eyed and as though he had not had enough sleep during the past night—or for several nights.

He slid off the verandah rail and said: 'Hullo, Vicky. No need to ask how you slept. You look offensively well. I hope the dogs didn't worry you? They're apt to be a bit noisy at intervals.'

'They did wake me a couple of times,' admitted

Victoria, seating herself at the table, 'but I was too sleepy to bother. What was all the noise about?'

'Nothing. Or anything! Trouble is, they usually run loose about the grounds at night, but the Markhams' spaniel is on heat, and Lisa asked us if we'd keep 'em locked up for the duration, as apparently they sit under her window and serenade her all night. So they've been shut up in one of the spare godowns, and they hate it. Have some coffee. Gran's having her breakfast in bed. She said to tell you she'd like to see you as soon as you're through with yours. I should take your time if I were you. She's not in the best of tempers.'

'Why? Nothing else has happened, has it? I mean—nothing else has been broken, or——?'

'No, nothing like that. It's just that Kamau never turned up last night, and she hung about waiting for him and got chilled to the bone, and lost her temper into the bargain. She doesn't like being kept waiting and she doesn't take kindly to having her orders disobeyed. He probably had an assignation with his girlfriend. Or else he's lost his nerve and gone A.W.O.L. for a few days! Gran's livid, and I can clearly see that this is going to be one of those days when nothing goes right.'

Zacharia appeared with a dish of buttered eggs and bacon, and Victoria helped herself and enquired if Eden was going out riding.

'I've been,' said Eden briefly. He rejected the eggs with every appearance of loathing, and pouring out a second cup of black coffee, returned to his seat on the verandah rail. 'When you've finished I'll take you along to Gran's room. With any luck she may have simmered down a bit, and it mightn't be a bad idea if we ganged up on her and tried to see if we couldn't persuade her to spend the day in bed.'

But neither hope was to be realized. Em was already up, and in an exceedingly bad temper. They found her seated in front of her dressing-table, wearing a pair of grey corduroy trousers topped by what appeared to be a fisherman's jersey in a painful shade of orange.

'Oh, it's you,' said Em without turning, addressing their reflections in the glass. 'Good morning, Victoria. I trust you had a good night—it's more than I had!'

She turned to speak in trenchant Swahili to Zacharia, who was peering into one of the cupboards, and added crossly: 'He's getting too old for the work. That's what it is. I shall have to pension him off.'

'What's he been doing now?' enquired Eden perfunctorily.

'Lost a pair of my red dungarees. And as one pair hasn't been ironed yet and another is in the wash, and the pair I wore yesterday are filthy, I'm reduced to wearing a pair of your father's old corduroys. Sheer carelessness. Oh, do stop rootling round in that cupboard, Zach! If they weren't there five minutes ago they aren't there now. Here, take these ones away and get them washed at once. You'd better boil them. And see that they're dried and ironed by this evening.'

She reached down and picked up the discarded dungarees and blouse that she had worn on the previous day, and making a bundle of them, flung them at the old Kikuyu who caught them deftly and carried them away.

Eden put a coaxing arm around his grandmother's shoulders and said: 'Snap out of it, Gran. You can't tear a strip off everyone in the house on Victoria's first day here. It'll give her a wrong impression. Don't be cross, darling. It's bad for the blood pressure.'

'I'm not cross. I'm furious! Zach thinks that Kamau went off to meet that *ndito* of Lisa's last night instead of waiting for me. If he did, then of course she would have told him that she'd talked to Lisa, and naturally he wasn't going to face me after that. Just wait until I get my hands on him, that's all! I gather he's gone to help cut lucerne in the east field this morning; thinks he can keep out of my way, I suppose. I've told Zach I wish to see him the moment he gets back.'

Em pinned on a diamond brooch and catching sight of Victoria in the looking glass, turned about to study her approvingly.

'How nice you look, dear. I'd forgotten that you were so pretty. Have you had some breakfast? Good. Well now I'm going to show you the office and give you some idea of what there is to do, and then we'll do a tour of the house and the gardens, and after luncheon——'

'After luncheon,' cut in Eden firmly, 'I am taking her out in the launch. Unless you propose to keep her nose to the grindstone from the word "Go"?'

'No, of course not. I want her to enjoy herself. Certainly take her out on the lake. She will like that. And we must arrange a few expeditions—picnic parties, so that she can see something of the Rift. I see no reason why we should mope indoors. Let me see—you are going to take a look at the new bore hole this morning, aren't you? Then we shall see you at luncheon. Come along, dear.'

She swept Victoria out, and the remainder of the morning was devoted to the programme she had outlined. Eden had been delayed, so luncheon was late, and young Mr Hennessy of the police, accompanied by two police askaris, arrived halfway through the meal, and was kept waiting. 'It will do him no harm to cool his heels on the verandah,' observed Em tartly; and she had lingered over the coffee until the hands of the grandfather clock pointed at twenty minutes to three, before going out to see him.

'I wouldn't be in Bill Hennessy's shoes this afternoon for all the coffee in Brazil!' said Eden, taking Victoria's arm and hurrying her down a path that wound between a colourful wilderness of plumbago and wild lupins towards the lake. 'She can't forget that she knew him when he was a sticky little schoolboy, and to have him questioning her servants in the name of the Law is adding insult to injury. Look out for those thorns.'

He opened the gate into the shamba and ushered Victoria into a lush, green wilderness where the warm air was heavy with the scent of orange blossom and drowsy with the hum of bees, and the damp ground squelched under her sandalled feet.

'I suppose that's the trouble with Gran,' continued Eden. 'When you get to her age there's hardly anyone left whom you didn't know when they were children. Makes it difficult to take them seriously. She must feel like a governess in a schoolroom full of irresponsible brats. All the same, I get a bit tired of being treated as if I were still in the Lower Fourth. If Gran would only realize that I was now an adult she'd put me in as manager in place of that waster, Gilly. Damn it all, I may as well learn how to run it, considering that I shall own the place one day. That is, unless Gran cuts me out of her will and leaves it to you instead.'

'To *me?*' exclaimed Victoria, startled. 'What nonsense! Why should she do any such thing?'

Eden shrugged his shoulders and preceded her through another gate into a shadowy forest of banana palms. 'Ask me another. Why does Gran do anything? Because she wants to. Besides, she's a bit of a feminist, our Em. She may think you'd do more for *Flamingo*—and for Kenya—than I would. The female of the species being more deadly than the male—and all the rest of it.'

'Rubbish!' retorted Victoria. 'You know quite well that she adores you. She always has. She only snaps at you to try and disguise the fact; and fools nobody.'

Eden laughed. 'Perhaps. All the same, it's quite on the cards that she may have thought that I was taking my responsibilities as Heir to the Throne too lightly, and doesn't think it will do me any harm to realize that if I don't watch my step she can nominate another candidate. She's a Machiavellian old darling.'

'But *you* don't think that?' said Victoria, troubled.

'I mean, even supposing she did—and she wouldn't!—you don't think that I'd do you out of *Flamingo*, do you?'

Eden stopped, and turned to smile down at her, and her heart did a foolish check and leap. He said: 'Wouldn't you, darling? I wonder. You might think that it would serve me right.'

A tide of colour rose to the roots of Victoria's brown hair and she said confusedly: 'Don't be silly, Eden! I never thought—I mean— Well, we made a mistake. That was all. But we're still friends.'

'Are we?' asked Eden soberly. 'Are we really, Vicky?'

'Of course,' said Victoria, making a determined grab at lightness. 'I'm like Aunt Em. I can't forget that we were allies against Authority in the days when you were a beastly little boy with scratched knees and a dirty neck.'

But Eden refused to follow her lead. He said, unsmiling: 'Thank you, Vicky.' And reaching out he took her hand, and before she realized what he meant to do, he had lifted it and kissed it.

Victoria fought down a strong impulse to snatch it away and run, and an even stronger one to stroke his bent head with her free hand. Heroically resisting both, she said briskly: 'Do you think we could take some of these bananas on the boat with us? It's years since I picked one straight off the bunch.'

'They're not ripe,' said Eden a shade sulkily. He turned and walked on down the path, only to stop again a few minutes later with an impatient exclamation. 'Damn! The hippo have been in again. It's just ruddy idleness on Gilly's part; he won't see that the fences are properly made. What the hell's the use of a single strand of wire, even if you do run a mild electric current through it? It hasn't apparently even stopped the remnants of the Mau Mau gangs from keeping open an escape route round the lake!'

Victoria said: 'Do you think there's anything in it? Gangs hiding out in the *marula*, I mean?'

'No. Though I suppose it's just possible that the odd man who is still on the run spends a day or two there. There couldn't be a better hiding place, could there? Just look at it!'

He waved a hand in the general direction of the papyrus swamps that reared up like a solid grey-green wall between the shamba and the Lake. A weird, waving jungle, so dense that a man forcing his way through it, his ears filled by the noise of his own passage, might pass within a yard of another who stood still, and never know it. It stretched for miles along the lake shore, and during the Emergency the gangs had cut their own secret paths and built solidly constructed hides in it.

Years earlier Gerald DeBrett too had cut a wide pathway through the papyrus, and laid down a duck-board to the lake edge where he had built a wooden boat-house supported on piles and sheltered by the reeds. It was weather-beaten now, and ramshackle, but Em had kept the approach to it in tolerable repair, and it housed a small rowing boat, a battered punt and a neat white motor launch.

'We had to have a guard on this all through the

Emergency,' said Eden, casting off and poling the launch down a narrow channel between shadowy walls of papyrus. 'Damned nuisance it was too. Greg got pretty crisp about it. He wanted it pulled down and the boats holed or dragged up somewhere where they couldn't be used, to prevent the Mau Mau using them. But Gran wouldn't hear of it. She fixed up a roster of guards. Myself, Gus Abbott and half a dozen of the loyal Kikuyu. Even poor old Zach was pressed into service, but he was far more afraid of handling a gun—and of the hippo—than he was of being murdered. Kamau refused to take a gun at all. He pinned his faith to a panga; and got a chap with it, too! Caught him trying to cut a boat loose, and slashed at him in the dark. Cut his head clean off, and carried it triumphantly up to the house in the morning. Alice fainted all over the coffee cups, but Gran didn't turn a hair.'

Victoria said shuddering: 'You don't mean he actually *showed* it to them?'

'He certainly did. He was as pleased as Punch about it. And with reason! For it turned out to be one of the top Mau Mau brass, "Brigadier" Gitahi, no less. There was a nice fat price on his head too, which was duly handed over to Kamau, with the result that the entire labour force of *Flamingo* were beautifully tight for at least a week afterwards. Now let's see if we can get this engine to start.'

The launch glided free of the papyrus and the floating weed beds, and they were in hot sunlight again, with the wide expanse of the lake spread out before them. Bright blue lilies spangled the water, and there was a continuous quack and ruffle of birds: stately white pelicans, numerous as swans on the Liffey; spoonbills, dab-chicks, cormorants, wild duck and herons.

A huge head adorned by two wildly agitated ears rose up on the port bow, regarded them with austere disapproval, and sank again. 'Too many hippo in the lake,' observed Eden, frowning. 'It's quite time we shot some. One or two make rather pleasant local colour, but twenty or thirty of them can do as much damage to the lakeside shambas as a plague of locusts. Look—there are some flamingo. They must be on their way to Elmenteita. They don't often come to Naivasha. Beautiful, aren't they?'

'Lovely!' said Victoria on a breath of rapture. 'You know, I used to think of all this, and wonder if it could posibly be as beautiful as I remembered it to be. But it is. Every bit as beautiful!'

'So in spite of everything,' said Eden, 'you're glad you came back?'

'What do you mean? "In spite of everything",' demanded Victoria defensively.

'Me—Alice—Gran rapidly going off her rocker. A resident poltergeist, and the police almost permanently on the premises,' said Eden bitterly.

'Oh, Eden, I'm sorry!' Victoria lifted a flushed and contrite face. 'I keep on forgetting about Alice. I'm a selfish pig!'

'No you're not, dear. You're refreshingly normal. And thank God for it! To tell you the truth, Vicky, I can't quite believe it myself, and when I'm away from the house it all seems like a nightmare that I shall wake up from. It's only when I get back to the house that— Oh, hell! Let's talk about something else, shall we?'

'Yes, *let's!*' said Victoria gratefully. 'Where are we going, by the way? And whose is that house up on the hill over there?'

'Drew Stratton's. Chap who collected you from the Airport yesterday.'

'Oh,' said Victoria in a repressive voice, and after a moment or two of silence enquired: 'Do you mean his house, or where we are going?'

'Both.'

'Oh,' said Victoria again, betraying a marked lack of enthusiasm.

Eden threw her an amused glance. 'You don't sound wildly enthusiastic. Didn't you take to our Mr Stratton?'

'He didn't take to me. In fact I rather think that he went out of his way to be rude. Is he a confirmed misogynist, or something?'

'Not that I know of. And as everyone in Kenya knows everyone else's innermost secrets, you can take it that he is neither.'

'Merely mannerless, I suppose,' said Victoria with some acidity.

'You have got your knife into him, haven't you?'

'I have never,' said Victoria with dignity, 'taken kindly to being disliked and disapproved of at sight and for no reason.'

Eden laughed. 'Don't tell me it's ever happened to you before, because I won't believe it! You must have got hold of the wrong end of the stick. Everyone likes Drew.'

'I can't think why, when he's obviously conceited and egotistical, as well as being boorish and entirely lacking in manners, and——'

'Here! Hi!' said Eden. 'Give the poor chap a chance! You can't knock our local hero-boy, you know. He's one of our leading citizens. In fact we point to him with pride.'

'Why?' demanded Victoria frostily. 'Because he lounges around with a gun on his hip and drives too fast, I suppose?'

'Then you suppose wrong. To start off with he's Kenya-born, and his grandparents were two of the real pioneers—like Delamere and Grogan and old Grandfather DeBrett—and in a young Colony that means something! He lost both his parents before he was twenty, and having copped a packet in the way of wounds and decorations during the Normandy landings, came back to find that his manager had let the place go to rack and ruin, and there was a load of debt instead of the fat profits that other farms had been making during the war years. A lot of men faced with that sort of mess would have sold up and got out, but Drew flatly refused to part with a single acre of his land. Said he knew he could pull it out of the red. And did. He must have lived on cattle food and *posho* for God knows how long, and he worked like ten men. And then just as things were really beginning to look up, the Mau Mau business broke...'

Eden looked broodingly out across the lake and was silent for so long that at last Victoria said impatiently: 'Go on. What happened to him then?'

'Who? Oh Drew. Nothing much, if you mean

to his place. The Strattons have always employed Masai, and Drew was practically brought up in a *manyatta*. He's blood-brother to every ochre-painted *moran* in the Colony, and so the Mau Mau gave him a wide berth. But he's one of the "*My country, 'tis of thee*", brigade, and he handed over the management of the estate to old Ole Gachia, with instructions to keep it on an even keel, and offered his services to the Security Forces. He ended up by more or less running his own show, and used to go out with a pseudo gang, despite the fact that he's as blond as a chorus girl.'

'What's a "pseudo gang"?' asked Victoria, intrigued.

'Didn't you ever read your papers? They were the boys who pretended to be terrorists. Learnt all the jargon and dressed themselves up for the part—and blacked themselves all over, if they were British. They used to push off into the forests to make contact with the gangs. Drew had a hand-picked bunch of his own. Pukka devils, from all accounts. They pulled off some astonishing coups, and had a pleasant habit of cutting a notch in Drew's verandah rail for every kill. It made an impressive tally, and I am credibly informed that although the Emergency is officially a thing of the past, there is still an occasional new notch there. We'll take a look and see. Here we are. Stand by for the bump.'

He switched off the engine, and as the launch lost speed, manoeuvred it expertly alongside a small wooden jetty that thrust out into a narrow bay whose steep banks blazed with flamboyant and vivid cascades of bougainvillaea. A long flight of steps wound upwards from the jetty and passed between banks of roses and flowering shrubs, to come out on a gravel path which followed the curve of a stone wall buttressing a grassed terrace in front of a long, low, single-storeyed house whose wide verandah was shaded by flowering creepers.

Mr Stratton might employ Masai on his estate, but his house servants were coast Arabs, and a dignified white-robed figure, whose face might have been carved from a polished chunk of obsidian, greeted the visitors, and informed them that the Bwana should be immediately notified of their arrival.

'What a heavenly view!' said Victoria, leaning on the verandah rail and looking out across a vast panorama of lake and tree-clad hills and far rolling grassland ringed by blue ranges that shimmered like mirages in the afternoon sun. Her eye fell on a long row of notches cut into the wood of the rail, and she drew back sharply, the pleasure on her face giving place to disgust.

'What did I tell you?' said Eden, following the direction of her gaze. 'Quite a nice line-up.'

'*Nice!* You call that nice? Why, it's appalling! And—and barbaric! Chalking up a record of dead men!'

'Of dead murderers,' corrected a dry voice behind her.

Victoria whirled round, her cheeks flushing scarlet. Mr Stratton, dressed in impeccable riding clothes, was standing in the doorway of a room that opened on to the verandah. He was looking perfectly amiable, and his bland gaze travelled thoughtfully from Miss Caryll to her cousin.

'Courtesy call, Eden?'

'Business, I'm afraid. Those Herefords of yours. Gran wants me to have a look at them before we clinch the deal.'

'Of course. She said something about it yesterday. They're in the paddock just behind the house. You'll find Kekinai out there. He'll tell you anything you want to know. I'll entertain Miss Caryll until you're through.'

Eden looked doubtfully at Victoria, and then all at once a malicious smile leapt to life in his eyes, and he said: 'Good idea. I won't be long.' And left them.

Victoria made a swift movement as though she would have followed him, but Mr Stratton, either by accident or design, had moved forward in the same moment and barred her way. 'Cigarette?' he enquired, proffering his case.

'Thank you; I don't smoke,' said Victoria curtly.

'You won't mind if I do? Tea will be along in a minute. Or would you rather have a cold drink? It's quite a pull up from the lake on a hot day.'

Victoria disregarded the offer and said, stammering a little: 'I'm sorry that you should have heard w-what I said. About the notches. I didn't mean to be r-rude.'

'There's no need to apologize for your views,' said Drew gravely.

'I'm not. Only for letting you hear them.'

'My feelings,' said Drew, 'are not so easily

wounded. So you think I'm appalling and barbaric because I allow the boys to cut a tally of their kills on my verandah rail, do you? You are not the only one. There are uncounted thousands of soft-hearted and fluffy-minded—and abysmally ignorant—people who would agree with you.'

'Thank you,' said Victoria sweetly.

'Don't mention it. Unlike you, I meant to be rude. You see, Miss Caryll, I get a little bored by people who broadcast views on something that is, to them, only a problem on paper, and one which does not touch them, personally, in any way. We each have something that we love deeply and are prepared to fight for and die for, and kill for! and I wonder just how many of the virtuous prosers, if it was the agony of their own child or wife or lover, or the safety of their own snug little surburban home that was in question, would not fight in their defence?'

Victoria said: 'I didn't mean that. I meant this sort of thing—cutting notches. Making a game of killing.'

'It wasn't a game. It was deadly serious. The men we were after had deliberately bestialized themselves by acts and oaths and ceremonies that were so unspeakably filthy and abominable that the half of them have never been printed, or believed by the outside world. If any of us were caught—and a good many of us were—we knew just how slowly and unpleasantly we should die. You cannot conduct a campaign against a bestial horror like the Mau Mau with gloves on. Or you can!—if you have no objection to digging up a grave in the forest and finding that it contains the body of your best friend, who has been roasted alive over a slow fire after having certain parts of him removed for use in Mau Mau ceremonials.'

Neither Drew's face nor his pleasant voice had altered, but his bland blue eyes were suddenly as hard and blank and cold as pebbles, and Victoria was aware with a sense of shock that he was speaking of something that he himself had seen—and could still see.

She said hesitantly and inadequately: 'I—I'm sorry.'

The blankness left Drew's eyes and he tossed the end of his cigarette over the verandah rail and said: 'Come here; I want to show you something.'

He took her arm in an ungentle grasp, and turning her about, walked her over to the far end of the verandah and stopped before the upright post that supported the corner of the roof. There were notches on that too. Each one cut deep into the flat of the wood pillar.

'Those are our losses,' said Drew, and touched them lightly. 'That one was Sendayo. We used to play together when we were kids. His father worked for mine when they were both young men. That was Mtua. One of the best men we had. They cut his hands and feet off and pegged him out where the safari ants would get him. That one was Tony Sherraway. They burnt him alive. This one was Barugu. He was a Kikuyu whose entire family—parents, grandparents, wife and children—were murdered in the Lari massacre, where the Mau Mau set all the huts in the village on fire and clubbed and panga'd the people as they ran out. Barugu worked for us for a year before they got him, and what they did to him is not repeatable.'

He released Victoria's arm with an impatient gesture and said: 'Why go on? They won't mean anything to you. Or to anyone else. But cutting a tally of kills helped the morale of the others. They also got a bit of satisfaction out of chalking up that score, and out of knowing that if one of them went, he would be amply avenged.'

Drew turned away and stood looking out across the beauty that lay below and around him, his eyes narrowed against the sun glare, and presently he said: 'It's no good trying to treat Africans as though their processes of thought were the same as Europeans. That is the way of madness—and politicians!'

Victoria said doubtfully: 'But it *is* their country.'

'Whose?' demanded Drew, without turning his head.

'The—the Africans.'

'Which Africans? All this that you can see here, the Rift and most of what is known as the White Highlands, belonged, if it belonged to anyone, to the Masai. But it is the Kikuyu who claim the land, though they never owned a foot of it—and would have been speared if they'd set a foot on it! The place was a no-man's-land when Delamere first came here, and the fact that cattle and sheep can now be raised here is entirely due to him and men like him. And even they didn't just grab the land. The handful of Masai then inhabiting it voluntarily exchanged it for the enormous territory that tribe now holds.'

'But——' began Victoria, and was interrupted.

'All the chatter about "It belongs to them",' said Drew, 'makes me tired. Sixty years ago Americans were still fighting Red Indians and Mexicans and grabbing *their* land; but I've never heard anyone suggesting that they should get the hell out of it and give it back to the original owners. Our grandfathers found a howling wilderness that no one wanted, and which, at the time, no one objected to their taking possession of. And with blood, toil, tears and sweat they turned it into a flourishing concern. At which point a yelping chorus is raised, demanding, in the name of "Nationalism", that it be handed over to them. Well, if they are capable of running this on their own, or of turning a howling wilderness into a rich and prosperous concern, let 'em prove it! There's a hell of a lot of Africa. They can find a bit and start right in to show us. But that won't do for them. It's the fruit of somebody else's labour that they are after.'

He flung out a hand in the direction of the green lawns and gardens, the orchards, outhouses and paddocks: 'There was nothing and nobody here when my grandfather first saw this. This is the fruit of his labour—and of my parents', and my own. I was born here, and this is as much my home as Sendayo's. I want to stay here, and if that is immoral and indefensible Colonialism, then every American whose pioneer forebears went in a covered wagon to open up the West is tarred with the same brush; and when U.N.O. orders them out, we may consider moving!'

He turned to face Victoria and for the first time

since she had met him, he smiled. It was a disquietingly attractive smile, and despite herself she felt a considerable portion of her hostility towards him waning.

He said: 'I apologize for treating you to a grossly over-simplified lecture on the Settlers' point of view. Very tedious for you. Here's the tea at last. Come and pour out.'

He kept up an idly amiable flow of small-talk until Eden returned, and after that the conversation took a strictly technical turn, and Victoria allowed her attention to wander.

'An over-simplified viewpoint.' Perhaps. Yet she could still remember her father telling her tales of her grandfather's early days in the great valley. The gruelling toil under the burning sun. The laborious digging of wells and the struggle to grow grass and crops and to raise cattle. The first glorious signs of success—of the 'wilderness blossoming like a rose'. The years of drought when first the crops and then the cattle died, and ruin faced them—and was stared down and outfaced by men who refused to be beaten. The first roads. The first hospitals. The first railway. The first schools... It could not have been easy, but the sweat and the toil and the despair and determination that it had cost had made it doubly dear, and Victoria found herself remembering a line from the theme song of *Oklahoma!*—that exhilarating musical about another pioneer state which barely a century ago had also belonged to 'painted savages'.

'We belong to the land, and the land we belong to is grand.'

She was aroused from her abstraction by Eden saying: 'Look, Drew, if you're driving over to see Gilly, why not come back in the launch with us, and let your driver take the car round to *Flamingo?* Then you can have a word with Gran about the deal. Just as well to get it settled.'

Mr Stratton, having agreed to the suggestion, went off to change out of his riding clothes, and Eden cocked an interrogatory eyebrow at Victoria and said: 'How did you get on with the detestable Drew? Sorry I had to leave you like that, but you wouldn't have enjoyed inspecting cows and calves, and I took it that you wouldn't actually come to blows! Do you mind having him as a passenger on the way home? I want him to have a word with Gran, and this seems a good way of seeing that he gets it.'

'Of course I don't mind. Why should I?' enquired Victoria loftily. 'I'm not so prejudiced that I can't sit in a boat with him. And in any case you will be far too busy discussing milk yields and foot-and-mouth for either of you to notice whether I am there or not.'

Eden laughed and reached out to pull her to her feet. 'Did we bore you? Forgive me, darling. I promise to keep off shop in future whenever you're around.'

Something in Victoria flinched at his casual use of an endearment that had once meant so much but which now came so easily and so meaninglessly to his tongue. She removed the hand that he still held, and said lightly: 'If I'm to be of any use to Aunt Em, the more I know about milk yields and foot-

'Are you cold? Or was that someone jumping over your grave?'

Victoria started as though she had been sleep-walking, and was suddenly angry with an unreasoning and defensive anger born of the sharp unease that had momentarily possessed her.

'Must you mention graves after what has happened here? I should have thought we could at least have kept off——' She stopped and bit her lip.

Drew's eyebrows lifted and his blue eyes were unpleasantly satirical, but his voice remained unruffled. 'I stand corrected. Very tactless of me. My apologies, Eden.'

'What's that?' said Eden, jerked out of abstraction as Victoria had been. 'I'm sorry. I didn't hear what you said.'

'Nothing of any importance. It doesn't look as though your grandmother is in, does it? Or else she's locked the dogs up.'

'More likely that the police have locked up all our labour!' said Eden bitterly. 'There don't seem to be any cars about, so at least Bill and his boys have pushed off—which is some comfort!'

At the top of the verandah steps he paused to listen, his head lifted and his face strained and intent. But no one moved in the silent house, and the normal cheerful noises from the kitchen and the back premises were conspicuous by their absence.

Something of his disquiet communicated itself to Drew Stratton, who said with unwonted sharpness: 'There's nothing wrong, is there?'

Eden's strained rigidity relaxed and he gave a short and rather uncertain laugh. 'No. No, of course not. I was only wondering where everyone had got to. Place seems a bit deserted this evening. I'll go and rout out Zacharia and some drinks.' But he made no move to go, and the hand that he had laid on the verandah rail tightened until the knuckles showed white through the tanned skin.

Somewhere in the house a door slammed and Victoria jumped at the suddenness of the sound.

'Somebody appears to be at home,' observed Mr Stratton dryly. 'Unless that was your poltergeist.'

Eden's hand dropped from the rail and he turned an appalled face. 'But it couldn't be!—not now. I mean——'

He whirled round and had started for the nearest door at a run when Em appeared at the far end of the verandah:

'Eden! Thank goodness you're back! I've been worried to death.' Her voice sharpened as she took in his expression. 'What's the matter? You haven't—heard anything have you?'

'No,' said Eden with a crack of laughter that held more than a trace of hysteria. 'Not a sound. That's what was worrying me. The whole place was as quiet as a tomb and I suddenly got the horrors, wondering if anything had happened to you. Where is everyone? Don't tell me that young Bill Hennessy has arrested the whole boiling—live stock included? What have you done with the dogs?'

'Locked them up,' said Em and sat down abruptly and heavily in one of the verandah chairs. 'They didn't take to the askaris.'

She appeared to notice Drew and Victoria for the first time and nodded absently at them. 'Good evening, Drew. Didn't see you. Eden brought you, I suppose? Well, I can't talk cattle with you today. It'll have to wait. I'm too upset. Did you have a nice trip on the lake, Victoria? Eden, go and tell Zacharia to bring the drinks. I need something. Brandy, for choice!'

'Bill been giving you a bad time, Gran?' enquired Eden. 'You should have let me stay and deal with him. Come on, tell me the worst. Are half our staff behind bars? Is that why the place is so quiet this evening?'

'No. Nothing like that. He only wanted to ask a lot of silly questions, and I let him get on with it. It isn't the police. It's Kamau.'

'Why? What about him? Don't tell me he really *does* know something after all?'

'I don't know,' said Em tiredly. 'Eden, *do* go and call Zach! I'm sure we could all do with a drink.'

Eden departed, and Drew said: 'Kamau? Isn't he the one who scuppered that Mau Mau "Brigadier" and scooped in a fat reward? Do the police think that he knows something about the murder?'

'No. I mean, yes, he's the one who killed Gitahi. Lisa thought he might know something...' Em recounted the tale, adding that Kamau had failed to meet her on the previous night. 'And when I sent for him this morning— Oh, *mzuri*, Zacharia. Put it down there. No, no, the Bwanas can help themselves.' She waved the old man away, and Eden dispensed drinks.

'Go on,' said Drew. 'You sent for him this morning?'

Em accepted an exceedingly stiff brandy and soda

from her grandson and gulped down half of it before replying. 'They said they thought he'd gone off to cut lucerne, and now it doesn't look as if he did.'

'Bolted, I suppose,' said Eden succinctly.

Em lowered her glass and looked at him sharply. 'Why do you say that?'

'Well, it's the obvious conclusion, isn't it?'

'That's what the Police say. In fact they said just what you said yesterday: that he might have done the murder himself, and now that this girl, Wambui, has told on him, he's lost his nerve and run for it.'

'But you don't believe that,' said Drew slowly.

'No.'

Eden banged his glass down on the tray with such violence that the bottles jumped and rattled. 'Why not? The same old reason I suppose. "My Kukes are loyal!" My God, they ought to have that written up in letters of gold right across the Rift—and headed "Famous Last Words"! Why shouldn't it be the answer? *Someone* did it, and it all ties up with the other things that happened in the house—the poltergeist and the poisoning of Simba. Whoever was responsible for that must have been employed here, or working with an accomplice who was, and if Kamau had no hand in it why has he run away? Tell me that!'

'Because he may think he knows who did it, and is afraid.'

'Afraid of what?'

'Of his own life, of course! Really, Eden, you're being very stupid today. Suppose he *was* watching from the bushes and saw everything? Suppose he even recognized the murderer?'

'In the dusk? At that range?' said Eden scornfully. 'Don't you believe it, Gran! The distance between where he was standing and the spot where Alice was killed is well over fifty yards. And it was getting dark. For all we know, the marks he left may have been made hours earlier—or else they were made by an accomplice keeping *cave*. If Kamau really knows anything about this business it's either because he himself did the murder or connived at it!'

'I don't believe it,' said Em obstinately. 'That's just the sort of conclusion the police jump at—and Gilly and Hector and Mabel. Because it's the easiest one that offers. It's my opinion that Kamau *did* know something, and was sufficiently frightened by what he saw to keep his mouth shut, but couldn't resist throwing out hints to his girl. But I didn't think he'd run away, or that the police would immediately leap to the same silly conclusion that you appear to have leapt to!'

She sipped her drink and glared indignantly at her grandson over the rim of her glass. '*Men!*' said Em scornfully, and directed a speaking glance at her niece. But Victoria's attention had been momentarily distracted by the behaviour of Mr Stratton.

Drew had been sitting on the verandah rail within a foot of her, leaning back lazily against one of the pillars. He looked relaxed and at peace with the world, and appeared to be taking no more than a polite interest in the discussion, until something in

Em's last sentence had jerked him to attention. Victoria did not know why she was so sure of this, for he had made no noticeable movement. Nevertheless she was aware that he was no longer relaxed but had abruptly stiffened into alertness, and that he was sitting very still.

She glanced sideways at him and saw that his eyes were wide and very bright and that they held a curious look of astonishment, as though some new and startling thought had suddenly presented itself to him. It was a look that for some reason disturbed Victoria, and she turned quickly to stare at her aunt as though she might find there some clue as to what had caused it. But Em's face was as aloof and sulky as an elderly bloodhound's, and there was nothing to be read there but her scornful impatience with the limited intelligence of all people who did not think as she did.

Eden said: 'Oh, all right, Gran. Don't let's argue about it. We shall always be on opposite sides of the fence over this. You are quite prepared to believe that everyone else's Kikuyu servants are untrustworthy, but never your own. Hector and Mabel are just as bad. Look at the way Hector behaved in '54 over that knife.'

Em said sharply: 'I will not have you talking scandal, Eden! It was an accident, and you know it. Hector and Mabel are old friends of mine, and——'

'And like Kamau can do no wrong,' finished Eden. 'I know, darling. Sorry I spoke. Have another drink. You've finished that one. What about you, Drew? Have the other half.'

'I've still got it, thanks,' said Drew. 'Have Hector and Mabel been over here this afternoon, Em?'

'Yes,' said Em, handing over her glass to be refilled. 'Mabel brought me a bottle of her chutney. A peace-offering, I think. Dear Mabel. She's such a kind-hearted, sensible person except when she gets on to the subject of Ken. Which reminds me, Eden; Ken was here just after you left. He wanted to know if that Luger of yours was still for sale.'

Eden looked slightly surprised. 'He must be mad. He knows quite well that I flogged it in Mays only about ten days ago. He was there! Besides, he wouldn't have been able to get any ammunition for it.'

'Oh well, perhaps I got it wrong. He may have wanted to know if Mays still had it. I'm afraid I was a bit sharp with him. I found him riding right across the lucerne patch behind the labour lines. He didn't expect to see me down there—let alone Hennessy!—and he stammered and stuttered like a schoolboy caught with his fist in the cake tin. Mabel ought to send him to the coast for a spell. Or better still, take him there herself. The boy is a bundle of nerves.'

Eden said shortly: 'The further away she takes him, and them, the better. I hope you were sufficiently sharp with him to discourage any more visits for the time being.'

'Ken is unsnubbable. You ought to know that by now. Lisa took him off my hands. She came over to borrow some sugar, and took him back with her. It's odd that two people like Hector and Mabel should have produced a child like Ken. He's not really the right type for Kenya.'

'Judging from his capacity for falling in love with other men's wives,' said Eden acidly, 'I should have thought he had at least one of the necessary qualifications.'

'Don't be cheap, dear,' said his grandmother severely. She selected a cigarette from a box on the table beside her, and Drew slid off the verandah rail and went over to light it for her.

'Gilly been around today?' he enquired idly, snapping on the lighter.

'I expect so. He's around so often that I don't notice any more. Thank you, Drew.'

Drew returned the lighter to his pocket and observed that he had not realized that Gilly was so hard-working.

'It's not always work,' said Em with a short laugh. 'My Bechstein is a good deal better than his own piano. He comes over to play.'

Eden muttered something under his breath that was uncomplimentary to Mr Gilbraith Markham, and a frown passed over Em's face. She said: 'I know you think I'm an old fool to keep him on, but God knows what would become of him if I didn't. He's very little use as a manager, and not really a good enough musician to keep himself in any sort of comfort—let alone Lisa!'

Eden said coldly: 'That's nonsense. He was offered a perfectly good job with a dance band. A more than adequate salary, with accommodation thrown in. What is more, Lisa was all for his taking it: Nairobi is far more her cup of tea than the Rift.'

Em looked at him with mingled affection and regret. 'You haven't inherited a particle of feeling for music, dear, have you? It's odd, when your father and all my mother's side of the family had such a love for it. All the Beaumartins have been musical, but it's missed you. If it hadn't, you couldn't talk like that. Gilly is enough of a musician to consider that playing in a dance band would rank with prostitution. He'd prefer to starve.'

'Don't you believe it! Gilly is far too fond of himself. He'd have taken it all right, if you hadn't fallen for all that high falutin' stuff and offered him Gus Abbott's job in order to save him from 'Prostituting his Art'. And if he'd put in as little work with the dance band as he has here, he'd have got the sack inside a week. Probably less! Yet he has the nerve to suggest that you put him in to manage the Rumuruti estates now that Jerry Coles wants to retire.'

Em said softly: 'Perhaps his reasons for wishing to remove to Rumuruti are domestic rather than financial.'

'*Domestic?* Why Lisa simply loathes the idea of going there.'

'Quite,' said Em dryly.

Eden stared at her for a moment, obviously puzzled by her tone, and then flushed hotly in sudden comprehension, and turning his back on her busied himself once more with the tray of drinks.

Em said placidly, but with a wicked twinkle in her eye: 'But I am unlikely to give it to him. You see, I should miss hearing him play.'

'Was he playing here today?' asked Drew.

'I don't think so. I didn't hear him. But then I went down to the labour lines with Bill Hennessy and his askaris, and I wouldn't have heard him from there. I'm getting too deaf.'

Em sighed and shook her head impatiently, as though the infirmities of old age were tormenting flies; and then all at once she stiffened in her chair, listening.

A car was coming up the long, rutted drive between the acacias and the spiky clusters of sisal, and Em rose hurriedly. 'If it's anyone else offering condolences, tell them I'm out. Or ill!'

'Don't worry,' said Eden, 'it'll only be Drew's car. His driver was bringing it round.'

But it was not Mr Stratton's car. It was Mr Gilbert's, and a moment later, accompanied by the Markhams, he walked on to the verandah; and at the sight of his face they all came quickly to their feet.

Greg dispensed with formalities and came straight to the point: 'Hennessy tells me that one of your Kikuyu boys has disappeared. Kamau.'

He ignored Drew, Eden and Victoria, and addressed himself solely to Em, while behind him Lisa fidgeted and twisted her fingers, her pretty face sulky and apprehensive, and Gilly leaned against a verandah pillar with a studied negligence that was belied by the avid interest that was plainly visible in his restless eyes.

Em said coldly and defiantly: 'Yes. And I presume, as you have brought Lisa and Gilly with you, that you know why.'

'Hennessey told me why. It seems that you told

him of Mrs Markham's visit to you yesterday, and I came down to see what I could get out of this woman Wambui.'

Lisa gave a little whimpering sob. 'I wish I hadn't said anything to anyone! I *wish* I hadn't! I only thought that Lady Emily ought to know.'

Mr Gilbert ignored the interruption. He said: 'I got quite a lot out of her, but before we go any further I'd like to have your own account of exactly what happened yesterday; from Mrs Markham's arrival to the time you decided that Kamau wasn't going to turn up. Also what action, if any, you took about it this morning.'

Em looked at Greg Gilbert's grim unsmiling face, and her shrewd old eyes were puzzled and wary. She said slowly: 'Let me see——' And for the second time that evening described Lisa's visit and the happenings of the hours that followed it, ending with her enquiries that morning as to Kamau's whereabouts, and her discovery, when Hennessy and his askaris had gone down to the labour lines to question the African employees and their families, that no one had seen him since Zacharia had delivered her message to him on the previous afternoon. Except, presumably, Wambui?

'No, she didn't,' said Lisa with an air of conscious virtue. 'I made a point of seeing that she couldn't get away last night. I thought that you should have every chance to speak to Kamau first, and as I said to Hector——'

She checked suddenly, her eyes and her mouth blank circles of dismay.

Greg turned with a swiftness that startled her,

and said brusquely: 'You told me that you had not mentioned this to anyone else. Not even your husband.'

'Least of all her husband,' interpolated Gilly with an edge to his voice.

'Shut up, Gilly! Did you tell Hector Brandon, Lisa?'

Lisa's large violet eyes filled with tears and she said querulously: 'Don't bark at me, Greg! There's no need for you——'

'*Did* you?'

'Well—well, yes. But only in the strictest confidence. After all, I've known Hector for years, and I knew he wouldn't let it go any further. And I was very worried. You don't seem to realize——'

'When did you tell him? Before you'd been over here, or afterwards?'

'Oh, afterwards. Because of course by then I was sure that Lady Emily would get it all out of Kamau, and then everything would be all right. I mean, at least we'd all *know*.'

'Hmm,' said Greg disagreeably. He stared at her long and meditatively until she reddened under his gaze, and then turning away abruptly he addressed himself again to Em:

'We've got search parties out looking for Kamau, and with luck we should pick him up without much trouble. He's probably made for the Reserve. But even when we get him I doubt if we'll get much more out of him than we got out of Wambui.'

Em said tartly: 'You certainly won't if you start off by sending out your askaris to arrest him as though he'd done something criminal, when all he is guilty of is telling his girl-friend that he thinks he knows something about the murder.'

'I'm afraid he told her more than that,' said Greg quietly.

Em stiffened suddenly and once again her eyes moved from Greg to Lisa, and she said haltingly: 'But Lisa, you told me——' and stopped.

Lisa dragged at her handkerchief until the fabric tore, and her voice was high and hysterical: 'I didn't know there was any more! I tell you I didn't know! I had no idea—she just said that he—he knew something. But if I'd known what it was I wouldn't have said a word! Eden, you *know* I wouldn't——'

Eden said in an entirely expressionless voice: 'I'm afraid I don't know what you're talking about. Perhaps Greg will be good enough to explain.'

'Yes,' said Em harshly. 'If you have anything to say, Greg, let us hear it and get it over.'

Mr Gilbert surveyed her thoughtfully, and there was something in his expression that frightened Victoria. He said slowly and deliberately: 'Wambui told Mrs Markham that Kamau had hinted that he knew something about Mrs DeBrett's murder. That was not true. He had done a good deal more than hint, but she was afraid to admit to anything else because his story is too fantastic to be believed.'

He paused, as though collecting his thoughts, and Em said grimly: 'Go on.'

'Kamau's story,' said Greg, 'is that on Tuesday evening he waited for Wambui as usual among the bushes near the knoll, and that shortly after he got there he saw Mrs DeBrett arrive and start picking roses; so he lay low and waited for her to go away. But she sat down on the fallen tree and stayed there until it was nearly dark, and he began to get tired of waiting and must have made some movement in the bushes, for she jumped up as though she was alarmed and began to run away. And then, he said, he saw someone coming to meet her. Someone whom she knew, and ran to. And who killed her.'

'No!' cried Lisa, her voice shockingly shrill after Greg's quiet and unemotional tones. 'She made it up! She must have done! I don't believe it!' She burst into noisy sobs, but no one had any attention to spare for her, for they were looking with a fixed and fascinated intensity at Greg Gilbert.

Eden said loudly: 'If he saw who it was, why didn't he say so at once?—when he was questioned with the others? Why didn't——'

Em made a swift impatient gesture of the hand, silencing him, and Greg said slowly, frowning down at the matting as though he preferred not to meet the painfully intent stares that were fixed on him: 'Wambui says it was because he recognized the murderer, and was afraid.'

'Go on,' repeated Em, harshly and imperiously. 'Who did he say it was?'

Greg removed his gaze from the matting and looked up, meeting her gaze squarely.

He said softly: 'You, Em.'

10

There was a moment of complete and utter stillness, as though everyone on the verandah had been temporarily deprived of the power of speech or movement. The blood drained out of Em's face leaving it yellow and drawn and incredibly old, and she sat down heavily and abruptly as though her legs could no longer support her.

The protesting creak of the wicker-work chair broke the silence with the effect of a stone dropped into a quiet pool, and Eden said furiously: 'What the hell d'you mean by making accusations like that! By God, I've a good mind to——' He took a swift stride forward, and Drew said sharply and compellingly: 'Be quiet, Eden! You're only making matters worse.'

He reached out and caught Eden's arm, jerking him back, and Greg said: 'I am not making any accusations—at the moment. I am merely repeating something that I have heard at second hand. Well, Em? How about it?'

Eden shook off Drew's restraining hand and said: 'Don't answer him, Gran! If he's going to believe every silly fairy story cooked up by a half-witted African farm-hand, you'd better wait until you can see your lawyer!'

Em paid no attention to him. She looked at Greg with eyes that were blank with shock, and said slowly and as though it were an effort to speak: 'What do you want me to say? That I did not kill Alice? But telling you so is not proof, is it? And I was here in the house that evening, so I suppose from your point of view I could have done it.'

'Gran, for God's sake!' begged Eden.

'Oh, Eden dear, *do* stop being so silly! Drew is quite right. It really does not help at all to lose our heads and shout—or collapse into tears, like Lisa. Surely we can behave in a rational manner? Sit down, Greg. You had better tell me what you propose to do about this—this extraordinary statement.'

Mr Gilbert drew up a chair and sat down facing her. He said: 'We can't do much about it until we pull in Kamau and get him to verify it. What I want you to do is to give me an exact account of what happened that evening. Yes, I know we've been into this before, but I want it once again. You'd been out shooting, and got back just before six. What did you do then?'

'I changed,' said Em patiently.

'Into what? That Japanese job with storks all over

it that you were wearing when I arrived later that night?'

'No, of course not! That was a kimono. I changed into a house-coat. Yellow, if you want to know. But I had to take it off because——' She stopped suddenly, and after a brief pause said: 'Because it had blood all over it. Yes... I can see that that doesn't sound good. But I couldn't help it. I'd tried to carry her up to the house, and—well, you saw her.'

'Yes,' agreed Greg briefly. 'What did you do then? After you'd changed into the house-coat?'

'I came into the drawing-room for a drink, and saw Lisa's note asking for a lift into Nairobi—I'd left it on the piano—and Alice went over to tell her that I'd give her a lift when I went in to fetch Victoria.'

'What did you do when she'd gone?'

'Went out to tell Zach and Cookie about cutting up the kongoni, and after that I saw the dogs fed, and gave Majiri the curtains and covers from Victoria's room to wash—the water's always extra hot in the evenings, because of the baths. Zach came round just before half-past six and turned on the lights, and I told him to leave the drinks in the drawing-room. And then I played the piano.'

'Until when?'

'Until around eight o'clock, when he came in to say that Alice was still not back, and should he serve dinner? I hadn't realized it was so late, and I called the dogs and went off to fetch her. *Must* I go over all that part again?'

'No. That's not the really important time from

your point of view, as she must have been killed around seven o'clock, and you say you were playing the piano from six thirty onwards. That in itself is a reasonably good alibi.'

'Why?' enquired Em with an attempt at a smile. 'You've only my word for it.'

Greg consulted the notebook they had seen on the previous day, and said: 'Not quite. Seven of your servants stated independently that the "Memsahib Mkubwa" had been playing during that time, and had not stopped for more than a minute or two at most. Certainly not long enough to murder Alice and then change into fresh clothes, as presumably even old Zacharia would have noticed bloodstains on a yellow house-coat! It couldn't have been done in under ten to fifteen minutes, and on a cross-check of the evidence you never stopped playing for anything like that.'

'You've forgotten something,' said Em dryly. 'I have an extremely good radio-gramophone, and not one of my servants would know the difference.'

Eden said hoarsely: 'Gran, are you mad! Listen, Greg, she doesn't realize how serious this may be. She ought to have a lawyer. Drew, can't *you* stop this? Can't you make her see some sense?'

'Your grandmother,' said Drew, 'appears to me to be seeing it with extreme clarity. It would only be a question of time before someone else thought of that one, so she might just as well mention the radiogram herself.'

'Exactly!' said Em approvingly. 'Everyone knows about it—and about such things as long-playing records, too! I can see no point in laying claim to an alibi that is obviously as full of holes as a sieve. Besides I don't need one. I know quite enough about Kenya to know that no jury in this country is going to take such a charge seriously. And so does Greg! Because everyone knows me. If they did not, it might be possible to get a conviction on such evidence. After all, I am still tolerably strong—strong enough to kill a little weak defenceless creature like Alice who would have been too surprised to——'

Em's voice failed suddenly and she covered her face with her hands as though to blot out the horror that her own words had conjured up: the picture of Alice standing helpless and appalled in the dusk, too stunned with shock to scream or run. A strong shudder shook her bulky body and presently she lifted a ravaged face and staring, haunted eyes, and spoke in a voice that was barely more than a hoarse whisper:

'I've seen a lot of bad things in my time. Men who were mauled by lions or trampled by buffalo or rhino. And—and there was Gus Abbott too. But they were men. I suppose that made it different. It's silly to feel like this. But—but she couldn't bear wounds and blood. I used to tell her that she shouldn't mind. But when I saw her that night, I minded too. I minded...'

Eden said: 'Don't, Gran! Please——!' His face was as drawn and ravaged as her own, and, for a moment only, ugly with remembered horror. The sight of it seemed to act on Em like a douche of cold water, and she straightened her bowed shoulders with a palpable effort and said remorsefully:

'Forgive me, dear. I'm behaving very badly. But then this is all so absurd. I wish I knew why Kamau should have said such a thing. Perhaps Wambui made it up?'

'I don't think so,' said Greg. 'I can usually tell when I'm being spun a yarn. I'd say she was speaking the truth. But was Kamau?'

'Yes,' said Drew, abruptly and positively.

There was a simultaneous gasp from at least four throats, and Em shrank back in her chair and stared at him in horrified disbelief.

Mr Stratton viewed his audience with undisguised impatience and said: 'There's no need to look at me as though I'd gone off my head. The thing stands out a mile. Of *course* he was speaking the truth—or what he thought was the truth. Just take a look at Em. She's a nice, bright splash of colour, isn't she? And she's been dressing like that ever since I was in rompers! Eden has already pointed out that the distance between the bushes and the spot where Alice was killed is rather more than fifty yards, and it was getting dark. So all that Kamau saw was someone wearing the sort of hat and clothes she wears, and naturally he thought it was Em. Bet you any money you like I'm right!'

'No takers,' said Greg with a wry smile. 'I ought to have seen it myself.'

'But *why?*' demanded Eden vehemently. 'Why should anyone try and pin it on Gran, when she's the very last person who'd be likely to do it?'

Drew shrugged and said: 'Perhaps that was why. Because no one would credit it.'

'No,' said Greg slowly. 'I imagine that the reason

was even simpler than that. Anyone, male or female, could wear that sort of outfit and get away with it, because no one would give them a second look. It also provided an excuse for being seen in the gardens at that hour, for if anyone happened to see the wearer, they'd take it for granted that it was Em. It was the perfect disguise. And that of course is the answer to the riddle of the verandah cushion!'

'How do you work that out?' demanded Em, thereby temporarily depriving Mr Gilbert of his composure.

'Well . . . er . . . I thought—padding?' he suggested cautiously.

Em looked bewildered but Lisa unexpectedly went off into a gale of giggles, and Em, turning to look at her, remarked coldly that they would all like to share in the joke: any joke.

'I'm s-sorry,' gasped Lisa, wavering helplessly between relief and hysteria. 'I suppose I shouldn't laugh, but it's so f-funny! He means your b-b-bosom! A man wouldn't have one, but you have! *Ha, ha, ha, ha!*'

Instinctively and simultaneously every eye was focused upon Em's imposing frontage, and the next minute they were all laughing as helplessly as Lisa—and for much the same reason. Only Em, like Queen Victoria, declined to be amused, and announced austerely that she saw nothing to laugh at.

'You wouldn't, darling. You're behind it!' said Eden, and collapsed into renewed mirth.

Em folded her hands in her lap and waited with a dignified display of patience for the laughter to subside.

'I apologize,' said Greg, mopping his streaming eyes and recovering himself. 'On behalf of us all. Extremely silly and unnecessary, but for some reason it's done me a power of good. Seriously, Em, that cushion worried me. But it's quite obvious that whoever impersonated you was too slim to be convincing, and needed a bit of—well, building up. Hence the cushion. Now what about those clothes? How many pairs of those red overalls have you got, and have you lost any recently?'

Victoria gave a startled gasp and Em said grimly: 'I never thought of that! I should have four pairs of them, but one can't be found.'

'Could it have been missing for some time?'

Em shrugged. 'Perhaps. I wouldn't have noticed, and I don't suppose Zacharia would have done either until an occasion like this morning, when three pairs happened to be in the wash at once.'

'Supposing someone wanted to steal a pair, would it have been easy or difficult? For an outsider, for instance.'

'I should say only too easy. All the washing is hung up on the lines behind the kitchen, and anyone could remove something from a line if they waited for the right moment. The odd thing does occasionally vanish—generally dish-cloths. But Zach ought to have noticed something like a pair of my dungarees. Except that he's getting old—like me.'

Mr Gilbert frowned thoughtfully at the small notebook that lay open on his knee, and presently said: 'By the way, in spite of what you said on the subject of alibis, I think you may turn out to have a cast-iron one after all. Can you remember what you were playing on the piano that evening?'

'Yes,' said Em, her face suddenly bleak. 'I was playing Toroni's concerto. *The Rift Valley Concerto*. There isn't any record of that. Not any longer.'

'So I understand. It was broken by the poltergeist, wasn't it? And I also seem to remember that there was only the one record, and that it isn't on sale, or available to the general public. Am I right?'

'Yes. He had it made for me in New York. But then none of my servants would know the difference between one tune and another, I'm afraid.'

Greg said: 'That's where you're wrong. The average African has a better ear for music than one would imagine, and that particular piece not only had a good many tribal tunes and rhythms incorporated into it, but I gather that Toroni composed it here at *Flamingo*, on your piano; and that you yourself have played it pretty frequently of late. Anyway, three of your servants say that you were playing "Bwana Toroni's songs". So you see it's not such a bad alibi after all. We shall have to check it of course, for form's sake: cable New York and make sure that you couldn't have got hold of a duplicate, and that sort of thing. And if their answer clears you, then the thing is buttoned as far as you are concerned.'

'I rather think that it's buttoned without that,' remarked Gilly unexpectedly. 'In fact you can save yourself the expense of a cable, and the F.B.I. a headache.'

'How's that?' demanded Greg, turning quickly to face him.

Gilly abandoned the pose of disinterested spectator, and strolled forward, his hands in his pockets.

He said: 'Drew'll tell you that I met him at the gate in the hedge just after he'd seen Alice off, and we both heard Em playing that thing. He pushed off, but I didn't. I sat on the concrete block just outside the gate for a goodish while. Until it was dark.'

'You *what?*' demanded Greg incredulously. 'Why the hell didn't you tell me this before? You mean that you were there after seven? Surely you must have heard *something*. A cry, or——'

Gilly cut him short. 'I didn't hear anything! You forget that the knoll is away to the right, and there are trees and bamboos and heaven knows what between it and the gate. But there is a fairly clear line between the gate and the house, and I could hear the piano. I sat there for quite a time, listening to Em tackling that piece. I know it a damn sight better than she does; every bar and every note of it! And you can take it from me that it wouldn't make any difference if you discovered that there were half a million of those records in existence, and all of them in Kenya!'

'Why?' demanded Greg tersely.

'Why? Because I'm enough of a musician to tell the difference between Em's rendering of the concerto, and Toroni's. That's why!'

Gilly transferred his gaze from Greg's relieved face to Em's tight-lipped, rigid mouth and basilisk stare, and laughed.

'I'm sorry, Em. I know that touches you on the raw. But let's face it, you're a pretty poor performer when it comes to the piano, while Toroni was in a class by himself. And if you think I couldn't go into the witness box and swear to the difference between your playing of the concerto and his—and be believed—you're even less of a musician than I take you for. Well?'

The fury died out of Em's face but she continued to eye him with considerable hauteur, and after staring at him in disdainful silence for a full minute, she said coldly: 'As both Greg and Eden seem to think that I could do with an alibi, I shall not argue with you.'

'It may be a useful thing to have handy,' observed Greg, and added briskly, 'And now the next thing is to go after that missing pair of overalls.'

'You are not going after them tonight,' snapped Em. 'At least, not in this house. I don't care what you do in the grounds. Or anywhere else! But I have had quite enough alarms and excursions for one day, and I propose to have an early supper and go to bed. Good night.'

She heaved herself up out of her chair and withdrew with the dignity of a Dowager Empress concluding an audience, leaving a somewhat conscience-stricken silence behind her. It was broken by Eden, who opened a bottle of soda water with an irritable violence that sent it frothing over the matting, and informed Gilly that this time he really had put his foot in it.

'If there is one thing that Gran is vain about,' said Eden, 'it's her playing. You may have given her a cast-iron alibi, but she won't thank you for it. She'd probably have preferred to stand trial! So if you find yourself queueing up at the Labour Exchange in the near future, you'll know why. You'd better get yourself a drink while the going's good. It's probably the last you'll get on the house.'

'Rot!' said Gilly. He giggled light-heartedly, and taking advantage of the offer, poured himself out a double whisky, gulped it down neat, and refilled his glass. 'Your grandmother may have been a tolerable amateur pianist in the days of her youth—though personally, I doubt it. But though her appreciation of good music is still Grade A, her performance, when compared to someone like Toroni's, is on a par with a pianola's. As for booting me out, *phooey!* Bet you she gives me a rise! After all, what's injured pride compared to a stretched neck?'

'Point is,' said Eden, 'that as she'll never believe in the possibility of the latter, she will have plenty of indignation to spare for the former.'

'You underrate her intelligence,' grinned Gilly. '*Skoal!* She may be a vain old peacock, but she's no fool. Sheerest stroke of luck that I didn't trot straight back to the house that evening. Very nearly did! But I'd had just about enough of Hector and Mabel for one day, and I didn't want to run into them; so I stayed where I was and listened to Em massacring that concerto. Stroke of luck!'

Greg slid the notebook into his pocket and said: 'Look, Eden, do you think I could have a word with Majiri and Zacharia without running into Em again—about those dungarees? I shall have to send Bill Hennessy down tomorrow to go into the question in more detail of course. That'll turn his hair white!'

'As long as you steer clear of the cook,' said Eden, 'I don't care who you see. But cheese and biscuits for supper on top of all this would be the last straw. All right, come on.' They departed, leaving Victoria to the society of the Markhams and Mr Stratton.

The sun had set and the gardens were no longer gaily coloured and noisy with bird song, but cool and green and quiet, and a bat swooped out from under the eaves and flitted along the silent verandah.

Lisa stood up and said in a bright, brittle voice: 'So it was all a storm in a teacup. I can't imagine why Greg should have insisted on our coming over with him. So embarrassing! And quite unnecessary, as it happened.'

Gilly poured himself out a third whisky and observed dispassionately that it provided an interesting and unexpected sidelight on his wife's character to find that she could refer to a brutal murder as a storm in a teacup, and that she knew quite well why Greg had brought them over. 'Or you should know. After all, you were the one who started this hare. Besides, you were quite prepared to believe that she'd done it. Don't tell me you weren't!'

Lisa said indignantly: 'Gilly, I do wish you wouldn't talk such arrant nonsense. Drew and I know you well enough to know when you're joking, but Miss Caryll might take you seriously.'

'And how right Miss Caryll would be! You also produced a very, very neat little theory as to *why* Em should have done it, didn't you?'

'Gilly, be quiet!' Lisa rounded on her husband, her eyes brilliant with anger.

'And a damned good theory, too, if I may say so,' said Gilly, ignoring her. 'Except for one small but vital point that you have overlooked.'

'*Gilly!*' Lisa's voice was imploring, and she dragged at his arm. 'It's getting late. Let's go home.'

'Pipe down, Lisa. Drew's interested; aren't you Drew? Interesting case—very. Drew doesn't believe that any stray Mau Mau thug did this, any more'n I do—or Greg, or Em. Much as they'd like to believe it, Lisa my love. But they don't know what I know.'

He began to giggle, and Drew said: 'What do you know, Gilly?' But the question had been asked too sharply, and the slightly vacuous expression that whisky had brought to Gilly's face was replaced by wariness and a trace of malice.

'We aren't discussing me,' said Gilly. 'Discussin' Lisa's theory about Em. Em and Alice. We all think that Em was fond of Alice—in a patronizing Protect-the-Weak the poor-kid-can't-help-it sort of way. But suppose we were wrong? Supposing that underneath all that surface affection she hated her guts? That it was all an act, and she was really jealous of her—because of Eden, or because one day she would be mistress of *Flamingo?* It's no secret that Em's nuts about Eden and dotty on the subject of *Flamingo*. She'd do anything for either of them—even murder! That was Lisa's theory. And mark you, granting the premise, perfectly feasible. I don't suppose that Em has ever heard that song about *You can't chop your momma up in Massachusetts*, but she'd be quite capable of chopping up a granddaughter-in-law in Kenya if she judged it to be necessary. Law unto herself; that's Em! All the same, Lisa doesn't notice things...'

'What sort of things?' This time Drew's voice was deceptively casual.

'Oh—this and that. Or maybe she does? She's a sly little thing, Lisa. All women are sly. Ever noticed that, Drew? You will—you will! Take Mabel, for instance... asked if she could take a couple of pineapples home on Tuesday evening, just after Alice left, and went off to pick 'em. Lisa never noticed that she came back without any. And shall I tell you why? Because Lisa had been out too. Down to the shamba, *she* says, to get some tomatoes. Though what she wanted 'em for is anybody's guess—we had roast duck and cauliflower for supper. She thinks *I* don't notice things, but I do!'

Lisa made no comment, but Victoria saw her eyes widen in surprise and become fixed and intent. Gilly wagged his head sagely and helped himself to yet another drink, and Drew said curtly: 'Haven't you had enough of that?'

'Enough of what?' demanded Gilly. 'Women—or Em's whisky? If the former, certainly. But no one can have too much of Em's whisky. First because it's good, and secon'ly because it's Em's; on the house! *Prosit!*'

He took a deep gulp, and lowered his voice to a confidential undertone: 'Ever struck you, Drew, that all the time Greg was talking about alibis for Em, he hadn't noticed that no one else has one either? You, for instance. You say you went off home when you left me. Did you? Mabel says she was picking pineapples. Oh yeah? Hector walked home by the path that runs along the top of the shambas—so he says. Eden's supposed to have been driving around somewhere, and Lisa's wandering round the tomato patch. But is there an alibi in the bunch? Not on your life!'

Drew said amiably: 'That's quite a point. We might start with you. Can you prove one?'

Gilly looked startled. 'Prove what?'

'That you sat on that lump of concrete for half an hour or so and didn't hear a thing?'

Gilly put down his empty glass hurriedly. 'Here! Who says I didn't hear anything? I heard Em playing—I heard that damned concerto of Toroni's.'

'That's what *you* say. But Em had already told us what it was that she had been playing, and the evidence of three of her servants confirmed it. You might have decided to use that information as an alibi for yourself. Or you might still have heard it, but from a good deal nearer! See what I mean? So if I were you I'd lay off all these heavy hints that various people are in need of alibis. Because the obvious inference is that they must each have had a reason for wishing Alice dead, and that you know it. Which is dangerous bunkum.'

'But I do——' began Gilly. And stopped. He made a nervous grab at his glass, and then changed his mind and pushed it away so violently that it toppled off the table and splintered into pieces on the verandah floor.

Lisa said briskly and with a trace of satisfaction

in her voice: 'Now look what you've done! That's one of Em's crystal set, and she won't be a bit pleased. Or do you think that if we just tiptoe away and leave her to find it she'll put it down to the poltergeist?'

She accompanied the remark with a high-pitched tinkling laugh; but her face as she bent to pick up the broken pieces was white and frightened, and Victoria, stooping to help her, saw that her hands were shaking uncontrollably.

A light clicked on in the dining-room behind them, and a warm yellow glow fell across the verandah from the windows and the open door. And instantly it was evening no longer, but dusk: the garden shadowy with nightfall and the sky already sprinkled with pale stars.

Lisa deposited the bits of broken glass on the tray and said: 'Would you tell your aunt that it was an accident, and that we're so sorry? Oh, and she did say something about a picnic on the twenty-ninth. It was arranged before—before anything happened of course, so it may not be on. Would you ask her to let me know about it, because I'm afraid we must rush. Drew, you're coming over to collect those papers, aren't you? You'd better stay to supper as it's so late. It's only ourselves and Ken Brandon. He's rather in a state, poor boy, and it might take his mind off things if we had some bridge.'

Drew said firmly: 'No thank you, Lisa. An evening spent coping with an adolescent who is "in a state" is not in my line. Besides, I must get back.'

'Don't blame you,' said Gilly feelingly. 'Good

night, Victoria.' He nodded absently at her and followed his wife down the steps and out into the violet dusk.

Victoria watched them go, and then turned to look at Mr Stratton, who had not moved. She was unaware that at that moment her face was as white and as frightened as Lisa's had been—or Gilly's. But Drew, looking down at it, was unaccountably disturbed.

He said abruptly: 'You're scared, aren't you.'

'A—a little,' admitted Victoria. And having admitted it was immediately aware of a diminution of that fear.

'Of what?'

'I don't know. The house—the things that have happened in it. But you don't believe in ghosts, do you?'

'Not in this one,' said Drew grimly. 'That is, if you're referring to the poltergeist.'

'I don't either. It all sounds too——'

She hesitated, wrinkling her brows, and Drew said: 'Too unghostly?'

'I was going to say, "too planned"; as though someone had worked it all out very carefully to a—a sort of pattern. I think that is what is frightening.'

'Why? Because you think that no African would have planned something like this and carried it through? If that's what you think, you're wrong. It's just the sort of tortuous scheme that would appeal to them. But there's nothing to be afraid of now, for if there ever was a plan, or a pattern, Mrs DeBrett's death completed it. It's finished.'

He had spoken with complete confidence, but

almost before the words were out of his mouth he realized with a sudden sense of shock that he did not believe them. How could anyone assert with confidence that Alice's death had put an end to the things that had happened at *Flamingo*, while her killer was still at large? *It is only the first killing that is difficult*. Greg had said that only yesterday...

A bird fluttered among the hanging creepers at the verandah edge, and Drew saw Victoria start at the sound and bite hard on her underlip; and was surprised to find himself suddenly and savagely angry. With Em for bringing the girl out here. With Eden for permitting it. With Greg and Gilly and Lisa for frightening her. And most of all with himself—for caring whether they did or not!

11

Breakfast was barely over on the following morning when young Mr Hennessy and his police askaris descended upon *Flamingo*.

Em interviewed them briefly on the verandah and dismissed them to the kitchen quarters and the labour lines in charge of Eden, there to pursue their enquiries into the disappearance of Kamau and a pair of scarlet dungarees.

An hour later Gilly had appeared with a batch of files, and she retired with him into the office, having refused her niece's offer of assistance.

Victoria, left to her own devices, fetched a hat and went out to explore the garden, and she had been following a narrow path that wound through bushes of bougainvillaea, plumbago and orange trumpet flower when she came suddenly upon a stranger. A middle-aged woman in a green cotton dress who wore a battered wide-brimmed double terai hat jammed down over a riot of grey curls, and who appeared to have lost something, for she was bending down and peering anxiously about her.

'Can I help?' enquired Victoria.

The woman jumped violently, and said in a breathless voice: 'Oh dear, how you startled me! I believe there's a puff adder in there. They are such dangerous creatures. You must be Victoria. I used to know your parents—oh, years ago. You wouldn't remember me. I'm Mabel Brandon. Our place, *Brandonmead*, is just over there——' She gestured vaguely to the west with one hand and began to move on down the path, still talking, so that Victoria had perforce to follow her:

'We have a sort of mutual right-of-way between *Flamingo* and our land,' said Mrs Brandon. 'It saves us going miles by road. There's a track that runs right round this side of the lake across at least a dozen estates. I believe it used to be a game track once. There was any amount of big game in the valley when we first came here. Rhino and lion and buffalo, and even elephant. But of course they're gone now. Just as well really. It would have made farming impossible. Of course lions still come over sometimes from the Masai territory, though they get killed off very quickly. I believe one was seen at Crater Lake only last year. We must take you there. Em said something about a picnic. But she will have cancelled that of course.'

Mrs Brandon had quickened her steps as she talked and now she was walking quite briskly. Almost as though she did not want Victoria to linger among the bushes and was hurrying her away from them, talking trivialities to distract her attention from the fact.

The path took a sharp downward curve and came out upon a long belt of open ground, where a narrow trolley line ran parallel with the shamba and carried the heavy piles of maize and vegetables and bananas up to the higher ground where the *Flamingo* lorries were loaded. Mrs Brandon paused irresolutely and murmured something about running up to see Gilly.

'He won't be there,' volunteered Victoria. 'He's up at the house with Aunt Em.'

'Oh,' said Mrs Brandon doubtfully. 'Well perhaps I might call in there: just for a minute or two. No, don't let's go back that way——' She left the path and struck upwards again, following the trolley line, and they came out among a grove of acacias, one of which was being cut up and converted into charcoal.

Mrs Brandon sat down on the fallen trunk, and removing her hat, fanned her hot face with it and enquired conversationally if Victoria was glad to be back in Kenya, and how did she find Em? 'Personally,' said Mrs Brandon, 'I don't think that she is looking at all well. But then all this has been a terrible blow to her. And now I hear that one of her boys has run off. Kamau.' She paused expectantly, but receiving no reply went on to ask what Mr Gilbert had made of Wambui's story.

'What story?' asked Victoria innocently.

Mrs Brandon's pleasant face flushed and she shifted uncomfortably. But she was not to be deflected. 'The one she told Lisa. That it was Em who had killed Alice. Quite ridiculous of course, but—well, it does raise a question, doesn't it? I was never *quite* sure that Em really liked Alice. And Africans are so quick to spot these things. They're very observant. If Kamau thought that Em disliked her, that might have put the idea into his head—that Em killed her. It would have seemed quite natural to him. The wish being father to the thought. If—if you see what I mean.'

'No,' said Victoria, 'I'm afraid I don't. Mr Gilbert says it's quite obvious that Kamau thought he saw her do it.'

'But that's ridiculous!' protested Mrs Brandon.

'Of course it is,' said Victoria cheerfully. 'But Mr Gilbert thinks it was someone wearing the sort of clothes and hat that Aunt Em wears. He says it would have been the best possible disguise, as even a smaller person or a thinner one could have worn it, since no one would have looked twice.'

'A thin person,' repeated Mabel stupidly. And suddenly sat bolt upright, struck by the same thought that had struck Greg Gilbert. 'The cushion! So *that* was why—! Oh no, it isn't possible. It isn't!'

'What isn't possible?' enquired Victoria, puzzled.

'Prints,' said Mabel confusedly. 'It wasn't a plain one. It——' She seemed suddenly to recollect herself, and stopped short, biting her lip and presently smiled a little stiffly and said: 'It's difficult to know what to think, isn't it? One does not like to think that one's own servants may be under suspicion, and Em's have always been so staunch. It must be heartbreaking for her. For of course it must be one of the *Flamingo* servants. It could be no one else. What does Greg intend to do about it?'

'I don't know,' said Victoria with perfect truth, and firmly changing the subject, enquired: 'What are those odd looking mud heaps with smoke coming out of them?'

'Charcoal,' said Mabel briefly. 'Does Em think——'

'*Charcoal?* But it's mud and turf!'

'The charcoal is inside,' explained Mabel patiently. 'When a tree dies we cut it up into lengths and then put mud all over it in a huge mound—all those trenches are where the earth and turf were dug out—and when it's covered a slow fire is started at one end which burns away for weeks, and when that's out the charcoal is ready. They're really sort of home-made kilns. Does your aunt think that whoever murdered Alice was really wearing a pair of her dungarees? I mean, surely she must know if a pair is missing? It wouldn't be easy to steal them.'

Victoria gave it up. 'But there is a pair missing,' she said, resigning herself. 'And Aunt Em says it would have been quite easy for anyone who wanted a pair to take them off the washing line. I had a look this morning, and it would. In fact you could have had one yourself today if you'd felt like it. That path you were on passes it quite close.'

'Oh,' said Mrs Brandon, momentarily disconcerted. 'Yes, I suppose it would be possible. It's very careless of Em to have her lines where she can't see them. It encourages pilfering. But the hat—is one of her hats missing too?'

'I don't think so. But one floppy hat would look exactly like another in the dusk, wouldn't it?'

Mrs Brandon's gaze fell on the wide-brimmed double terai she held, and she dropped it as though it had stung her, and then stooped hurriedly and picked it up. She jammed it back on her dishevelled curls and stood up, and said in a rather breathless voice: 'It's dreadfully hot here, isn't it? All those kilns—Shall we go back to the house? Em may have finished with the office work by now, and I should like some shandy.'

She led the way between the acacia trees, and across a waste of parched grass strewn with rough lava boulders towards a green belt of trees and bamboos that screened the gardens; and on arrival at the house went off to telephone her husband.

Victoria departed in search of cold drinks and discovered Eden in the dining-room similarly employed—though he appeared to favour something stronger than shandy.

'Hullo, Vicky. What'll you have? Scotch or rye. Or what about a gin and ginger? You'd better get down to some steady drinking, because the odds are once again heavily in favour of a bread-and-cheese luncheon. The entire household staff are having hysterics over the question of Gran's pants. What a party!'

Victoria laughed and said: 'I've got Mrs Brandon

here. She's telephoning her husband to fetch her. She says she'd like some shandy, and I'll have some too. Is there any ice?'

'Lots. I've just collected a bowl from the 'fridge. Also some beer, so you're in luck. I presume Mabel is here with the object of collecting all the latest dope. Has she been cross-questioning you?'

'Yes,' admitted Victoria ruefully. 'I tried to dodge it, but it wasn't any use. She's madly curious.'

'She's scared stiff!' corrected Eden, mixing beer and ginger beer in a jug.

'Scared? But why?'

'Because her darling son had a juvenile crush on my wife,' said Eden.

'But that's no reason——' began Victoria, bewildered.

'No?' Eden added ice cubes, and filled a tankard, pushed it across to Victoria. 'You don't know Mabel! She's nuts about her ewe lamb, and it's my guess that she's been bitten with the crazy notion that Alice having repulsed him, he may have seen red and gone for her, preferring to see her dead rather than lost to him. All very dramatic and Othello-ish, and utterly ridiculous! I don't say that Ken mightn't have done that. In fact he's precisely the type of hysterical young ass who from time to time figures in the Sunday papers as having waylaid his ex-love, and bashed her with his own (and identifiable!) spanner, because she'd thrown him over. But what Mabel hasn't the sense to realize is that if he'd done it, he'd have shot himself five minutes later! Unless of course he had some totally different and entirely unsuspected reason for wanting Alice out of the way, which is absurd. If only one could put that to Mabel it would save her making an ass of herself. But of course one can't.'

'Why not?' demanded Victoria with some heat. 'Because "it's not done", I suppose!'

'No, darling. Because I, personally, do not fancy having my eyes scratched out. Just you try hinting to Mabel that she has even allowed such a possibility to cross her mind. She'd deny it with her last breath and never forgive you for having suggested it. But it's there all right—panicking about in her subconscious, if nowhere else. Nothing else will explain why she has taken to thinking up excuses for haunting the place and asking endless questions, and generally behaving like a flustered hen. Darling Mabel. The best thing we can do for her is to add a double brandy to her shandy.'

He mixed himself a stiff John Collins and lifted his glass to Victoria. 'Well, here's to you, darling. Don't let any of this get you down. You're too sweet to get involved in such a miserable business. Keep out of it, Vicky.'

Was there, or was there not, a note of warning in his voice? something more than the mere wish to save her from distress? The uncomfortable thought darted swiftly through Victoria's mind like a small fish glimpsed in deep water, and perhaps it had shown in her face, for Eden set down his glass, and crossing to her, put his hands on her shoulders and looked down into her eyes:

'I can't bear the idea of you getting mixed up in our troubles—in any troubles. And if only I were still strong-minded and self-sacrificing, instead of being weak-willed and abominably selfish, I'd insist on your leaving. But I'm not going to, because you are the one bright diamond in my present pile of coke.'

He smiled down at her, and once again, as it had on the previous day, Victoria's heart seemed to check and miss a beat. His hands tightened on her shoulders and the moment seemed to stretch out interminably.

'Oh, Vicky,' said Eden with a break in his voice, 'what a fool I've been!'

He released her abruptly, and picking up his glass and the jug of shandy, said: 'There's Mabel. Let's go and drink outside.'

He turned away and walked out on to the verandah, and Victoria, following more slowly, found Em and Gilly emerging from the hall door.

'Ah!' said Mr Markham enthusiastically, observing the tankard in her hand. 'Liquor! Just what I stand in need of after devoting an entire hour to the subject of milk (a dreary beverage and one I never touch). Would there be anything stronger than beer in the offing, Eden?'

'You'll find all the usual things on the sideboard in the dining-room,' said Eden. 'Help yourself.'

'Thanks, I will. What about you, Em?'

'Nothing, thank you. I dislike drinking at midday,' said Em grumpily, plumping herself down in a wicker chair.

'You don't know what you miss!' said Gilly blithely, and disappeared into the dining-room.

Mabel accepted a tankard of shandy and sat down on a long wicker divan that stood against the wall, its back formed by a row of three boldly patterned cushions—the fourth being presumably still in the possession of the police. She subjected her hostess to a worried scrutiny, and said anxiously: 'You don't look at all well, Em. You ought to get Dr North to give you a tonic.'

'Thank you, Mabel, I have no desire to fill my stomach with useless nostrums. I am merely tired, that is all. Tired of office work and silly questions and having the police permanently on the premises upsetting my servants. Is young Hennessy still here, Eden?'

'No,' said Eden. 'Having thrown the cook-house into hysterics he has retired to write up a report, and we shall probably have Greg here as soon as he's read it.'

'Did he get anything out of the servants?'

'Nothing but indignant denials and a suggestion that the dogs are responsible. Oh, and several missing dish-cloths that turned up in one of the huts. One of the *totos* had evidently been making a collection of them. No sign of your dungarees, however.'

'Where are the dogs today?' enquired Mabel, bending to peer along the verandah as though she expected to find them concealed under the chairs.

'Locked up,' said Eden. 'And they can stay there! They don't take to police on the premises, any more than Gran does.'

'Sensible animals,' observed Em morosely. 'Gilly, here's your wife. Get her a drink. Good morning, Lisa. What is it now?'

Gilly, who had emerged from the dining-room

with a glass in one hand and a bottle of gin in the other, returned to fetch a second glass as Lisa came up the steps looking cool and spruce and pretty in a full skirted dress of pale blue poplin patterned with daisies. He returned with a gin and lime for his wife, and Lisa said: 'I only came over to ask about the picnic. I suppose you *are* postponing it?'

'What picnic?' enquired Em. 'Oh, yes. I remember. We were going to take an all-day picnic tomorrow to show Victoria something of the Valley. No, I see no reason why we should postpone it. It will do us all good to get away from the house for a day—and from the police! Mabel, you and Hector were coming, weren't you? And Ken. Then that's settled. Where shall we go?'

'Crater Lake,' suggested Mabel. 'I was telling Victoria about it just now. It's rather a fascinating spot, Victoria. A lake in the crater of an old volcano. They say it's bottomless, and——'

She was interrupted by the arrival of a Land-Rover containing Hector Brandon and a slim youth wearing the familiar garb of the Angry Young Men—a pair of exceedingly dirty grey flannels and a polo-necked sweater. A lock of his dark hair flopped artistically over a forehead not entirely innocent of the spots that adolescence is apt to inflict upon sensitive youth, and he possessed a pair of hot brown eyes, thin and passably attractive features, and the general air of a misunderstood minor poet.

So this, thought Victoria, was the boy she had caught a glimpse of driving furiously along the lake road on the morning of her arrival, and who had reportedly fallen so disastrously in love with Alice DeBrett.

She had been so intrigued by the unexpected arrival of Ken Brandon that she had not noticed that there had been a third man in the Land-Rover, and only became aware of it when Drew Stratton sat down beside her and observed amiably that it was a nice day.

Victoria started and bit her tongue. 'What? Oh, it's you. I didn't know you were here. What did you say?'

'I made the classic opening remark of the socially disposed Englishman. I said it was a nice day. It's your move now.'

Victoria eyed him with some misgiving and said: 'I didn't know you were coming here this morning.'

'Would you rather I hadn't? I'm afraid it's a bit late to do much about it now, but I shan't be staying long.'

Victoria flushed pinkly. 'You know quite well I didn't mean it like that. I was only surprised to see you.'

'Pleasantly, I hope?'

'No!' said Victoria, regarding him with a kindling eye. 'I don't think it's ever particularly pleasant to meet people who dislike you; and you don't like me at all, do you? You made that quite clear from the moment you first saw me. Why don't you like me?'

Drew returned her indignant gaze thoughtfully and without embarrassment, and paid her the compliment of disdaining polite denial. He said: 'Because of Alice DeBrett.'

'*Alice?* But I didn't even know her! I don't think I understand.'

'Don't you? I thought I'd been into this once already. You are a very pretty girl, Miss Caryll, and you were once engaged to her husband. I don't know why you broke it off, but whatever the reason, you cannot really have supposed that she would welcome your arrival as a permanent fixture in the household?'

Victoria stiffened and found that her hands were shaking with anger. She gripped them together in her lap and enquired in a deceptively innocent voice: 'And were Mrs DeBrett's feelings so important to you, Mr Stratton?'

She looked with intention at Ken Brandon, who was talking moodily to Lisa Markham, and Drew noted the look and interpreted it correctly. He said dryly: 'I wasn't in love with her, if that is what you mean. Can you say the same about her husband?'

The angry colour drained out of Victoria's face and once again, as on the previous night, she looked young and forlorn and defenceless—and frightened. The indignation and the rigidity left her, and she said in a voice that was so low that he barely caught the words: 'I don't know. I wish I did know. Did you think that I came out here to try and take Eden away from her?'

'No,' said Drew, considering the matter. 'She told me that your aunt had asked you to come. But I thought that knowing how she herself must feel about it, you might, perhaps, have refused.'

'You're quite right,' said Victoria, still in a half whisper that appeared to be addressed more to herself than to Drew. 'I should never have come. But— I wanted to come back to Kenya. Mother was dead and I had no one but Aunt Em. I wanted to—to belong again, and come home; and I wouldn't let myself think about Eden. He was married, and it was all over. I don't think I ever thought at all about Alice as a person. She was just something that proved it was all over, and made it safe to come. But now it's different...'

Drew looked away from her to where Eden's unstudied grace and startling handsome profile were outlined against the brilliant sunlight of the garden, and was startled to find himself wrenched by a physical spasm of jealousy and dislike. He said disagreeably: 'Because now he is free? Is that what you mean? But that should make everything pleasantly simple for you.'

Victoria shook her head without lifting it. It was only a very slight gesture, but somehow it revealed such a gulf of unhappiness and bewilderment that he was shocked out of his anger. He said: 'I'm sorry. That was rude and officious of me. And none of my business. Shall we talk about something else?'

He began to tell her about a film unit that had recently arrived in Nairobi, until Em interrupted him with an enquiry relative to the picnic and the rival merits of Thermos flasks and kettles.

'Not kettles,' said Hector. 'Don't care for lighting fires. Weather's been pretty dry, and we might do no end of damage. Are we going to do any shootin'? Have to bring a gun if we are. Just as well to bring one or two anyway, just in case. After all, one never knows. May be the odd hard-core terrorist hidin' out in those parts. There was always a rumour that the gangs had a hide somewhere near Crater Lake. Better to be on the safe side. And we might get a pot at a warthog or a guinea-fowl.'

'We must make a list,' announced Mabel, 'so that we don't leave anything behind. Has anyone got a pencil and paper?'

'Why worry,' enquired Eden lazily. 'As long as we take plenty of food and drink and enough rugs to go to sleep on afterwards, that's all we're likely to need.'

Mabel regarded him with friendly contempt and remarked that that was just like a man. There were dozens of things that must be taken on a picnic: a flit gun and a fly swatter, a first-aid kit, matches, snake serum——

Eden laughed and turned to Victoria. 'So now you know what you are in for, Vicky. Snakes in the grass and warthogs in the undergrowth, and the odd terrorist lurking on the skyline. A nice, peaceful, Kenya afternoon! You needn't bother with the first-aid kit, Mabel. We always keep one in the Land-Rover. Bandages, lint, bottle of iodine—the works! I don't think we run to morphia and forceps, but possibly you can provide those.'

'As a matter of fact, I can,' retorted Mabel, unruffled. 'I don't believe in being unprepared for emergencies in a country where emergencies are apt to arise, and I always carry a bottle of iodine with me in my pocket. You've no idea how easily a scratch can turn septic in this country. But so far neither Hector nor I have ever had blood-poisoning.'

'Well neither have I, if it comes to that,' said Eden with a grin. 'And without the benefit of iodine! Don't tell me that Hector and Ken carry round the stuff too?'

'Of course they do. It's an elementary precaution that I insist upon. One should really carry permanganate as well.'

'What for? Medicating the drinking water, or washing the salad?'

'Snake-bite, of course. Serum is a bit bulky to take around, syringe and all. But permanganate is better than nothing. If you cut the wound across and rub the crystals in at once it can be very effective.'

'Look, Mabel,' said Eden earnestly, 'let's call off this picnic and go to a cinema instead. The whole thing sounds far too hazardous to me. My idea of a picnic is a peaceful afternoon spent flat on my back in the shade, after eating heartily of cold chicken, stuffed eggs, sausage-rolls and salad, topped off with coffee cake and several pints of beer. I am prepared to put up with flies and ants, but not with having myself carved up with a penknife and doctored with permanganate of potash!'

'Not in the least likely to happen,' said Hector reassuringly. 'Hundred-to-one chance. Though I'm not saying that Crater Lake hasn't got a bad name for snakes. Saw a mamba there once when I was a youngster. Came at me like the wind. Ugly brute. Fortunately I had m'shot-gun. Blew its head off. Very lucky shot.'

Eden covered his eyes and bowed his head on his knees, and Gilly burst into a roar of laughter to which Em added her rich chuckle, while even Ken Brandon momentarily, abandoned his Byronic gloom and permitted himself to smile.

Hector said huffily: 'It was not in the least amusing I assure you. If I'd missed it—well, that would have been the end of me. And it's a very painful way to die, let me tell you! Seen a chap do it. Blue in the face—writhing and twisting. Not at all funny.'

His son's reluctant smile broadened into a grin, and he said: 'Come off it, Dad! You're terrifying the girls. Lisa doesn't like snakes. Do you, Lisa?'

'No,' said Lisa with a shudder. 'Horrible things! Mbogo says that there are a pair of puff adders in a hole under the big acacia by the gate. He says he's seen their tracks in the dust. *Ugh!*'

Mabel gave a sympathetic shiver and said: 'There seems to be a plague of them this year. We're always passing dead ones on the road that have been run over by cars. It's the only thing I don't like about the Rift—the snakes. Hector and Ken don't seem to mind them. They collected them for the venom centre once. That place where they keep snakes and collect the poison for serums.'

'In that case,' said Gilly, 'any intelligent snake should give us a wide berth on Wednesday.' He waved his glass and chanted:

'You spotted snakes, with double tongue,
Thorny hedge-hogs, be not seen;
Newts, and blind-worms, do no wrong;
Come not near—there are Brandons about!'

'I can't see what you've got to be so cheerful about this morning,' said Lisa crossly.

'Can't you, my sweet? Well I'll let you into a secret. I've got a lovely surprise for you. Em's sending us off to Rumuruti when Jerry Coles leaves. How do you like that?'

There was a sudden startled silence. Eden sat bolt upright, while Lisa stared at her husband in open-mouthed, ludicrous dismay, and Drew's blond brows lifted in surprise. Even the Brandons seemed taken aback, and only Em remained tranquil.

The effect of his pronouncement appeared to afford Gilly considerable amusement, but Lisa's gaze had flown to Eden and she said involuntarily: 'Oh no! It isn't true! We can't——'

'Of course It's true,' said Gilly cheerfully. 'Why are you all looking so surprised? I've been trying to blarney Em into nominating me for the job for weeks, and she's seen reason at last. I received the accolade this morning. Manager of DeBrett Farms, Rumuruti. That's me. Or it will be. Aren't you going to congratulate me, Eden?'

Eden's mouth tightened into a narrow and ominous line and he stared at Gilly for a dangerous minute, and then turned to his grandmother. 'Is this true?' he demanded harshly. 'Have you really promised him Coles's job? *Have you?*'

'Come, come, my dear boy,' reproved Hector, intervening with all the tact of a charging rhinoceros. 'Must remember that you're speakin' to your grandmother!'

Drew said very softly: 'Ware wire, Hector!' but

Eden did not appear to have heard the interruption. '*Have you?*' he insisted, his eyes on Em.

Em looked long and deliberately from Eden to Lisa, and back again, and said calmly: 'Certainly, dear. On consideration it seemed to me an excellent idea. I admit that I once thought otherwise, but circumstances alter cases. And in the present circumstances I consider that it may prove to be a very satisfactory arrangement after all. To *everyone*. Victoria dear, you have not yet told us if there is any particular spot that you would prefer to visit rather than Crater Lake?'

Victoria, disconcerted at finding herself suddenly drawn into the conversation, disclaimed any preferences, and was perhaps the only person present who interpreted Em's apparently inconsequent query as an attempt to change the conversation. Eden glanced quickly at her, and then at Lisa, whose desperate gaze was still fixed on him, and there was, suddenly, comprehension and something that might almost have been relief in his face.

The rigidity went out of his slim figure and he relaxed in his chair, and Gilly, who had been watching his wife with bright observant eyes and a smile that was tinged with malice, said: 'Aren't you pleased, dear? I thought you'd be delighted! Promotion. More pay. Nice house. New faces—I hope. You'll love it!'

Lisa said nothing. She looked away from Eden at last, her face white and wooden and her mouth a tight scarlet line, and it was Hector who spoke.

'Must say,' said Hector judicially, 'I'm surprised.

Shouldn't have said you were up to it, Gilly. If you don't mind my speakin' frankly.'

'But I do mind,' said Gilly. 'And, speaking frankly, I don't consider that it is any of your dam' business. Which reminds me——' He turned his back on Hector, and addressing Ken said conversationally: 'I've been meaning to ask you, Ken. Was that Kerry Lad you were riding on Tuesday evening? Because if so, you really should enter him for the open jumping at the Royal Show. There can't be many hunters who can clear that hedge and the wire on the boundary side of my garden without coming to grief. You should have a walkover.'

Ken Brandon did not reply, and for the second time that morning a stricken silence descended upon the verandah. But now it was the boy's face that was as white and still as Lisa's had been, and the affectation and the Byronic pose fell away from him. He stared at Gilly like a hypnotized rabbit and licked his dry lips, and then Mabel had risen swiftly and was standing between them, her cheeks pink and her grey curls quivering:

'I don't know what you're talking about, Gilly,' she said in a calmly cheerful voice. 'Ken was riding White Lady on Tuesday. Wasn't he, Em? And she's no good over the sticks.'

'I didn't mean when he came over the first time,' said Gilly softly. 'I meant later on.'

'He wasn't out later on,' said Mabel positively, and turned to Lady Emily: 'We really must be going, Em. Thank you for the shandy. It was delicious. Where are we going to meet tomorrow? I suggest you all come along to us about eleven, as we're on your way, and then we can sort ourselves out and go on from there. Drew, you'll come won't you? Yes, of course you must. We won't take no for an answer. We fixed up who brings what food, didn't we? Then that's all right. Come on, Ken dear. Goodbye, Victoria. It's nice to have met Jack's girl. Can we give you a lift, Drew? Oh—but that's *your* Land-Rover, isn't it?'

'Yes,' said Drew, rising and stubbing out his cigarette. 'I am an uninvited guest at this party. I would appear to have the only transport that does not break down at awkward moments. Which has its disadvantages.'

His smile robbed the words of any offence, and the tension in the atmosphere decreased almost visibly. 'That's right,' confirmed Hector. 'Afraid we broke down. That damned clutch again. Drew picked us up. Wasted his morning, I'm afraid. Hope you won't mind givin' us a lift back, Drew?'

'Not at all, sir. Delighted. Goodbye, Em. Are you really expecting me to turn up at this picnic tomorrow?'

'You heard what Mabel said,' retorted Em with something that in anyone else would have been described as a sniff. 'She "won't take no for an answer". So naturally I shall expect to see you there.'

'All right,' said Drew resignedly, 'though frankly—if I may borrow a favourite word of Hector's—if I had any sense I'd remove myself to Nyali or the Northern Frontier until the situation here was less electric.'

'Greg wouldn't let you go,' announced Em a trifle grimly. '*You* haven't got an alibi either!'

The Land-Rover departed in a cloud of dust, and Eden, who had been watching the Markhams as they walked away across the garden, said slowly: 'What was Gilly getting at—about Ken riding across our land on Tuesday evening? Do you suppose he was here?'

'Yes,' said Em shortly. 'I imagine he did it fairly frequently, and for no better reason than the time-honoured one of passing the house in which his lady lived. Infatuated youth has done that sort of thing—and will go on doing it!—for centuries. But Ken is young enough and foolish enough to try and hide the fact, and Gilly is trading on that to tease him—and Mabel. It's a very silly thing to do, and I shall have to speak to Gilly. Drew is quite right. Too much electricity. I don't like it. I don't like it at all!'

She sighed heavily, and rising from her chair walked away down the verandah, muttering to herself after the manner of the old.

The remainder of the day had passed peacefully enough, but Victoria slept little that night. She lay awake hour after hour, worried at first by personal problems, but later by fear. For as the slow hours ticked away, the house that had seemed so silent began to fill with innumerable small stealthy sounds, until at times she could have sworn that someone was creeping about the darkened rooms—tip-toeing across the floors and easing open doors very softly so that the hinges should not creak.

She had locked her own door when she went to

bed, and had been ashamed of herself for doing so. But as she lay awake in the darkness, straining her ears to listen, it occurred to her that it was no use locking your door against a ghost, and that if there were such things as poltergeists it might be in her room at the moment, watching her and chuckling at her fear.

Beyond her window the garden had been white with moonlight, but even there it had not been silent, for down in the papyrus swamps birds were calling; crying like gulls on a windy day; though there was no wind, and it was night.

Were there really still remnants of the Mau Mau gangs hiding in the swamp?—desperate, hunted, hungry men who were being fed in secret by those who were, by daylight, faithful and trusted servants of the settlers whose estates bordered the lake?

Several times during that long night the dogs had growled and barked and scratched at the door of the disused storehouse in which they were locked, and though there might be a trivial reason for that—a rat scuttling in the roof, or a prowling cat—might they not be barking at a man creeping out from the labour lines with food in his hands, to meet a shadow who had come up through the darkness of the shamba and the papyrus swamp? A shadow who had perhaps killed Alice DeBrett——?

12

The Land-Rovers bumped and bounced and jolted over the unmade lake road, trailing the inevitable dust clouds behind them like smoke from an express train, and the morning was hot and blue and brilliant.

The country was more rugged here, near the foothills of the Mau, and oddly shaped hillocks that had once been the cones of volcanoes jutted up out of the plain, turning from green to darkest midnight blue as an idling cloud shadow would engulf one and silhouette it blackly against the surrounding blaze of sunlight.

There was little game to be seen at this hour of the day, for in the hot noonday the great herds of zebra and gazelle that grazed across the open ranges in the early morning and the late afternoon had retired to the shade of the trees. But in a grove of acacias outside a small village a troop of baboons howled and leapt and danced among the branches as the Land-Rovers passed.

The picnic party had arrived separately at the Brandons' farm, and had there sorted themselves out into three Land-Rovers. Ken Brandon and Lisa in Drew Stratton's, Em with Mabel and Hector, and Victoria and Gilly with Eden.

Eden's complement had also included Thuku, Em's African driver, and old Zacharia who had been brought along to deal with such tedious but necessary chores as the cleaning of dirty knives and dishes, the disposal of debris and the repacking of depleted baskets. The Brandons had also brought their driver, Samuel, for it was still not considered safe to leave a vehicle unguarded in the remoter parts of the Rift, and both Samuel and Thuku carried loaded shot-guns.

'There's Crater Lake,' announced Gilly, breaking a silence that had lasted for several miles. 'Or rather, there's the rim of the crater. Over on the right——'

'But there's no road,' objected Victoria.

'Lor' bless you, we don't need roads in this country,' said Gilly. 'What do you take us for? Sissies? I admit that this appalling chain of rocks and potholes that we have been bouncing along for the last umpteen miles or so calls itself a road, but you won't notice any appreciable difference when we take to the open range. Here we go!'

As he spoke, Eden drove the Land-Rover off the dust-laden road and across a long stretch of open country that sloped upward towards high ground crowned with rocks, candelabrum trees, thorn scrub and thickets of wild olive.

'See what I mean?' demanded Gilly, returning violently to his seat from hitting his head on the canvas roof. Victoria, who had inadvertently bitten her tongue, nodded dumbly and braced herself to withstand a sharp list to starboard as they roared up a steep cattle track that climbed over rocks and roots, and came at last to a stop in a small clearing where the two Land-Rovers that had preceded them were already parked.

'Well, that's as far as we can go,' said Eden, applying the brake and wiping the dust out of his eyes. 'We walk from here.'

Gilly descended and went round to the back of the car to superintend the removal of the beer, and Eden jumped out and reached up to lift Victoria down.

He held her for a full half-minute before he released her, and Victoria, looking into the grey eyes that were so near her own, was astonished to realize that her pulse had not quickened nor her heart missed a beat, and that for the first time in her life she was looking at him as though he were a friend, or a cousin, instead of the glamour-gilded Hero of all Romance that he had been to her for so many years.

Her feet touched the ground, and feeling it rough and solid under her shoes it was as if she had touched reality at long last and relinquished her grasp upon illusion.

Eden released her, but she did not move away. She stood in the hot sunlight looking at him gravely and intently, and he smiled his charming quizzical smile and said lightly: 'What is it, Vicky? Learning me by heart?'

'No,' said Victoria slowly. 'I know you by heart. I think that's always been my trouble. I've never known you any other way.'

'You mean, never with your head? Then don't start now, darling. You mightn't like me with your hard little head, and I couldn't bear that.'

He lifted her hand and kissed it, and then suddenly his face changed. The warmth went out of his eyes and he dropped her hand, and Victoria, turning, saw that Lisa and Drew had walked back to the cars and were standing within a few yards of them, having obviously witnessed the brief scene. It was also equally obvious that neither of them was pleased. Drew looked blank and bored and thoroughly disagreeable, and Lisa looked frankly furious.

It was, somehow, a deeply embarrassing moment out of all proportion to the triviality of the occasion, and facing Lisa's white-faced, tight-lipped jealousy and Drew's cold eyes, Victoria found herself blushing as hotly as though she had been guilty of some gross impropriety. She looked away and became aware that Gilly too was an interested spectator. He had come round from the back of the car and was leaning against it, studying his wife with detached interest as though she had been some stranger whom he had not previously met. His gaze took in her ultra-feminine and un-picnic-like garb, and once again there was comprehension and malice in his face, as though he were perfectly aware for whose approval she had dressed.

His glance slid past her and came to rest on Victoria, neat and slim in slacks and shirt, and he said meditatively and in the manner of one speaking a thought aloud: 'You know, she's good, this girl: she uses her head. Lisa'll have to work fast. Very fast!'

Eden said coldly: 'What are you babbling about, Gilly? Have you got the stuff unloaded?'

'I was musing, like Polonius, on the frailty of human nature,' said Gilly. '*Whose violent property fordoes itself, and leads the will to desperate undertakings, as oft as any passion under heaven*—and if you were referring to the beer, yes. I have unloaded it and it is on its way up. Hadn't somebody better stay and keep an eye on our transport, just in case the odd terrorist is still using this salubrious spot as a hide-out?'

Drew said briefly: 'Thuku can stay around.' And taking Lisa by the arm he turned her about and started back up the steep slope, the others following in single file behind him.

Lisa had not spoken, but Drew, holding her arm, could feel that she was shivering as though with ague, and he said sharply: 'Hold up, Lisa! If you don't look where you're going you'll end up with a broken ankle. Here we are——'

They had come out on a bare expanse of broken rock, and below them, ringed by the steep sides of the crater and bordered by a jungle of scrub and acacias, lay a little green lake. The eeriest place, thought Victoria, looking down on it, that she had ever seen. And the most silent.

The sky overhead was clear and blue, but the lake did not reflect it, and the whole cup of the crater was as green and dark and still as though a cold cloud shadow had fallen directly upon it. Victoria shivered, and drawing back from the edge of the cliff, said doubtfully: 'It looks rather an unfriendly place, doesn't it?'

'*A Daniel come to judgement!*' said Gilly. 'My opinion exactly. A morgue. However, don't worry, a few drinks will brighten your viewpoint considerably—and mine. And if you're worrying about the dangers of the African bush, Hector, Eden and Ken are all Grade A marksmen, while Drew has Annie Oakley beat to a frazzle. Anything she could do, he can do better. You are as safe as houses—except for the flies. And Mabel and her flit gun will probably be able to repel those. Let's go.'

Victoria laughed a little shamefacedly, and Drew, after favouring her with a brief, frowning glance, turned and led the way along the rim of the crater to a point where there was a fairly easy route down the cliff to the trees and the lake edge.

They met the Brandons' driver, Samuel, coming up the narrow track having helped carry down the baskets, and found Em, Mabel and Hector comfortably ensconced on rugs and ground sheets in the shade while Zacharia unpacked the luncheon.

Ken Brandon, who had been on a solitary ramble, reported that he had seen the pug marks of a leopard in a patch of wet mud at the far side of the lake, and that there was the skeleton of a big warthog among the bushes. He exhibited one of the enormous curved tusks, and said: 'Look at that! Must have been the great-grandfather of all warthogs. I've never seen tusks that size before.'

The air of embittered gloom had temporarily left him, and he looked boyish and refreshingly normal as he handled the yellowed chunk of ivory.

'Leopard kill?' enquired Drew.

Ken shook his head. 'No. The bones are complete. Old age probably. Or perhaps he was wounded somewhere on Conville's range, and came here to die.'

'Or got bitten by a snake?' suggested Gilly.

Ken dropped the tusk on to the ground and the animation went out of his face. He said: 'Perhaps,' in a colourless voice, and went to sit beside Lisa, who moved over to make room for him.

It was well past two o'clock by the time Zacharia had washed up in the scummy water of the lake, and assisted by Samuel had carried the picnic baskets back up the cliff path to the cars.

Hector departed to inspect the leopard's spoor and the skeleton of the warthog, while his wife produced a voluminous cretonne bag and settled down to some knitting, and Em, who had thoughtfully provided herself with a cushion, announced her intention of resting for at least an hour.

The remaining members of the party had gone off to explore the crater—with the exception of Gilly who, having drunk two bottles of beer on top of seven pink gins, had quarrelled with Hector, been offensive to Ken Brandon and been spoken to sharply by Em, and had retired with a rug and a flit gun to sleep it off behind a clump of bushes. Lisa's sandals, however, were not made for exploring, and she had clung to Eden's arm and they had fallen back and got separated from the others, so that Victoria found herself left with Drew Stratton and young Mr Brandon. Neither of her companions evinced the slightest desire to talk, and Victoria only noticed that Ken had removed himself elsewhere when they had made an almost complete circuit of the crater and she had turned to ask him where he had seen the leopard's pug marks.

'He left us about ten minutes ago,' said Mr Stratton, bored. 'Is there anything else you want to see?'

'Not here,' said Victoria with a shiver. 'I don't think I like this place. And I don't think it likes us. It's too quiet.'

She turned her head, listening, and in the silence they could hear faintly but distinctly, and coming from somewhere twenty or thirty yards ahead and out of sight, a sound that after a moment or two she identified as snores. That would be Gilly Markham—or Em! The snores ended on a loud snort, and after an interval of silence began again, and Victoria turned back to Mr Stratton and enquired uneasily if he really thought that there might be a leopard in the crater?

'Possibly,' said Drew, without interest. 'There are hundreds of hiding places among the rocks, and those pug marks were fairly new. Which is one reason why you can't be left to wander round here on your own.'

Victoria stood still and stared at him for a fulminating moment. 'If that means that you feel that you have to stay around in order to protect me, you needn't bother. I shall be quite safe, and I don't want to explore any more.' She sat down on a convenient boulder, with chin in the air, and added coldly: 'Don't let me keep you.'

Drew looked at her thoughtfully for a full half-minute, and then he shrugged his shoulders slightly and turned away.

Victoria watched him go with a mixture of resentment and apprehension, and was strongly tempted to call him back. Not because she anticipated any danger from leopards or terrorists, but because she did not like being left alone in this eerie and disquieting spot, even though she knew that nine other people were presumably within call, and at least three of them—Aunt Emily, Mrs Brandon and Mr Markham—less than thirty yards away. But Drew had disappeared among the thick belt of trees and she could no longer hear the bushes rustling as he moved. She sat quite still, listening; but no one seemed to be moving anywhere in the crater, and the silence flowed back into it, filling it as a cup is filled with water.

It was not in any way a peaceful silence, but a stealthy, all-pervading stillness that contained a disturbing quality of awareness. And suddenly, and for no reason, she was afraid. Where had everyone else got to? Had they all stolen away and left her alone in this horrible place? She must find them again. She would walk over to the trees where they had picnicked, and sit beside Aunt Em and Mrs Brandon and listen to the comforting click of Mrs Brandon's knitting needles.

But she found that she could not make the first move to break that brooding silence, and when at last she heard movements among the trees the sounds were as frightening as the silence had been, for there was about them the same disquieting suggestion of stealth; as though someone—or perhaps several people?—were moving within the crater with infinite caution and the minimum of noise.

Once a stone rattled down from the cliffs with a small metallic clatter that was uncomfortably reminiscent of the chatter of teeth, and then a twig cracked, and Victoria turned quickly: but there was no one there. Only the trees and the shadows and the rank grass—and a flicker of movement that might have been imagination or a bird flitting between the leaves.

'Who's there?' called Victoria, astonished at the huskiness of her own voice. 'Is anyone there?'

The words seemed astonishingly loud in the silence, but no one answered her, and a minute or two later the undergrowth rustled as though something or someone was moving stealthily away. The soft sound grew fainter until it was submerged at last by the silence, and though there were no more sounds Victoria did not move. She sat quite still, listening intently, while the sun moved slowly down the sky and the deep blue shadow of the cliff crept forward across the cup of the crater. Only when it touched her did she give herself a mental shake and stand up.

I'm behaving like an idiot, thought Victoria with disgust: sitting here working myself into a panic over nothing, just because everyone else has very sensibly done what Aunt Em and Mrs Brandon have—gone to sleep! And with that thought courage flowed back and her fears seemed childish, and she began to walk along the marshy margin of the lake towards the spot where they had picnicked. She had almost reached it when a sound that was painfully associated with her recent flight out from England assaulted her ears, and she stopped in sudden distaste. Mr Markham, having awoken from sleep, was obviously—and regrettably—engaged in parting with his lunch and the excess of alcohol with which he had insulted his long-suffering stomach.

Victoria turned and tiptoed away again, feeling for the first time deeply sorry for Gilly's wife, and she was halfway round the far side of the lake when Hector Brandon came out of the bushes a few yards ahead of her and waved cheerfully, and a moment later Lisa Markham joined them. They found Ken Brandon taking photographs with a large box camera, and as they reached the little clearing where they had picnicked, Drew came down the cliff path and Eden strolled out from between the tree trunks.

Em was asleep—her hat tilted well over her nose—and Mabel's busy needles were silent while their owner snored gently.

'A pretty and peaceful picture,' commented Eden. 'But unless we're going to have tea here, it's time we moved on. Wake up, Gran darling!'

Em grunted like a startled warthog, and sitting

up with a jerk that dislodged her hat, glared at her grandson.

'I wish,' she said crossly, 'that you would all go away and let me have a short rest. Surely you can amuse yourselves somewhere else for half an hour?'

'You've been resting, darling. And for well over an hour! It's getting on for half-past three.'

'That's right,' confirmed Hector, who had been rousing his sleeping wife. 'Time we were makin' tracks. Here are Zach and Samuel to carry up the rugs. Better let 'em take your cushion too. Hope we haven't left any bottles about. Where's Gilly?'

'Still sleeping it off, I expect,' said Eden. He raised his voice and called out: 'Hi, Gilly, wake up! We're off! Ken, go and rout him out.'

'Rout him out yourself,' said Ken sulkily.

Eden raised his brows, and the boy coloured hotly and said: 'Oh, all right,' and plunged round the clump of bushes behind which Gilly had retired for his afternoon nap. They heard him give an exclamation of disgust and mutter in an undertone, 'Tight again!' and then, loudly: 'Hi, Gilly—we're going: wake up! *Gilly——!*'

There followed an indescribable gasp, and the next minute he was back again, his face sickly white and his eyes wide and staring. 'I—I can't wake him! I think he's having a fit.'

Drew departed at a run, closely followed by Hector, and the remainder of the party, rounding the bushes, found him on his knees beside Gilly's recumbent body.

Gilly was shivering violently, and Drew looked

up and said curtly: 'It looks like an attack of fever. Has he ever had malaria, Lisa?'

'No,' said Lisa, staring in white-faced distaste at her husband's shuddering body. 'I don't think so. But he did once have——' She checked herself abruptly and bit her lip

'D.T.'s,' finished Hector bluntly. 'Yes, we know. Perhaps you're right.'

'Nonsense!' said Em crisply. 'He may have had too much to drink, but he certainly wasn't *that* drunk. Must be malaria.'

'He's not hot,' said Drew, laying a hand on Gilly's sweating forehead.

Em bent down to touch him, and drawing back with a gasp, struck with her stick at something that had lain concealed by a fold of the rug.

'Look out!' shouted Hector, leaping forward. '*Snake!*' He snatched the stick from her hand and beat at the puff adder that had been curled up near Gilly's arm, and Ken Brandon ran in with a broken branch, and lifting the limp, battered thing, flung it far out so that it fell with a splash into the silent lake.

Mabel said: 'He's been bitten—*look!*' And plumping down on her knees she pointed a trembling finger at two small purplish punctures on Gilly's bare forearm, from one of which hung a small drop of blood, already congealed. 'Get the serum, Ken! Run——! It's in the pocket of the car. Quickly!'

Ken turned and ran, stumbling through the bushes and panting up the cliff path, and Drew, who had not spoken, pulled back the lid from Gilly's eye, and after a quick look, thrust his hand inside the open-necked shirt, feeling for the heart beat. He said: 'Have we any brandy?'

Hector jerked a small silver flask from his pocket and handed it over without a word, and Drew forced the liquid between Gilly's quivering lips while Em, who had torn the chiffon scarf from her hat, wound it tightly above the puncture marks in a tourniquet, and demanding a sharp knife, made a deep cross-cut from which the blood welled sluggishly.

Gilly made no sound beyond the shuddering breaths that another attack of shivering forced from him, and Em dropped the knife into the grass and said frantically: 'What on earth is Ken doing? Mabel, where's that permanganate you talked about? He'll die before Ken gets back with the serum! Do something, can't you!'

'It's in the car,' gulped Mabel. 'With the rest of the first-aid kit. But I've got some iodine——' She fumbled in the pocket of her skirt and produced a small bottle.

'It may be better than nothing,' said Em, and poured the contents over the cut.

The minutes ticked by, and except for Gilly's laboured breathing the afternoon was so quiet that it seemed to Victoria that those who watched him must be holding their breaths; and in the silence she heard someone's teeth chatter.

Em burst out desperately: 'Eden, for goodness sake go and see what's keeping Ken. He must have——' And then Ken slithered down the cliff path bringing a young avalanche of stones with him, and crashed through the bushes to arrive hot and panting.

Em snatched the syringe from him, and filling it, plunged it into Gilly's arm above the wound, and they waited breathlessly, watching the pallid face, while Mabel chafed his limp hands and the shivering lessened until at last he lay still. His colourless face twitched, and the brandy that Drew had been forcing down his throat trickled from the corners of his mouth.

Drew put down the flask and felt for Gilly's heart again, and after a full minute he stood up and brushed the broken grass from his knees.

'He's dead,' said Drew curtly.

Mabel gave a hoarse cry and Lisa broke into shrill hysterical laughter that was somehow worse than any screaming or tears would have been.

Em stood up swiftly and slapped her across the face with the flat of her palm, and the laughter broke off in a choking gasp.

'Take her away, Mabel!' said Em sharply. 'Take her back to the car.' She turned on Drew and said: 'Don't talk nonsense! Of course he isn't dead. It's only the reaction from the serum.'

'Yes, I should say that was probably the last straw. His heart couldn't stand any more. He's dead all right.'

'No!' said Em hoarsely. 'No!' She looked dazedly at the syringe that she still held, and then threw it from her in a sudden convulsion of horror, while Eden, pushing her aside, went down on his knees beside Gilly, feeling for his heart as Drew had done.

After a minute or two he lifted a drawn and ravaged face, and Lisa, seeing it, said hysterically: 'He is dead, isn't he? *Isn't he!* Oh God, what a fool I've been! Gilly!—Gilly!'

Em said angrily: 'Mabel, I asked you to take her away! *Is* he dead, Eden?'

'Yes,' said Eden briefly, and got slowly to his feet.

They stood looking down at Gilly's thin, bony face with its clever forehead and weak chin, and it seemed to sneer up at them; the mouth half open and pulled down at one corner, and the pale eyes glinting through their lashes as maliciously as they had in life.

Lisa said in a sobbing whisper: 'He isn't dead. He's laughing at us! He's laughing——'

Mabel put an arm about Lisa's waist. Her pleasant gentle face was grey and shrunken, and she looked as though she were going to be sick. She said in a quavering voice: 'Come away, dear. Drew, give me that brandy.'

Drew picked up the flask and handed it over, but Lisa refused to drink from it. She wrenched herself free, gasping and panting. 'No—no, I won't! How do I know it isn't poisoned? Drew gave it to him and he died! How do I know it didn't kill him?'

'Oh, for God's sake, Lisa!' said Eden, exasperated. 'Pull yourself together! Here, Vicky, give Mabel a hand and get her away from here.'

But Victoria was not listening to him. She was watching Drew who was looking at Gilly as he had once looked at Em on the verandah at *Flamingo*. As though some new and startling thought had suddenly presented itself to him. It was a look that had disturbed her then; but coming on top of the shock of Gilly Markham's death it frightened her as Gilly's death had not done, and she backed away from him, and groping for support, found a tree trunk behind her and leant against it, cold and shivering.

Drew turned abruptly away and stooped to search among the grasses, and when he straightened up again they saw that he was holding the syringe that Em had thrown away. The needle was broken and the glass appeared to be smashed, but he handled it with the extreme caution of a man who holds a live bomb, and wrapping it in his handkerchief, put it very carefully into his pocket and bent again to hunt very carefully in the tangled undergrowth.

Em said tersely: 'What is it, Drew? What are you looking for?'

'The needle,' said Drew. 'We may need it.'

'What for?' demanded Hector impatiently. 'Can't use that thing with a broken needle! Stands to reason. Come on, let's get out of here. How are we going to get him up the cliff?'

Drew paid no attention and continued his search, and Em said heavily: 'Eden and Ken should be able to manage it. The rest of us had better get back to the cars.'

She turned away, and pushing Mabel and the sobbing Lisa ahead of her, moved off through the bushes, walking very slowly and as though she were feeling for each step.

Victoria did not move. Partly because she felt incapable of movement, and partly because horrified curiosity had rooted her to the spot. Why should

Drew think that it was important to find a useless thing like a broken piece of needle? And why were Hector and Eden watching him with such rigid apprehension? Why didn't they take Gilly back quickly to the cars? Surely they should get him to hospital as soon as possible? He *could* not be dead! Not just like that. There must be something that a doctor could do. Why didn't they do something—instead of watching Drew Stratton and looking so—so tense and strained and wary?

Something moved just behind her, and she whipped round, her heart in her mouth, but it was only old Zacharia calmly collecting the rugs and the ground sheets and various odds and ends that had not been taken away earlier with the picnic baskets.

Drew gave up at last, and turning to the three silent men who had watched him, he said curtly and incomprehensibly: 'They'll want that clasp knife, too. Where has it got to?'

The remark was meaningless to Victoria, but it was instantly obvious that it was clear to Eden, Hector and Ken. Eden's face took on a blankly wooden look that Victoria knew, and Ken gave an audible gasp, while Hector's bronzed features flushed darkly and he said explosively: 'Now look here, Stratton—you keep out of this! We don't want any more hysterical nonsense of that sort. I'll forgive it in Lisa. She's his wife—bound to be upset. But I'm damned if I'll stand it from you! Now, let's get the hell out of here.'

Drew said: 'I'm sorry, Hector, but it isn't as simple as that, and you know it. We must have that knife.'

But the knife was not there. They searched the grass and the bushes and shook out the rug on which Gilly had lain, but there was no sign of it.

'We're wasting our time,' said Hector angrily. 'It's probably in Em's pocket. Let's stop fooling about and get the body away. That's the most important thing to do.'

But when they at last arrived at the cars, after a slow and difficult ascent out of the crater, neither Em, Mabel nor Lisa knew anything of the clasp knife.

'I left it down there,' said Em. 'I think I dropped it on the grass. You can't have looked properly.'

'We looked everywhere,' said Drew. 'Who did it belong to? Was it yours?'

'No. I asked for a knife and someone handed me one.'

'Who?'

'I don't remember. And what does it matter, anyway? Why are they putting Gilly in your car?'

Drew said: 'We decided that Eden and I had better take him into Naivasha. You'll have your hands full with Lisa.'

He turned to Mabel and asked if she still had Hector's flask of brandy.

'Yes,' said Mabel, handing it over. 'Though I'm afraid there isn't much left. I think there's a bottle of whisky somewhere if you'd rather have that.'

Drew pocketed the flask without replying, and was turning away when Em spoke softly behind him.

'You've forgotten the iodine,' she said.

13

It was close on five o'clock by the time they arrived back at *Flamingo*, and Em had sent for Dr North and attempted to put Lisa to bed in one of the guest rooms.

But Lisa had refused flatly and with hysteria to sleep at *Flamingo*. The prospect of spending a night in a house that harboured a poltergeist appeared far worse to her than that of returning alone to her own empty bungalow, and eventually it was decided that Mabel should go back with her and stay the night.

Em and Victoria had eaten supper in the candle-lit dining-room, and it was towards the end of that silent meal that Victoria had asked a question that had been troubling her for several hours:

'Aunt Em, what did you mean when you told Drew—Mr Stratton—that he had forgotten the iodine?'

Em looked up from the food that she had barely touched, and her face in the soft light was grey and bleak. As grey and bleak as her voice:

'Because he does not happen to be a fool.'

She pushed her plate away and stared unseeingly at the candle flame that wavered in the faint draught made by Zacharia as he passed silently around the table, and Victoria said uncomfortably: 'I don't understand.'

'No,' said Em slowly. 'You wouldn't, of course. There are so few poisonous snakes in England. But I expect Drew had seen someone die of snake-bite, and that is why he thinks that Gilly Markham was murdered.'

She had spoken the word quite softly and casually into the quiet room, but it seemed to Victoria as though she had shouted it, and that the whole house must echo with it. *Murdered . . .*

Em waved away the dish that Zacharia was proffering, and selecting a cigarette from a box in front of her, lit it from the nearest candle and leant back in her chair, her bulky figure slumped and shapeless.

Victoria said with a catch in her voice: 'But why? How can he think that? It *was* a snake, wasn't it? We all saw it. Does he think that someone put it there? But no one could have— He didn't say so. He didn't say anything! I was there the whole time, and he never said anything about it being—being——'

'Murder,' said Em. And once again the word was like a stone dropped into a quiet pool. 'He may not have used that word; but all the same, that was what he meant.'

'No!' said Victoria breathlessly. 'I don't believe it. If anyone had put a snake there on purpose it might not have bitten him. Or it might have bitten *them!* No one would risk it.'

'Oh, I don't suppose Drew thinks it was put there on purpose,' said Em impatiently. 'I imagine he thinks that someone who happened to have the means was quick enough to seize the opportunity, and make quite sure that Gilly did die. Stupid, really, because if he had been bitten the chances are that he would have died anyway. Personally, I think Drew is wrong. I think Gilly had a heart attack, and that is why he didn't cry out. But if I'm right, then either I killed him, or Drew did. And—and that is not going to be a very pleasant thought for either of us to live with.'

'*You!* You mean he thinks— You think——' Victoria's voice stopped on a gasp and she pushed back her chair and stood up, gripping the edge of the table. 'Aunt Em, you can't think he did it! You *can't!*'

'No, of course I don't,' said Em with a return of impatience. 'Sit down, child. I will not have hysterics. They do not help at all, and after Lisa I have had enough of them to last me a good many years. Neither does Drew think I did it—on purpose. But only two people touched Gilly. Myself and Drew. I made two cuts in his arm and gave him a full strength dose of snake serum, and Drew gave him a great deal of brandy. You cannot do that sort of thing to a man who is having a heart attack without killing him. And then again, if someone did give him poison to ensure that he died, then it was given in one of four ways. It might have been on the blade of the knife, or in the iodine, or the syringe, or in the brandy. Though of course there is always a fifth possibility: that he was given something at luncheon. But Zacharia had washed up all the glasses in the lake. I asked.'

Victoria sat down again and stared at her aunt. She said imploringly: 'It isn't true. They'll find out that it was only snakebite, won't they? The doctors will know. It *must* have been snakebite.'

Em shook her head. 'People who have been bitten by poisonous snakes do not die like that. It's a pity Drew was there. Probably no one else would have noticed details. Or if they had, they'd have kept their mouths shut.'

'But if it was murder——'

'There are some things that are worse than murder,' said Em wearily. 'Trials, hanging, suspicion, miscarriage of justice.' She stubbed out her cigarette and quoted in an undertone: '*Duncan is in his grave; After life's fitful fever he sleeps well; Treason has done his worst: nor steel, nor poison, Malice domestic, foreign levy, nothing, Can touch him further*. Hmm. Gilly was fond of quoting Shakespeare. That would have appealed to him I imagine. *Malice domestic* . . . I wonder——'

She relapsed into brooding silence, looking exhausted and ill, and Victoria eyed her in some disquiet and wished fervently that Eden would return. But although it was by now well past nine o'clock there was still no sign of him, and when Em had gone to bed Victoria went out into the dark verandah to listen for the car.

The moon was already high and the lawns and the trees were silver-white and patched with black shadows, and once again from somewhere down by the shamba and the papyrus swamp, birds were calling.

A bat flickered along the verandah almost brushing Victoria's head, and something moved in the shadows and sent her heart into her mouth; but it was only Pusser, the *Flamingo* cat, who had evidently been asleep in one of the wicker chairs.

Victoria was annoyed to find that her heart was racing and that she was breathing as quickly as though she had been running. Why didn't Eden come back? What were they doing—he and Drew? It was hours since they had left Crater Lake with Gilly Markham's body.

Somewhere in the house a clock struck ten, and the light in the dining-room, where Zacharia had been putting away the silver, was turned out. Victoria heard his shuffling footsteps retreating down the hall and then the sound of a door closing. And all at once the house was deathly quiet and only the night outside was full of small sounds.

Victoria clutched at the sides of her chair and glanced quickly over her shoulder at the open doorway that led into the hall, but the silent house seemed more frightening to her than the moonlit garden, and she stayed where she was, tense and listening, until at last she heard the faint, far-away purr of a car.

The sound grew louder and nearer, and presently

the yellow glare of headlights lit up the pepper trees and threw long black shadows across the sweep of the drive, and Eden walked up the verandah steps and checked at the sight of Victoria.

'Vicky! What are you doing here! You ought to be in bed. Did you wait up for us?'

'Us?' said Victoria. And saw then that Drew Stratton and young Mr Hennessy of the police were with him.

'Drew brought me back. It was his car. And Bill has been sent along to keep an eye on us and see that none of us makes a break for the border. They're staying the night. We thought it would be more convenient, as Greg wants to see us all in the morning. They can share the double bed in the blue room, and I hope one of them snores!'

He stopped by the hall door and said suddenly: 'There's nothing wrong, is there? Is Gran all right?'

'No. I mean, there's nothing wrong. Aunt Em went to bed. I stayed up because—because I didn't feel like going to sleep.'

'You look as though you could do with it, all the same,' said Eden as the light from the hall fell on her face. 'How's Lisa?'

'All right, I think. Aunt Em wanted her to stay here, but she wouldn't. Mrs Brandon is spending the night with her.'

'Good for Mabel. She won't enjoy it!'

There was a solitary table lamp burning in a corner of the drawing-room, and Eden switched on every other light and said: 'That's better! Vicky, I suppose you couldn't be a darling and rustle us up some coffee and sandwiches, could you? We've just driven back from Nairobi. I ought to have 'phoned, but I didn't want Em asking all sorts of awkward questions with half the Valley listening in on the party line.'

Victoria said: 'There's both in the dining-room. Aunt Em said you'd probably need something when you got back. Wait, and I'll fetch it.'

'Bless you,' said Eden, sinking gratefully into an arm-chair, 'and her. God, I'm tired!'

He lay back and shut his eyes, and looking down at him Victoria felt protective and maternal and as though, in some strange way, she had suddenly grown up.

She became aware that she herself was being watched, and turning her head met Drew Stratton's cool, level gaze. But tonight there was no hostility in his blue eyes; only interest and a faint trace of surprise. Victoria returned his look gravely, and then went away to fetch the Thermos flasks and the chicken sandwiches that Zacharia had left on the sideboard in the dining-room.

There was a light on in the hall, but the two long passages that led off it were full of shadows, and the house was as quiet as Crater Lake had been. Was it waiting for something to happen, as Crater Lake had waited? But that was absurd! thought Victoria impatiently. There was nothing wrong with the house; only with herself and her unruly imagination. *The fault, dear Brutus, is not in our stars, But in ourselves, that we are underlings*— Gilly... Gilly had been fond of quoting Shakespeare, and Gilly was dead. What was it that Em had said? *Nor steel, nor poison, Malice domestic . . . nothing, Can touch him further*. Yes, he was safe—if death were safety. But Eden and Aunt Em? and she herself, Victoria?—what about them?

Victoria shivered again, and setting her teeth, opened the dining-room door and groped for the light switches.

A single bulb in a red shade illuminated the sideboard but left the remainder of the room in shadow, and without waiting to turn on any more, Victoria collected a laden tray, and turned to see Drew Stratton standing behind her.

She had not heard him enter, and she was so startled that she would have dropped the tray if Drew had not taken it from her. He frowned at the sight of her white face and wide eyes, and said: 'What's the matter? Didn't you hear me?'

'No,' said Victoria breathlessly. 'You startled me.'

'I can see I did. You ought not to have stayed up. I suppose you've been sitting around alone, frightening yourself stiff?'

'Something like that,' admitted Victoria with a wan smile. 'What are you doing with that tray?'

'Making quite sure that the contents are as advertised,' said Drew. 'Though as I see that it wasn't only Eden who was expected, I imagine it's safe enough. Who made this? You?'

He had put the tray back on the sideboard and was unscrewing the cap of the Thermos.

'No. I suppose Zacharia did. Or the cook. Why?'

Drew did not reply. He removed the cork and poured a small quantity of coffee into one of the cups, smelt it suspiciously, and then put the tip of his finger into it and touched it cautiously to his tongue.

The import of the action was suddenly and horribly clear to Victoria, and she drew back with a gasp and put her hands to her throat: 'You c-can't— You can't think——' Once again she could not finish a sentence, for her breath appeared to have failed her.

Drew said: 'Seems all right.' He replaced the cork and turned his attention to the sandwiches, and after a moment or two said: 'How many people did Em order coffee for?'

'I—I don't know. She just said that Eden might want something when he came back, but she spoke to Zacharia in Swahili, so I don't know what she said.'

'*Hmm,*' said Drew thoughtfully. 'They all knew that as Eden had gone in my car, I'd probably be bringing him back. But there are four cups. If the extra two were Zacharia's idea, it shows that the old gentleman has more on the ball than one would imagine and had realized that someone from the police would come back with us. Which is interesting, to say the least of it.'

Victoria said huskily: 'Why have they sent a policeman here? Why not to the Markhams' bungalow? Why to us?'

'It isn't only to us. By this time there will not only be one at the Markhams' bungalow, but another at the Brandons.'

'Why? Is it— *Was* Gilly murdered?'

Drew replaced the sandwiches and looked up,

frowning. 'Now what gave you that idea?'

'Aunt Em said you thought he h-had been. Was he?'

'Yes,' said Drew briefly, and picked up the tray.

Victoria had hardly slept at all during the previous night and had endured a harrowing day, and the effects were telling upon her. She began to shiver violently, and Drew put the tray down abruptly and took her into his arms.

It was an entirely unexpected action, but an astonishingly comforting one, and Victoria found herself clinging to him as frantically as though he had been a life line in a cold sea. his arms were warm and close and reassuring, and presently she stopped shivering and relaxed against him; feeling safe for perhaps the first time since her arrival at *Flamingo*, and suddenly and surprisingly sleepy. She turned her head against his shoulder and yawned, and Drew laughed and released her.

'You know,' he said, 'this is painfully like one of those detective novels in which just as the plot is getting littered with clues and corpses, the heroine holds up the action for three pages with a sentimental scene. Are you coming into the drawing-room to drink coffee with us, or would you rather go to bed?'

'Bed,' said Victoria; and yawned again.

Drew accompanied her down the dark passage to her room, and having turned on the light for her, subjected the room to a careful scrutiny.

'No one in the cupboards or under the bed. And Bill Hennessy and I will be in the next room, and Eden only a few doors off. So you've nothing to panic about. I must get back or I shall have the police after me. You all right now?'

'Yes,' said Victoria, and smiled sleepily at him.

Drew took her chin in his hand and bent his head and kissed her quite casually and gently, and went away down the long dark passage, leaving her looking blankly at the panels of the door that he had closed behind him.

It was well past eight o'clock when Victoria awoke to the sound of knocking on her door, and unlocked it to admit an aggrieved Majiri who had apparently made several earlier attempts to rouse her.

The day, thought Victoria, blinking at the sunlight, could hardly be a pleasant one, but it was difficult to believe that horrible and frightening things could happen while the sun shone and the breeze smelt of geraniums and orange blossom, and the lake glittered like a vast aquamarine set in a ring of gold and emeralds. And yet Gilly was dead.

Duncan is in his grave . . .

She dressed hurriedly and went out to the verandah to find that Eden, Drew and the young policeman were already half-way through their breakfast, and that Em was having hers in bed.

Lisa and Mabel, both looking white and exhausted, arrived just as the breakfast things were being cleared away, escorted by a police officer who left them at the verandah steps and disappeared round the back of the house.

Mabel was wearing the same crumpled cotton frock that she had worn on the previous day, and she did not look as though she had slept at all, while for the first time in anyone's recollection Lisa Markham had paid little or no attention to her personal appearance. It was also equally evident that she was frightened.

Victoria had offered her some black coffee, and she had gulped it down thirstily, her teeth chattering against the rim of the cup, and replacing it clumsily on the table had let it fall to the ground, where it had smashed into half a dozen pieces.

It had been one of the Rockingham cups, but Lisa had offered no apology or even appeared to notice what she had done. Em, appearing on the verandah arrayed like Solomon in all his glory, had glanced at the broken fragments and made no comment. She had nodded at Mabel, Lisa and Drew, bestowed an affectionate kiss on Victoria and a more perfunctory one on Eden, and ignored Mr Bill Hennessy, who blushed pinkly and looked acutely uncomfortable. And then Hector and Ken had arrived with a third policeman who, after a brief colloquy with Mr Hennessy, also departed round the back of the house.

'I suppose you will all be staying to luncheon,' said Em morosely, surveying the assembled company without pleasure. 'If we are going to spend the entire morning being interrogated, we had better——'

She was interrupted by Lisa, who stood up abruptly and announced in quivering tones that she did not feel at all well: certainly not well enough to answer any questions today from Greg Gilbert or anyone else. That she had only come over because

Mabel had said she must, but if she had known that Greg was going to be so inconsiderate and unfeeling as to expect her to undergo a police grilling when——

Her spate of words grew shriller and higher, but any idea of her returning home was forestalled by the arrival of Greg Gilbert, two CID officers from Nakuru, several police askaris and an anonymous individual in a brown suit.

Greg confined his greetings to a single comprehensive nod that embraced everyone in the verandah, but the two CID officers were more punctilious. And then the entire party, with the exception of Mr Hennessy and the askaris, moved into the drawing-room, preceded by Em who seated herself regally in the wing-chair.

Greg refused a chair and stationed himself with his back to the windows, facing the half circle of anxious faces. His own face was blankly impersonal and his voice as devoid of emotional content as though he were reading the minutes of a board meeting to an assembly of total strangers.

He said: 'I imagine that you all know why I am here. An autopsy has been performed on Markham's body, and the doctor's report is quite definite. Gilly was not bitten by a snake, and there is the possibility that he was murdered!'

'No!' Lisa leapt to her feet, white-faced and gasping. 'You can't say that! You can't! It *was* a snake—we saw it!'

Mabel put out a hand and pulled her down again on to the sofa, murmuring: 'Lisa, dear. *Please!* Let him speak.'

Greg said: 'You may have seen it, but it didn't bite him.'

'We saw the fang marks,' said Em quietly.

'So Drew says; and Eden.'

'And I say it—and Mabel, and Ken,' put in Hector. 'Plain as the nose on your face!'

Greg shrugged. 'You saw two punctures that may have been made by anything; one of those double thorns off a thorn tree, for instance. Or if they were made by a snake, it was a snake that had either outlived its poison or emptied its poison sac. The autopsy showed no trace of snake venom, and it's my opinion that the snake you saw was a dead one.'

'But——' began Em, and checked; biting her lip.

Greg turned on her swiftly; 'Can you swear to it being alive? Did you actually see it move?'

Em hesitated, frowning. 'I thought I did. It moved when I hit it, but that might have been—'

'Of course it was alive!' boomed Hector. 'Why, I killed it! Dammit, I've got eyes!'

'But you have to wear spectacles for reading, don't you? And strong ones,' said Greg. 'And so does your wife, and Lady Emily.'

'That's different! Look—I wouldn't have wasted my time bashing a dead snake. Broke its neck and smashed its head.'

'And then threw it into the lake. A pity. If we could have got our hands on it, it might have told us quite a lot.'

'But——' began Hector, and stopped, as Em had done.

There was a brief and painful interval of silence, and then Ken Brandon spoke, his voice a deliberate drawl: '*I* threw it away. And what of it? Are you by any chance suggesting that I did it to destroy evidence?'

'Ken, darling!' begged Mabel in a strangled whisper. 'Don't be silly. *Please* don't be silly, darling.'

Greg favoured the boy with a long cool critical look and said softly: 'No one is accusing you of anything—yet.'

Mabel caught her breath in a small sobbing gasp and Hector took a swift stride forward, his chin jutting and his hands clenched into fists. 'Now look here, Greg,' he began belligerently.

Mr Gilbert turned a cold gaze upon him, and though he did not raise his voice it held a cutting quality that was as effective as the crack of a whip: '*I* am conducting this enquiry, Hector, and I will do it in my own way. All of you here are required to answer questions, not to ask them; and I would point out that there is a well-known saying to the effect that he who excuses himself, accuses himself. I have not, I repeat, accused anyone—yet. Will you sit down, please? No, not over there. Eden, give him a chair behind Mabel, will you. Thank you.'

Hector seated himself reluctantly, muttering under his breath, and Greg turned his attention back to Em:

'You were answering a question when Hector interrupted you. Are you quite certain that the snake was alive when you hit it?'

'No,' said Em heavily. 'It may have been, and it never occurred to me that it wasn't. I suppose we were all too worked up about Gilly to notice details, and puff adders are often sluggish creatures. But I wouldn't like to swear to it, because——' She hesitated for so long that Greg said: 'Because of what?'

Em sighed and the lines of her face sagged. 'Because I realized later that whatever he died of, it wasn't snake-bite.'

'Why?'

Em threw him a look of impatient contempt and said irritably: 'There is no need to treat me as though I were senile, Greg. You must know quite well that I have seen people die of snake-bite—and before you were born! It is, to say the least of it, an unpleasant death. Gilly didn't die that way; and if you want to know what I think, I think he had a heart attack; but because we saw the snake we jumped to the conclusion that it was snake-bite—and killed him.'

'By giving him that injection?'

Em nodded. 'Drew said it was probably the last straw, and he may have been right. If we'd left him alone he might have pulled through: people do survive heart attacks. But he didn't have a chance. It was seeing the snake—I didn't even think of it being anything else.'

'It wasn't your fault, Gran,' said Eden roughly. 'If you hadn't done it, someone else would. We all thought he'd been bitten. What did he die of, Greg?'

'Heart failure,' said Mr Gilbert calmly.

14

'What!' bellowed Hector, bounding to his feet and stuttering with wrath. 'Then what in thunder do you mean by interrogating us in this fashion? By God, Gilbert, I've a good mind to take this straight up to the Governor! You have the infernal impertinence to post one of your men in my house, and another to keep an eye on my wife and on poor Gilly's widow, when all the time Markham died a natural death from heart failure!'

Mr Gilbert waited patiently until he had quite finished, and for at least a minute afterwards, and his silence appeared to have a sobering effect upon Hector, for he said with considerably less truculence and a trace of uncertainty: 'Well? What have you got to say for yourself?'

'Quite a lot,' said Mr Gilbert gently. 'For one thing, most deaths are due to failure of the heart. What we do not know is *why* Markham's heart stopped beating. It is of course just possible that he was suffering from a heart attack when you found him. He drank fairly heavily—I'm sorry, Lisa, but that's true, isn't it?'

'Yes,' said Lisa. She had ceased to slump in a frightened heap in a corner of the sofa, and there was a look on her pale face that was curiously like eagerness. 'He always drank too much, but in the last few months he seemed to be much worse. I told him we couldn't afford it, and—and that it would kill him if he went on like this; but he only laughed.'

Greg nodded, but said: 'All the same, I don't believe he had a heart attack.'

'But surely—the doctors,' urged Mabel distressfully.

'The doctors say that his heart was flabby and full of blood, and that the symptoms described by Drew and Eden square with a heart attack. But they also square with something else—Acocanthera. *Msunguti*.'

Once again the words meant nothing whatever to Victoria, but in the sudden silence that followed them she became acutely aware that they held a meaning—and a singularly unpleasant one—for every other person in the room. Knowledge and shock—and wariness—was written plainly on six faces. Only Drew showed neither surprise nor wariness, but it was quite clear that he too knew the meaning of those two words.

Greg Gilbert looked round the room as though he expected someone to speak, but no one moved or spoke. They did not even look at one another.

They looked at Greg as though they could not look away, and their bodies were still with a stillness that spoke of tensed muscles and held breath.

Greg said slowly: 'I see that you all know what that means. Except Miss Caryll; which is possibly a good thing for her. For your information, Miss Caryll, I am talking of arrow poison. Something that is only too easy to come by in this country and which produces death—by heart failure—in anything from twenty minutes to two hours. Unfortunately it also produces no detectable symptoms, so unless we can produce other evidence the autopsy verdict on Markham will have to stand as "heart failure due to unknown causes". A verdict with which I, personally, am not prepared to agree.'

'Why?' demanded Em harshly. 'He might well have had a heart attack. He'd been drinking far too much, and he was three parts drunk by lunch-time yesterday—the autopsy must have shown that, too! And he was too thin and too highly strung. He lived on his nerves. Why do you have to believe the worst, when there is no shadow of proof to support it?'

'But there is a shadow of proof,' said Greg gently. 'The fact that three things which might have proved that it was a heart attack are all missing. We had a squad of our men down at Crater Lake at first light, and they went all over the ground with a small tooth comb—and a magnet. But though they found the broken half of the needle, they didn't find the knife you slashed Markhams' arm with, or the bottle of iodine you doctored it with. Or the snake that may or may not have bitten him. Odd, to say the least of it.'

Ken Brandon leant forward, his hands gripping the arms of his chair so tightly that his knuckles showed white, and said in a high strained voice that had lost all traces of a drawl: 'Why do you keep harping on that snake? What would *you* have done with it? Put it in your pocket? I didn't even know that it would fall in the lake! It was a fluke, I tell you! I——'

Hector said brusquely: 'Shut up, Ken! I'm not letting you say anything more without a lawyer. And if the rest of you have any sense you won't answer any more questions either! If Gilbert is accusing one of us of murder—and it looks damned like it to me!—then he's got no right to expect us to answer questions until we have had legal advice.'

Greg surveyed him thoughtfully, and then turned to look at Em. 'That your opinion too, Em?'

'No, of course not,' said Em crossly. 'I'm no fool. Or at least, not so big a fool as Hector is making himself out to be. Lawyers! *Bah!* The only useful advice that any lawyer could give any of us is to speak the truth and stop behaving as though we had something to hide.'

'If that is to my address,' flared Hector, 'I have nothing to hide! *Nothing!* But I still say——'

'Be quiet, Hector.' Mabel had not raised her voice, but the three softly spoken words were drops of ice, and they froze Hector's torrent of words as ice will freeze Niagara.

No one had ever heard Mabel use that tone before; or had believed her capable of it. And Hector's instant and instinctive reaction to it was equally surprising. He stood for a moment with his mouth open, looking like some large and foolish fish, and then he shut it hurriedly and sat down, and thereafter only spoke when he was spoken to.

Mabel said composedly: 'You must forgive us, Greg. We are all a little upset. Of course we will answer any questions that we can. We all know that you are only here to help, and that it cannot be any less unpleasant for you than it is for us. I suppose you want to know all about the picnic? Why we went and how we went, and when. And what we ate, and things like that.'

Greg shook his head. 'I know that already. I heard it last night from both Drew and Eden. No. I want to know about the knife. And about the bottle of iodine. Em, you used the knife on Markham's arm, didn't you? Whose was it?'

Em met his gaze squarely and with composure, and replied without the least hesitation. 'My own.'

The two words were as coldly and quietly spoken as Mabel's had been, but they produced an even more startling effect. There was an audible and almost simultaneous gasp from several throats: a sound that might have been relief or apprehension or shock, and Eden spoke for the first time since they had entered the drawing-room:

'Gran, are you sure?'

'Of what?' enquired Em, continuing to look blandly at Greg Gilbert. 'That it was my knife, or that I know what I'm doing? The answer to both is "yes".'

For the first time that morning Mr Gilbert lost his calm. A flush of colour showed red in his tanned cheeks and his mouth and eyes opened in angry astonishment. 'Then why,' he demanded dangerously, 'did you say yesterday that you didn't know whose it was?'

'Did I?' enquired Em blandly. 'I can't have been thinking. We were all a bit——'

'Upset!' interrupted Greg savagely. 'So I have already heard. Now look here, Em, I'm not going to have any of this nonsense. That wasn't your knife, and you know it. Whose was it? You won't do any good to anyone by playing the heroine and telling lies to cover up for someone else.'

'You mean for Eden,' said Em calmly. 'But he never carries a knife. Only a silly little gold penknife arrangement on a chain that Alice gave him one Christmas. And I doubt if you'll find any bloodstains or arrow poison on that.'

For a moment it looked as though Mr Gilbert were about to lose his temper as explosively as Hector Brandon had done, but he controlled himself with a visible effort, and said quite quietly: 'I am not going to warn you of the consequences of deliberately obstructing the police, because you must be well aware of them. You also don't give a damn for the police or anyone else, do you? You're like too many of the Old Guard in that. You think that you can be a law unto yourselves. But that's where you're wrong. You can't have your cake and eat it too.'

He looked round at the ring of strained faces and added grimly: 'And that goes for all of you. You cannot let a murderer escape justice just because you happen to know him, or he is a relative or a friend. I do not believe that knife belonged to Lady Emily. The way I heard it, she asked for a knife and was handed one. Quite possibly she did not notice at the time who handed it to her, and she certainly told Stratton yesterday that she did not know whose it was. She has now, for reasons of her own, decided that it was hers. But there were half a dozen of you watching her, and one of you must remember where she was standing and who was next to her; and if the knife was not her own, one of you must have given it to her. That person had better speak up at once.'

No one spoke, and the silence lengthened out and filled with sullenness and strain and taut emotions, until suddenly and unexpectedly Eden laughed. It was an entirely genuine laugh and therefore the more startling. He leant back in his chair with his hands in his pockets, and said lightly:

'"Hands up the boy who broke that window!" It's no use Greg. This isn't the Fifth Form at St Custards, and you can't gate the entire class for a month if the culprit won't own up. Maybe that knife really was Gran's.'

'Maybe,' said Greg sceptically. 'Very well, then. If it was, let's have a description of it.'

'Certainly,' said Em briskly. 'It was a three-bladed knife that once belonged to Kendall. It had a horn handle with his initials cut on it, and the small blade had been broken off short. I often take it with me when I go picnicking or shooting. It's very useful. I had it in my pocket.'

'I see,' said Greg through shut teeth. 'Can you confirm that, Eden?'

Eden had been looking at his grandmother with an expression that was something between doubt and the effort to recall an elusive memory, and he started slightly on being addressed, and said hurriedly: 'Yes. Yes of course I can. It generally stays in the hall drawer. I've seen it a hundred times.'

'And it was the knife your grandmother cut Markham's arm with?'

Eden's face changed as though a mask had dropped over it, and he said in an entirely expressionless voice: 'I'm afraid I don't remember. If she says it was, then presumably it was. We were all looking at Gilly at the time.'

'Were you!' said Mr Gilbert grimly. And he turned again to Em: 'What did you do with it after that?'

'I put it down—or else I threw it on one side. I'm not sure.'

'And poured iodine on the wound? I'd like to hear about that.'

Em described the incident in some detail, but professed not to remember what she had done with the bottle.

'Then you didn't hand it back to Mrs Brandon?'

'I don't think so. I probably just dropped it too. It was empty.'

Mabel Brandon dabbed her eyes with a handkerchief and blew her nose with determination, and looking across at Em she smiled a little tremulously and said, 'Thank you, Em. I—I know you do remember, and that you're only saying that to keep me out of it. But I'm not going to hide behind you.

She did give it back to me, Greg. I took it from her and put it down somewhere, and I didn't think of it again until Drew asked me what I'd done with it.'

Greg turned slowly and looked at Em, and it was noticeable that she returned his look with less assurance.

'Well, Em?' said Greg softly.

Em's mouth twisted into a wry and somewhat shamefaced smile.

'I'm sorry Greg. Yes, I knew Mabel had taken it. But I also know that she didn't kill Gilly, and I can't see that she need get mixed up in this horrible business just because she always carries around a bottle of iodine in case of accidents.'

'That,' said Greg, still softly, 'is the point. She always carries one, and everyone knows it. And that is why this may be a Mau Mau killing after all.'

'What!' The exclamation came loudly and simultaneously from half a dozen throats, and in a flash the atmosphere in the room changed as though a current of electricity had been switched off, and muscles that had been tense with strain and apprehension relaxed in sudden relief.

'I knew it!' cried Lisa; and began to sob loudly. 'I knew it would be all right!'

Em turned to gaze at her in disapproval, and observed coldly that she was glad that Lisa considered that everything was now all right: it was at least an original view of the case.

'I didn't mean Gilly being dead,' sobbed Lisa. 'Of course that's awful. It's just that I thought Greg might find out——'

'Lisa!' said Drew sharply and compellingly.

He had not spoken before, and his intervention checked Lisa, who gulped and turned to look at him.

'Whatever you were going to say—don't,' said Drew; and grinned at Greg Gilbert's furious face. 'Sorry, Greg, but I'm against shooting sitting birds. And in any case, from your last remark I gather we may all be out of the red, though I don't quite see how you can involve the Mau Mau in this one.'

Mr Gilbert said ominously: 'If you prompt anyone, or interrupt anyone again, Stratton, I shall get you ten days in the cells, if I get the sack for it!'

'And I'll go quiet,' promised Drew equably. 'What is this Mau Mau angle?'

'I should have thought it was obvious enough,' said Greg coldly. 'Hector is still doing a lot of useful interrogation work, and someone may have been laying for him—or for his wife or son. It would have been easy enough to substitute a solution of arrow poison for the iodine, and the next time any of them had a cut or a scratch Mabel would have doctored it from that bottle, and that would have been that. It's a possibility that we can't ignore.'

'And the knife?' enquired Em crisply.

'Same thing. Except—if it *was* your knife—it might conceivably have been a trap laid for either you or Eden.'

'No. Not for us,' said Em thoughtfully. 'The dogs. I have often used it to cauterize sores on the dogs, and it would have got one of them. Like—like Simba.'

Mabel said: 'So Gilly was killed by mistake. It

should have been Hector or Ken—or me! Or one of Em's dogs.'

'Or the first person you happened to doctor with iodine or who happened to cut themselves on my knife—and who might just as well have been an African,' pointed out Em dryly. 'It sounds very far-fetched to me, and it still doesn't explain the disappearance of the knife and the bottle. Where does that fit in?'

'It doesn't,' confessed Greg. 'It doesn't even fit in with my own theory of the crime.'

'And what is your theory? Or do you prefer to keep us in the dark?' enquired Em acidly.

Greg looked meditatively at the carpet for a mintue or two without speaking, and then allowed his gaze to travel with deliberation along the half circle of intent faces that watched him so anxiously. And it is doubtful if he missed even the smallest change in any one of them.

He said slowly: 'No. There is no reason why I should not tell you, for although I believe that I am right, I can't prove it. I think that Gilly Markham died from the effects of arrow poison, and that his murder was carefully planned in advance. Everyone here, and everyone in the Rift for that matter, knew that he drank too much and could be trusted to drink too much even at a picnic, provided the drink was there; which it was. I believe that someone took a dead puff adder to Crater Lake yesterday, and sometime during the afternoon, while Gilly was asleep, placed it beside him and gave him a jab in the arm with some sort of pronged instrument that had been liberally coated with arrow poison. Something that would leave a wound similar to the mark of a snake's fangs.'

Lisa was the first person to speak. She said in a strained voice that was barely a whisper: 'But—why that way? The snake?'

'Because although arrow poison is not detectable in an autopsy, there might well have been some of it left outside the wound. Enough to prove that it had been used. But the first thing anyone does when dealing with a snake-bite is to make a deep cut on or just above it. That's why it had to be a snake; because the murderer could count on someone removing the evidence in double quick time. It would not matter who did it as long as it was done—and of course it was done. That disposed of any superfluous poison, and the snake was an equally easy bet. No one stops to see if a snake is alive if it is found lying curled up in a life-like attitude beside a sleeping person. They take a bash at it with the first thing that comes handy, and the blows would have made it appear to be moving. Also, no one is going to pay very close attention to it when there is a dying man to attend to. So you see, it would have been fairly foolproof.'

'But you said it could have been the knife,' whispered Lisa. 'Or the iodine. You *said* so!'

'It could have been. Because those two things have inexplicably disappeared. But it is far more likely that the poison was administered at least half an hour before either of those things were used. Acocanthera frequently produces vomiting, and your husband had been sick. He was also found in a state of coma just after three-thirty.'

Mabel's hands twisted together against the skirt of her crumpled cotton frock, and she said distressfully: 'Oh no!—Oh, I do hope not! I mean—I heard him. Being sick. If I had gone to him at once I might have been able to do something. But I thought—well, he *had* had too much to drink, and I thought it would be better to keep away. If *only* I had gone!'

'It wouldn't have done any good. Not if my theory is correct. There's no antidote.'

'But you can't be right!' said Mabel, suddenly sitting bolt upright. 'No, of course you can't be. You can't jab someone in the arm without waking them up. He would have cried out. I should have heard him. And,' she concluded triumphantly, 'I didn't! I didn't hear a *sound*, and neither did Em. Did you, Em?'

'I'm afraid I was asleep,' confessed Em reluctantly. 'I didn't even hear him being sick, and I certainly wouldn't have gone to him if I had.'

Greg said: 'Markham was sleeping off a fairly outsize dose of alcohol; and before the discovery of anaesthetics it was the accepted thing to give a man half a bottle of whisky to drink before an operation or an amputation—to deaden the pain. If the jab was a quick one it might have done no more than jerk him awake for a few seconds, and the chances are that he would have dozed off again at once. What is it, Miss Caryll?'

'N-nothing,' stammered Victoria, startled. 'I d-didn't say anything.'

'But you thought of something, didn't you?'

'Yes. I—it was nothing, really. It was only that

while I was standing by the lake yesterday I heard someone snoring, and then they made a noise as though they had been woken up suddenly. You know. A—a sort of snort. I thought it was Gil—Mr Markham. But after a bit the snoring started again.'

'Hmm,' said Greg. 'What time was that?'

'I've no idea. Somewhere between half-past two and three I suppose.'

Greg turned to Mabel and asked her if she had also heard such a sound, and Mabel, looking a trifle conscience-striken, admitted to having dozed, though she had been woken later by hearing Gilly retching. 'But I didn't do anything about it. I remember thinking "*Really!* Pool Lisa." Or something like that, and the next thing I remember was Hector telling me to wake up because it was time we were going.'

'Hmm,' said Greg again, and was silent for so long that the tension became too much for Ken Brandon. His control cracked under the strain of that silence and his voice cracked with it:

'It's no good looking at me! I didn't go near him. I swear I didn't! I didn't even touch him. None of us did—only Stratton and Lady Emily. I'm not going to sit here and be accused of—of things, just because I threw away a dead snake! Dad was quite right. You haven't any right to do this. We aren't under arrest, and I'm going!'

He stood up clenching and unclenching his hands, and looking, for all his nineteen years, less like an Angry Young Man than a small boy who has flown into a temper to hide his fright.

'Oh *no,* Kennie darling!' moaned Mabel, wringing her hands. *'Don't* talk like that. Of course you didn't go near Gilly, darling. Greg knows that. We all know it. Stay here, darling. *Please!'*

Greg said patiently: 'Sit down, Ken. You're only making an ass of yourself, and I haven't accused anyone of anything.'

'Yet!' mimicked Ken savagely. 'That's what you said before, isn't it? *"Yet!"* But you will, won't you? Even though you haven't a shred of evidence! Even though you admit yourself that Gilly may have died of a heart attack. And what do you base your precious theory on? The fact that a knife and an empty bottle have been lost or mislaid. Why, they're probably both still there, trodden into the grass by your flat-footed, bone-headed askaris!'

'Oh no, Kennie. Don't, dear,' sobbed Mabel in a monotonous moaning whisper. But Ken Brandon was beyond listening to reason or his mother's pleas, and the words poured out of him in a childish spate of nervous rage:

'What the hell does it matter if they aren't found? You've as good as admitted that there's nothing wrong with either of them, haven't you? *Haven't you?* And that if Gilly was poisoned, it was done half an hour before anyone used the knife or the iodine on him. And yet you can produce a footling thing like that and call it evidence of murder! If that's all the evidence you've got, then you haven't got a case at all. Not a shadow of a case!—and no right in the world to haul us in here and talk like this to us.'

He paused for breath, and Greg said mildly:

'I told you that the disappearance of those two

things didn't square with any theory. But that is why I am interested in them: or rather, in why someone thought fit to remove them, and is now lying about it. There must be a reason for that, and it is my guess that whoever made away with them suspected murder—and the murderer—and having a shrewd idea as to how it had been done, jumped to the same conclusion that both Stratton and Lady Emily arrived at: that if it was Acocanthera, it was either on the knife or in the iodine bottle—and therefore hid them. But if it *was* murder, then the one person who would *not* have done that is the murderer; because such an action could only lead to suspicion of murder in what might possibly have passed as death from snake-bite, or, if questions were asked and an autopsy performed, from a heart attack due to heavy drinking. I am quite sure in my own mind that there was nothing wrong with either the knife or the iodine, and when we eventually find them we shall be able to prove it. That is why I am asking whoever made away with them to own up to it now. It must be one of you, and as it cannot possibly be the murderer, all that you are being asked to do is to clear yourself. And at the same time to help clear whoever it was that you suspected of doctoring either of those two things.'

Once again there was a strained silence in the room when he had finished speaking, but if anyone had intended to admit responsibility they were forestalled by Ken Brandon, who said loudly and scornfully:

'Oh no, you're not! You're not asking anything of

the sort. We're not all fools, though you're treating us as though we were. What you're trying to do is to get one of us to implicate someone else. That's it, isn't it? Maybe there wasn't anything wrong with that knife or the iodine. But someone thought there might be, and they must have had a damned good reason for thinking it. You'd want to know that reason, wouldn't you? Well we're not falling for that one. You can do your own dirty work! I'm going, for one. Come on, Mother, let's get out of here.'

Mabel stood up, pale and trembling, and behind her Hector too had risen; but slowly and reluctantly.

Mr Gilbert moved deliberately and without haste, and placed himself between Ken and the door. He said quietly: 'I'm sorry, Ken, but you can't go just yet. Don't make this any more unpleasant than it need be. Because if you try and leave, I shall have to put you under arrest for obstructing the police.'

'*Try* and leave? I'm going to do more than try! I'm not putting up with this any longer, and that's all there is to it. And just *you* try and stop me!'

He whirled round and made a dive for the open window, and Drew rose swiftly and hit him once and scientifically.

Ken Brandon crumpled at the knees and collapsed upon the floor, his nose bleeding profusely and a foolish smile fixed upon his face. And peace reigned.

'Oh, thank you, Drew!' gasped Mabel with real gratitude.

15

The remainder of the morning was as unenjoyable as the beginning, though less full of unpleasant surprises, and although Mr Gilbert and his entourage had departed shortly before one, the respite had been brief, for they had returned an hour and a half later.

This time the two C.I.D. officers as well as Mr Gilbert faced their audience, while the unobtrusive gentleman in the brown suit sat behind them, and judging from the soft and ceaseless scratching of pen upon paper, occupied himself in taking down their replies verbatim and in shorthand.

The questions that afternoon were mainly concerned with movements. They appeared to be merely routine ones, and often pointless, but one thing at least emerged from them. No one could produce an alibi that covered the period of time in which Gilly Markham could have been murdered, for the entire party, with the exception of Em and Mabel, had separated after luncheon. And even Em and Mabel could not alibi each other, since both at different times had vanished into the bushes for, as Em observed frostily, 'obvious reasons', and later both had slept.

Eden and Lisa, who had departed together, had quarrelled and separated. Not that either admitted to quarrelling, but it took very little intuition on anyone's part to fill in the gap in their respective stories. Lisa said she had 'just strolled about', and Eden said he had sat on a fallen trunk and 'thought he might have dozed'.

Ken Brandon asserted that he had left the crater to explore the far side of it, and had only returned just before the party reassembled, while Hector said that he had spent the best part of an hour searching among the rocks to see if he could pick up the track of the leopard whose pug marks they had seen at the lake edge.

Drew also had left the crater and gone for a walk, and Victoria, answering endless questions as to the sounds she professed to have heard that afternoon, could only insist that she had seen no one for half an hour after his departure, and thought that they might have been caused by some animal.

No one appeared to have paid much attention to time until well after three o'clock, and though Greg went over and over the details of that last twenty-five minutes of Gilly's life, it had proved impossible to build up an accurate picture of exactly where everyone had stood, or who had been standing next to whom, for only Em, Victoria and Drew had remained in approximately the same position throughout, and they and everyone else had been far too intent on the life-and-death drama that was taking place under their eyes to note the movements or expressions of other people.

'Can't you understand?' said Em, her voice flat with exhaustion. 'He was dying! And we knew he was dying. It never occurred to any of us that it was murder. Why should it? Perhaps if it had we would have watched each other instead of him. But it didn't.'

'Oh, yes it did!' Greg contradicted grimly. 'Three of you at least thought that it might be murder. Otherwise Stratton would not have hunted for that broken needle, or Mrs Markham refused to drink the brandy. Even you knew that something was wrong!'

Em said wearily: 'But I didn't think of murder until much later. Not until Drew started asking questions about the knife and said we must go back and look for it. I'd thought it was a heart attack, and that I'd killed him.'

'I wasn't thinking of you when I said "three people". The third was whoever removed the knife and the iodine bottle. Or if two people were involved in that, then that makes it four. Four people out of seven suspected that Markham had been murdered, and I'd like to know why. Perhaps you can give me your reasons, Mrs Markham? Why did you think that your husband might have been murdered?'

Lisa clutched the arms of her chair and half rose from it. 'I didn't! You can't say I did. You're just trying to get me to admit things I never said. You're twisting things! I — I'd seen Gilly die. Drew gave him brandy, and he died. I wasn't thinking straight. I didn't mean it that way. I only didn't want to drink because—because Gilly had drunk from it—and—and died.'

Greg shrugged his shoulders, and somewhat unexpectedly did not press the question. He turned instead to Drew and demanded his reasons for suspecting murder, but was interrupted by Eden who observed with some asperity that considering Drew had, to his certain knowledge, already answered that question at length on the previous night, and had, moreover, been asked to sign a typed copy of his statement, it appeared to him to be a pointless question and a waste of time.

'I never ask pointless questions,' said Mr Gilbert without heat. 'Well, Drew?'

Drew said, 'I knew it couldn't be snake-bite for the same reasons that Em gave you. I've seen men die that way. I've also twice seen a man die from the effects of a poisoned arrow, and as I did not know that the symptoms of heart attack were similar, heart did not occur to me, but *msunguti* did. Gilly had been perfectly well, though a bit tight, an hour earlier, and now he was dying. That was all there was to it.'

'Thank you,' said Greg briefly.

The remainder of the afternoon was merely a repetition of the beginning, with the sole difference that the questions were asked again, and answered, individually and behind the closed door of the dining-room.

It was well after five when Greg had finished with Victoria, who had been questioned last. He looked tired and grim and driven, for excepting only Victoria, these were all his personal friends: people he had known for years, and had dined with and danced with, and suffered with during the harsh years of the Emergency. But he faced them now with the bleak impersonal gaze of a stranger, and his voice was as detached and unfriendly as his eyes:

'I shall probably have to see you all again during the next few days, and until this business is settled I'd be grateful if you'd arrange not to be out, or anywhere where I can't get in touch with you at short notice.'

And then he had gone.

'Well thank goodness that's over!' said Em with a gusty sigh. 'And at least he isn't likely to be back tomorrow, which means that with luck we should have one peaceful day.'

But the following day could hardly have been termed peaceful.

Gilly's body had been brought back for burial, and having notified Mr Gilbert of their intentions, they had all attended the funeral, which had been marred by the behaviour of Lisa and, in a lesser degree, Ken Brandon. Lisa had gone off into screaming, shrieking hysterics and had to be forcibly removed, and Ken Brandon had quietly and unobtrusively fainted.

Drew had caught him as he fell, and had driven him back to *Flamingo*, together with Mabel. And Em, Eden, Hector and Victoria had returned some twenty minutes later, with the information that Lisa was back in her own bungalow under the care of the doctor's wife, and had been given a strong injection of morphia.

'What was it all about?' demanded Mabel, pallid and shivering. 'You—you don't think she can possibly have... No! No, of course not! One should not even *think* such things!'

'That Lisa might have done it?' supplied Drew. 'Who is to say what anyone else is capable of under certain pressures? Or even where one's own breaking point lies? But personally I'd cross Lisa off any list of suspects, because unless she's a remarkably good actress, that performance of hers at Crater Lake was genuine. She thought someone had murdered her husband all right, whatever she says now, and she thought the stuff might be in the brandy. Q.E.D.—she didn't do the job herself!'

'My dear Drew,' said Em with asperity, '*all* women are excellent actresses when circumstances force them to it; and the sooner men realize that, the better! But of course Lisa did not murder her husband—though I have no doubt there were times when she wanted to. There were times when I myself felt like it, and I, let me point out, was not compelled to put up with Gilly's company as Lisa was. She could quite possibly have been another Mrs Thompson. Someone who might talk or dream about doing away with an unwanted husband, in the way a child will invent long and improbable stories, but who would never really *mean* it.'

Drew said softly: 'They hanged Mrs Thompson.'

He refused an invitation to stay to luncheon, and left, followed shortly afterwards by the Brandons;

and Em, watching them go, had expressed a hope that they—and the police—would stay away from *Flamingo* for at least a week.

But it was a hope that was not to be realized.

Eden and Victoria had spent the afternoon out on the lake, and had returned in the peaceful, pearl-pink evening to find both Drew and the Brandons in the drawing-room again, and the house once more full of policemen. For Kamau, the lover of Wambui, had been found.

'It was the dogs,' said Em looking oddly shrunken in the depths of the big wing-chair, and hugging a woollen shawl about her shoulders as though she were cold. 'They've been kept shut up for days and only taken out on a leash, because of Lisa's bitch. But I—I couldn't keep them shut up for ever, could I? I suppose they smelt him . . .'

It had happened barely half an hour after Eden and Victoria had left. Em had heard the barking and had gone out with a whip and tried to beat them off. The dog boy had run out with the leashes, and Em had sent him for the askaris, and having left them on guard had returned to the house and telephoned Greg.

Mr Gilbert and several policemen had arrived within the hour, and what the ants had left of Kamau had been disinterred from a shallow grave among the charcoal kilns.

Greg's temper had not been improved by the discovery that Eden was out in the motor launch and could not be reached, and he had sent for the Brandons and for Drew, who had been questioned severally and separately as to their movements on the night of Kamau's disappearance.

'But why you and the Brandons?' demanded Victoria of Drew.

She had spent an unnerving half-hour in the dining-room answering endless questions, and had come out into the twilit verandah to discover Drew Stratton leaning against one of the creeper-covered pillars and smoking a cigarette.

Drew said sombrely: 'Because whoever killed Kamau presumably killed Alice DeBrett—and then killed Kamau because he had not only seen it done, but had talked about it.'

Victoria said in a small, shaken voice: 'But—but that's just what makes it so pointless. It would have been different if he'd been killed to stop him talking. But he'd talked already. He said it was Aunt Em!'

'I know. But we didn't hear that until the next day, did we? And by that time he was dead. If his girlfriend had only come clean straight away, instead of pretending that he'd merely hinted at knowing something, he might still be alive—though I doubt it. As it was, someone evidently thought it was worth while stopping his mouth permanently, and if it hadn't been for the fact that by a fluke, and because he was no mean pianist, Gilly was able to blow a hole through Wambui's story, your aunt would have been left in a very sticky position. She won't be in too good a one now. Not now that Gilly is dead.'

'Why not?' demanded Victoria anxiously.

'Because Gilly giving evidence on the one subject

that he was really at home in would have been able to convince any jury that he knew what he was talking about. But the same evidence, given at second hand by Greg, isn't going to sound nearly so convincing. And now there's this business of Kamau. God, what a mess!'

Victoria said: 'But they couldn't think Aunt Em had killed Kamau! No one could!'

'Why not?' enquired Drew impatiently. 'She had the best opportunity of anyone. She was meeting him that night by the gate into the shamba.'

'How can you say that!' blazed Victoria, stiff with anger. 'You haven't any right to! You're just being s-stupid and—and——'

'*Shh!*' said Drew with the flicker of a grin. 'There's no need to fly off the handle. You're not looking at this from the police viewpoint, which is purely concerned with hard facts and is not swayed—or is trying not to be—by the personal angle. You are only thinking of your aunt as someone you know and are fond of. But they have got to think of her as "X", who allied to B, or minus Z, may equal Y.'

Victoria said scornfully: 'Then they're just being stupid too! Suppose she did meet Kamau that night, and kill him? All right, how did she carry him from the gate right up to the place where they found him? And when she got him there, how did she manage to dig a grave and bury him? She's over seventy!'

'Seventy-two, I believe—and as strong as a carthorse. But that's beside the point. You're not using your head, Victoria. If Em had done it she wouldn't have needed to kill him by the gate. She could have invented a dozen excuses to get him to walk with her to the kilns, and dealt with him on the spot. And she wouldn't have needed to dig a grave. There were several there already. It must have been only too easy to topple a body into one of those trenches and cover it up with some of the loose earth that was lying around, and the fumes from the charcoal kilns would have interfered with the scent if tracker dogs were used.'

'But it was Aunt Em's dogs who found him!'

'Ah, that was different. He'd been underground for quite a few days by then.'

Victoria flinched, and Drew said quickly: 'I'm sorry. This is a beastly business for all of us, but the rest of us have at least seen or heard of worse things in our day. The Emergency wasn't a picnic!—though now I come to think of it, that's an unfortunate simile, isn't it? But you've been pitchforked into this from a safe and orderly existence, and it must be pretty unnerving for you. Wishing you hadn't come?'

'No—o,' said Victoria hesitantly. 'I don't think I could ever wish I hadn't come back to Kenya. But I wish I hadn't...'

She did not complete the sentence, but come to lean on the verandah rail beside him, looking out into the deepening dusk. There was something about Drew's mere physical presence that was reassuring, and as long as he was here the house seemed less frightening. She turned to look at him and said abruptly:

'Are you staying here tonight?'

'Yes. Greg wants all his suspects under one roof.

Or rather, under two: the Brandons are reluctantly parking out at Lisa's. Just as well really, as he seems to have roped in our respective house servants for questioning, and turned all our labour lines into the nearest thing to a concentration camp that I've seen outside one.'

'Then he does think it may possibly be an African after all?'

'Of course he does. He's no fool. They've been getting a far stiffer grilling than we have. You mustn't think that just because Greg has been hauling us over the coals that he hasn't had a squad of his boys doing exactly the same thing to every single African who works on this estate, or on mine or Hector's. There were even two of them who might have pulled off that picnic business. Zach and Samuel were actually down in the crater. And there is still "General Africa"—who is still at large and still unidentified, and who may yet turn out to be the snake in the grass. I don't believe that Greg has lost sight of that possibility for a moment. In fact he's quite capable of making all this display of suspecting one of us with the sole object of confusing the issue and making it look as though the enquiries in the labour lines are merely routine, and that it is the Bwanas who are really under suspicion.'

Victoria gave a little sigh that was partly relief and partly weariness. 'I didn't think of that. You must be right. After all, we couldn't *really* be suspects. Not you or the Brandons, anyway.'

'Why not? We all happened to be here or hereabouts on the night Mrs DeBrett was killed. *And* on the night that Kamau disappeared.'

'But the Brandons weren't even here then!'

'No. But they called at the Markhams' bungalow that evening. Gilly was out, but Lisa had just got back from here, and it seems that she spilt the works. Which means that any one of them could have got over here in time to head off Kamau. It's no distance at all by the short cut between *Flamingo* and *Brandonmead*, and there was a moon that night.'

Victoria said: 'But they wouldn't have got him to go with them. You said that Aunt Em could have made an excuse to get him to walk to the kilns, but he might not have gone with one of the Brandons.'

'Ever noticed that there's a trolley arrangement that runs from the shamba to the road, and passes within a few yards of the kilns? No one would have needed to do any carrying of corpses. Even you could have managed it without much difficulty.'

'*Me!* But——'

'No, I'm not accusing you of running amok with a hatchet, so there's no need to glare at me. Though I daresay Greg has had to consider that possibility.'

'What possibility?'

'That you and Eden might have cooked this up between you.'

Victoria looked at him, meeting his bland blue gaze thoughtfully and without anger. Studying his face in the dusk as if it had been a letter held up for her to read: a very important letter.

She said at last: 'And what do you think?'

'Does it matter?'

Victoria did not answer, and presently Drew said slowly and as though he were thinking aloud:

'People who are desperately and deeply in love

are probably capable of anything. There are endless examples in history and the newspapers to prove that love can be a debasing passion as well as the most ennobling one; and a stronger and more relentless force than either ambition or hate, because those can be cold-blooded things, but love is always a hot-blooded one. Men and women have died for it—or for the loss of it. They have committed crimes for it and given up thrones for it, started wars, deserted their families, betrayed their countries, stolen, lied and murdered for it. And they will probably go on doing so until the end of time!'

He stubbed out his cigarette against the rail and dropped it among the geraniums, and after a moment or two Victoria said meditatively and without turning her head:

'And you think I might be—capable of anything?'

Drew gave an odd, curt laugh. 'Not of murder. Or even of conniving at it. But of covering up for someone you were in love with, or even very fond of, yes.'

'Even if I knew they had committed a murder? A horrible murder?'

'No. Because you would never love anyone like that.'

Victoria turned to look at him. The last of the daylight was running out with the swiftness of sand in an hour glass, and now it was so dark that she could no longer see the lines in his face.

She said: 'Then at least you don't believe that Eden could have done it.'

'I didn't say that. For all I know, he may have done it; though I shouldn't say it was in the least likely. But then you aren't in love with Eden.'

Victoria did not say anything, but she did not turn away, and Drew said: 'Are you.'

It was an affirmation rather than a question, and as she still did not speak he took her chin in his hand, as he had done once before.

Victoria stood quite still, aware of a crisis in her life: of having reached the end of a road—or perhaps the beginning of one. And then a door at the far end of the verandah opened and the shadows retreated before a flood of warm amber light, and it was no longer dusk, but night.

Drew's hand dropped and he turned unhurriedly:

'Hullo, Eden. Has Greg finished with you at last? How much longer is he likely to be around?'

'God knows,' said Eden shortly. 'What on earth are you two doing out here in the dark?'

'Talking,' said Drew pleasantly. 'Any objection?'

'No, of course not! But there are drinks in the drawing-room if you want one. I've sent Gran to bed.'

'Did she go?'

'Yes, surprisingly enough. She's going to be the next person to have a heart attack if we don't watch it.'

'A genuine one?' enquired Drew. 'Or one of the kind that hit Gilly?'

'Oh, for Pete's sake!' said Eden angrily, and turning his back on Drew he took Victoria's arm. 'Come on, Vicky darling. You must be cold. Come and have a glass of sherry. Or let's finish off the vodka and get really tight.'

They found Mabel in the drawing-room, sipping a brandy and soda and watching the door. Hector, accompanied by Bill Hennessy, had returned to *Brandonmead* to collect various necessities for a night's stay at the Markham's bungalow, but Ken was still being questioned, and Mabel would not leave without him.

'What *are* they doing with Kennie?' she demanded unhappily. 'He's been in there for hours! They must know that he can't know anything at all about this. It isn't kind of Greg—and after all the years we've known him! Drew, don't you think you could go and tell him that we're all very tired, and couldn't he let us go home?'

'No, Mabel. I couldn't,' said Drew firmly, collecting himself a stiff whisky and soda and sinking into an arm-chair. 'It would not only be a pure waste of time, but I have no desire to receive a blistering snub. He'll stop when he feels like it, or when he's got what he wants, and not before.'

'But we shall all be here tomorrow, and the next day.'

'We hope,' said Drew dryly. 'Well, here's to crime.'

He lifted his glass and drank deeply, and Eden said furiously: '*Must* you make a joke of it?'

'Sorry,' said Drew mildly.

But Eden refused to be placated. His handsome face was taut with strain and his voice was rough with fatigue, anxiety and anger: 'In the present circumstances, that sort of remark is in bloody bad taste, besides being entirely un-funny!'

Drew raised his eyebrows and pulled a faint grimace, but forebore to take offence. He said amiably: 'You're quite right. I can't have been thinking. My apologies. Have an olive, Mabel; and stop watching that door. Ken will be along any minute now. Hullo, here's another car. Who do you suppose this is? the D.C.?'

But it was only Hector, returning from *Brandonmead* with an assortment of pyjamas, tooth brushes and bedroom slippers. He accepted a drink, and after a nervous glance at his wife said in a subdued voice that contained no echo of his former booming tones: 'Is Kennie still there? They're keeping him a long time. Surely they know the boy isn't feeling fit. Never known him to pass out like that before. He ought to be in bed, not being badgered with silly questions.'

'Then why don't you put a stop to it?' demanded Mabel, wavering on the verge of tears. 'You're his father. They're bullying him: I know they are. Oh, if *only* he'd never met her! Why did this have to happen just when it seemed that everything was going to be peaceful and happy again? I'll never forgive Greg for this—never!'

Hector said uncomfortably: 'He's only doing his duty, dear. Why don't you come over to Lisa's with me now? She won't have given any orders about supper, so we'd better go and see about it.'

Mabel burst into tears and said wildly that it was just like a man to think of his own stomach before the welfare of his son, and Drew got up and left the room.

He returned a few minutes later, looking particularly wooden and accompanied by a white and subdued Ken Brandon, and the reunited family removed themselves into the night.

'How did you work that?' enquired Eden with grudging respect.

'Stuck my neck out,' said Drew morosely, 'and was duly executed.' He drew his index finger across his throat in a brief expressive gesture. 'Greg is in no very pleasant temper, but at least it was preferable to having Mabel going on a crying jag.'

Mr Gilbert appeared in the drawing-room on the heels of this remark, and informed them curtly that he was leaving, but would be back at nine o'clock on the following morning. He would be obliged if they would all be in the house and available at that hour, and he was leaving Bill Hennessy to see to it.

He had refused a drink, and had left; and they had dined frugally on soup and sandwiches, for the majority of the house servants had spent the day being questioned at police headquarters, and Zacharia and Thuku, together with the cook, were being kept there overnight.

Victoria had retired to bed immediately afterwards, and had been accompanied to the door of her room by Eden. He had not searched her room as Drew had done, but he had asked her if she had any aspirins, and on hearing that she had, advised her to take two and get a good night's rest. And then he had kissed her. Not lightly, as Drew had done, but hard and hungrily, holding her close.

She had made no attempt to avoid his embrace; but neither had she returned it. And when he released her at last she had put up a hand and touched his cheek in a fleeting caress that was purely maternal, and there was relief and pity and sadness in her smile; as though she had been a much older woman who has found a page of a forgotten love letter, and is smiling a little ruefully at herself because she cannot remember the name of the boy who wrote it.

16

Mr Gilbert was not only true to his word, but regrettably punctual. It was exactly one minute past nine, and breakfast was still in progress, when the now familiar squad of police and C.I.D. men arrived at *Flamingo*.

But this time the proceedings were brief. Typewritten copies of statements made on the previous day were produced and they were asked to sign them, and that being done Mr Stratton and the Brandons were curtly informed that they could return to their own houses, with the proviso that they must stay within reach of a telephone and not leave the Rift until further notice.

'And that means that you can't suddenly decide to go off on safari to the Northern Frontier, Stratton. Or take a holiday to Malindi, Mrs Brandon. I want you where I can get in touch with you at short notice. I hope that is quite clear.'

'Painfully, thank you,' said Drew.

'Are we under arrest?' demanded Hector, who appeared to have recovered some of his former truculence.

Greg favoured him with a bleak stare and said: 'No,' and went away, armed with a stop watch and a pair of binoculars, to head what appeared to be a conducted tour of the grounds and the short cut between *Flamingo* and *Brandonmead*.

It had been decided after some discussion that Mabel would remain with Lisa for a few days, and Eden had escorted her back to the Markhams' bungalow. Em had gone off to deal with some domestic crisis, pausing only to say morosely: 'I won't ask you to stay to luncheon, Drew, because there probably won't be any. But you should find some beer in the dining-room—if the C.I.D. haven't removed it for analysis to make quite sure we haven't added arsenic to it!'

The door slammed behind her, and Drew laughed. But Victoria did not. Victoria was standing by the bow window, watching Eden and Mabel Brandon as they walked away down the narrow dusty path that led across the garden towards the plumbago hedge and the Markham's bungalow, and presently Drew said: 'What are you thinking about?'

He had spoken very quietly, as though he did not wish to break her train of thought, and Victoria answered him as quietly:

'Eden.'

A bee flew into the room and buzzed about it, and when it flew out again into the sunlight the room seemed strangely silent.

Victoria said, still looking out the window: 'You said last night that Eden might have killed his wife; and Kamau. You don't really think that, do you?'

'No. In fact I should say that the betting is about a hundred to one against, despite the fact that the first question that is asked in a murder case is *cui bono?*—who benefits? and, financially at least, Eden does. But then I've known him, on and off, for a good many years, and this affair doesn't fit in with anything I know about him. Eden isn't a fool. He's got plenty of intelligence, and despite all that sunny surface charm, a cool brain and more stubborn determination than most people would give him credit for. He would have known quite well, for instance, that he was bound to be the number one suspect; and why. And that being so he would, if he were guilty, have provided himself with a reasonably cast-iron alibi. Whoever murdered Alice DeBrett planned it pretty carefully—the fact that Em's red trouserings were stolen is proof enough of that!—and only someone who did not need an alibi would have failed to provide one. That, to my mind—and I think, to Greg's—washes Eden out. But I don't know what it leaves us with.'

Victoria said: 'Aunt Em, Mrs Markham, the Brandons, "General Africa"—and you.'

Drew laughed: a laugh that was singularly devoid of amusement. He said: 'I asked for that one, didn't I?'

And then the door opened and Em was back, looking tired and cross and harried, and addressing someone in the hall in vituperative Swahili.

She broke off on seeing Drew and Victoria, and shutting the door with a defiant bang, sank gratefully into the depths of the wing-chair and observed that had she but died an hour before this chance, she had lived a blessed time.

Drew turned his head rather quickly and looked at her with frowning intentness, his blue eyes narrowed and his brows making a straight line across his forehead, as though he were trying to recall some tag-end of memory. Victoria, who had forgotten any Swahili she had ever known, said: 'Who were you talking to, Aunt Em?'

'Myself,' said Em. 'It's the privilege of the aged.'

'In Swahili?' enquired Victoria with a smile.

'Oh, that. That was only Samuel: Hector's gun-bearer-cum-driver-cum-general factotum. I found him wandering round the hall, hunting for Mabel's knitting bag that he seems to think she left here. I told him that it wouldn't be here, it would be over at Lisa's if anywhere. He must have misunderstood her. What are you scowling about, Drew?'

'Hmm?' said Drew in a preoccupied voice. 'Oh—nothing much. Just an idea. I must go. Thanks for your enforced hospitality, Em.'

He walked to the door, opened it, and then hesitated as though he were reluctant to leave, and turned to look back at them, the frown still in his eyes and a strange unreadable look on his face that was oddly disturbing. As though he were puzzled and disbelieving—and afraid.

He stood there for at least a minute, looking from one to the other of them; and then he had shrugged his shoulders and gone away without saying anything, and they heard his car start up and purr away down the drive.

Em said uneasily: 'Something's worrying Drew. I wonder— Oh, well, I suppose this wretched business is getting us all down.'

It was shortly after his departure that they heard Greg's car drive away, but it was almost two o'clock by the time Eden returned. He had replied to Em's questions in monosyllables, been uncommunicative on the subject of Lisa, and refusing the dishes that Zacharia proffered, had lunched frugally off a biscuit and several cups of black coffee.

Em had retired to her room to rest, having advised Victoria to do the same. But Victoria had seldom felt less like resting, and she had wandered into the drawing-room, and sitting down at the piano had played scraps of tunes: playing to keep herself from thinking, not of the frightening happenings of the last week, but of the past and her own personal problems. But when she lifted her hands from the keys the thoughts were there waiting for her, and even her hands betrayed her, for they turned from Bach and Debussy to the trite, sweet sentimental melodies of songs that she had once danced to with Eden: 'Some Enchanted Evening'... 'La Vie en Rose'... 'Hullo, Young Lovers'... And an older tune that an older generation had danced to in the days before the war, and that Eden had taken a fancy to. *I get along without you very well*...

I get along without you very well;
Of course I do.
Except perhaps in spring——

But she had not got along without him very well. Not in spring or summer, autumn or winter...

'What a fool am I . . .!'

Her fingers stumbled on the yellowed keys in a jarring discord, for she had not heard Eden enter and she started violently when he touched her; spinning round on the piano stool so that she was in his arms.

He had not meant to touch her. He had been through a horrible and harrowing week, and had endured a recent interview with Lisa Markham that he did not want to think of ever again—and knew that he would never forget. He supposed that he deserved it, although all the initial advances had been made by her, and he had thought that she knew the rules and would keep to them. But it had been a mistake from the beginning, and now that he had seen Victoria again, it was a calamity.

He had not expected to see Victoria again, or wanted to. But he had not been able to protest against her coming, because to do so might have led to questions, and he had never discussed Victoria with either Alice or Em, and he would not do so now. He had tried to shut Victoria out of his mind and his heart, but it had not been easy. That sentimental song of the 'thirties, that they had discovered and played light-heartedly in the sober post-war years, had indeed proved prophetic. *I get along without you very well—of course I do—except perhaps in spring*...Or when a tune was played to which they had once danced. Or a girl wore a yellow dress. Or when a rose, or a scent, or a sound recalled Victoria...

And then Em had sent for her, and he had not had the moral courage to explain to Em why she must not come; though knowing that he would see her again he had realized at last, and with blinding clarity, that neither Alice nor any of the shallow, foolish affairs with which he had attempted to fill the void in his heart meant anything to him; that only Victoria mattered, and despite any barrier of blood he must have her. That he would risk anything to have her! If only he were free——

Victoria had arrived at *Flamingo,* and Alice was dead. He was free. But he knew that he must behave circumspectly. He could not court another woman, even one to whom he had once been engaged, within a few days or even a few months of his wife's death. He would have to wait. He would persuade Em to send him to Rumuruti, and when enough time had elapsed to blur the raw memory of Alice's death he would come back and ask Victoria to marry him, and take her away from the Rift and all its tragic associations until people had forgotten. Until then he would not even touch her again.

But he had walked into the drawing-room and found her playing the tune that had been peculiarly their own, and had touched her almost without meaning to. And she had whirled about and was in his arms, and he was holding her hard against him: decency, convention, common sense thrown to the winds and forgotten. Kissing her hair and whispering broken endearments; telling her that they would get married at once—they could keep it a secret and no one need know except Em. That he could not wait, and that nothing mattered now that they were together again.

He was not aware for several minutes that Victoria was struggling to free herself, and when he realized it at last, and released her, he thought that it was emotion that had driven the blood from her face, and shyness and surprise that made her jump up and back away from him.

Victoria said breathlessly: 'No, Eden! No, please don't! It's no good saying I don't care for you any more, because I suppose I always shall. But not in that way any more. It's all over, and I never realized it. Not even when someone told me so. I still didn't believe it. Until you kissed me last night. I wanted you to kiss me——'

Eden took a swift step towards her, his hands outstretched, and once again she backed away from him.

'No! Oh Eden, I'm so very sorry! But how was I to know that you meant it? You hadn't meant it before, and——'

Eden said: 'Darling, I don't know what you're talking about, and I don't care. But I always meant it—with you. Right from the beginning. And I mean it now.'

Victoria wrung her hands and her face crumpled like a child's when it is going to cry. She said pleadingly: 'No you don't. Please say you don't! You see, I thought you were only kissing me because–because you like kissing girls. Because it was a sort of–of game, and didn't mean anything. I knew that if you kissed me I'd know. And I did. He was quite right. It's all over. It's–it's as if I'd grown up at last. That's silly, at my age. I should have done it before. But I didn't. I'm so fond of you Eden, but I don't love you any more, and I'm not sure that I ever did, in–in the way that matters.'

'Who was right?' demanded Eden, white-lipped and seizing on only three words out of all those that she had said.

Victoria looked bewildered, and he repeated the question in a voice that startled her: '*Who was right!* Who have you been discussing me with? Drew?'

A tide of colour flooded Victoria's pale cheeks and her eyes widened in dismay. 'No–I mean–I ought not to have said that. I didn't mean to. Eden, don't look like that! I wasn't discussing you with him. Not in that way.'

'In what way, then? Since when have you been on such intimate terms with Drew Stratton that you can discuss your love affairs with him? No, I don't mean that! Don't let's quarrel, darling. I know I treated you abominably once–over Alice. But I had to do it. At least–I thought I had to, and that it would be the best thing for both of us. I can explain, if you'll let me. And I know that I can make you happy.'

Victoria shook her head and her eyes filled with tears.

'No you can't. Not now. I meant what I said, Eden. I don't love you any more. I'm free too. I realized it when you kissed me last night.'

Eden said harshly: 'Or when Stratton did? Has he kissed you?'

He saw the bright colour deepen in her cheeks and was aghast at the tide of sheer physical jealousy that rose and engulfed him, and over which he had no control. He had always had a quick temper and now he had to hit back: to hit blindly, and to hurt as badly as he himself had been hurt. He gave a curt, ugly laugh:

'So you've fallen for our Mr Stratton, have you? Very amusing! And after all those vows of deathless devotion you used to write me. Remember them? A letter a day—sometimes two. I kept them all. A whole box full. I couldn't bear to part with them, but I might as well send them to Stratton for a wedding present. Or you might like to send him a few? Any of the undated ones would do. It will save you time and paper, and the sentiments you addressed to me will do just as well for him, won't they? After all, if he's getting a second-hand love, he may as well get his love letters at second hand too!'

He laughed again, seeing the disgust and contempt in Victoria's white, frozen face and sparkling eyes, and having begun to laugh, found that he could not stop. He dropped into a chair and hid his face his hands, pressing them over his eyes as though he could blot out the desperate weariness, the shamed despair and the savage jealousy; and shut out the horrifying sound of his own senseless mirth.

It stopped at last, and he said tonelessly: 'I'm sorry, Vicky. That was a filthy thing to say. I didn't mean it. I don't know what got into me. I'm going to pieces these days–not that that's any excuse. Forgive me, dear.'

He dropped his hands and lifted a haggard face, to find that he had been talking to himself. The room was empty and Victoria had gone.

Fifteen minutes later, leaning against the window-sill of her bedroom, Victoria heard the sound of horses' hooves and saw Eden gallop past, heading for the open country and riding as recklessly as though he were in the last lap of a race. It was a relief to know that he was no longer in the house, and she hoped that he would stay away for an hour or two and give her time to think.

One thing at least was clear. She would have to tell Aunt Em that she could not remain at *Flamingo*. How *dared* Eden talk like that! How could he turn on her like a spoilt, vindictive character out of a third-rate novel? Had he really kept her letters? She had a momentary vision of Drew Stratton reading one, his blue eyes cold with scorn, and her face flamed at the thought.

'But Eden isn't like that!' said Victoria, speaking aloud in the empty bedroom.

He couldn't be like that! He couldn't have changed so much in just five years. She was used to his brief outbreaks of black rage. They had never lasted long and they had never meant anything; and when they were over he had always been desperately ashamed and deeply apologetic. No, he would never do such a cruel, vulgar thing as this.

But the thought of the letters persisted. Not so much because she was afraid that Eden would carry out his preposterous threat, but because of Greg Gilbert.

Who was to say that Mr Gilbert would not order another search of the house, and this time find her letters–and read them? There must be many undated ones, and he might well jump to the conclusion that she had continued to correspond with Eden long after his marriage. He might even think what Drew himself had suggested–that she and Eden had planned Alice's death between them. That Eden, and not Aunt Em, had sent for her.

Seized with sudden resolution, Victoria left the room and walked quickly down the corridor to pause outside the door that led into the wing that had been Alice's and Eden's, and where Eden now slept alone. But with her hand on the door knob, she hesitated.

These were the only rooms in the big, rambling house that she had not as yet seen. She thought fleetingly of Bluebeard's chamber, and found the thought a singularly unpleasant one. Supposing that there was something waiting for her on the other side of that door? The poltergeist, who had ceased its vandalistic pranks with the first taste of blood?

I mustn't go in, thought Victoria with sudden

conviction. If I do, I shall be sorry. They are Eden's rooms. I haven't any right to search someone else's rooms. Not even for my own letters——

And yet Mrs Thompson had been convicted on the strength of her letters to her lover, and they had, as Drew had pointed out, hung Mrs Thompson...

Victoria set her teeth and turned the handle of the door.

17

Alice's bedroom was a long, blue-and-white room that looked out over the rose garden. An impersonal room: neat and cool and without emphasis. A room very like its owner.

There was a blue-and-white bathroom, a small writing room containing a roll-top desk in addition to a rosewood writing table, and, finally, Eden's dressing-room, in which he apparently slept, for there was a camp bed made up in it. There were no photographs of Alice in the room, but a single small snapshot in a battered leather frame adorned the dressing-table. It was badly faded, for it had been taken many years before with a Box Brownie, and Eden had developed and printed it himself. A snapshot of a skinny little girl riding on a zebra.

Looking at it Victoria's resolution wavered. There was surely no need for her to hunt through Eden's belongings for her letters. She had only to ask for them, and he would give them to her. Unless Greg Gilbert found them first——

It was a sobering reflection, and Victoria abandoned hesitation. But fifteen minutes later she was compelled to admit that either Eden had lied about keeping her letters, or they were not here, and she was about to leave the room when her eye was caught by an inequality in the panelling on the wall behind the camp bed. She turned back, and pulling the bed away from the wall, saw for the first time that there was another cupboard in the room: a long low cupboard built into the wall, and probably intended as a toy cupboard for a small boy.

Victoria went down on her knees and opened it, to find that it ran back far farther than she had supposed, and was stacked with old boxes and suitcases. She regarded them with some dismay, for if they were full it was going to take her hours to go through them. But the first two or three that she pulled out were empty, and it seemed likely that the remainder would be.

A small cabin trunk, dragged out to the light of day, revealed a battered collection of birds' eggs and an old box camera that was undoubtedly the one with which Eden had taken the photograph of Victoria on Falda. Victoria shut it with a sigh and pulled out an incongruous and outmoded piece of luggage that could only have belonged to Eden's grandfather, Gerald DeBrett: a tin hat box of antediluvian design. It was empty except for a quantity of yellowing tissue paper, dead moths and D.D.T. powder, but Victoria regarded it with interest, remembering a similar relic of vanished days that had stood in a schoolfriend's attic: a hat box that had possessed a false bottom to it, in which, she had been told, ostrich plumes could be packed. This one too was made to the same pattern, and without thinking, she pressed the almost invisible catch that revealed the hidden space.

There were no ostrich plumes, but there was something else. A flat package wrapped very carefully in several folds of soft silk.

Victoria never knew why she should have unwrapped it, for it could not have been what she was looking for. The action was purely automatic, and for a moment the object that lay revealed merely surprised her, and she was about to replace it when her hands checked and her heart seemed to stop, and she sat back on her heels, staring at it, wide-eyed and rigid, while a hundred frantic thoughts whirled round in her brain, falling into fantastic patterns and breaking up into chaotic fragments that did not make sense.

The poltergeist... Who was it who had said: 'I'll start believing in evil spirits only when someone has eliminated all possibility of the evil human element.' Drew——! And Drew had said too, 'Who can say what anyone is capable of under certain pressures?'

A dozen things that she had seen or heard during the past week, isolated incidents that had seemed to have no connection with each other, took on shape and meaning: a horrible meaning. But it was the malice in it that frightened her most. Em must be made to suffer the loss of her dearest possessions, starting with the small but cherished things and working up to greater things. Her dog. Her grandson's wife. Her pride and her good name. And at the last there would still be blackmail.

But would Em allow herself to be blackmailed? From what Victoria knew of her, Lady Emily, faced with such a threat, would be just as likely to take the law into her own hands, and shoot the blackmailer and take the consequences, rather than submit. Had the 'poltergeist' thought of that? Or had that malicious brain overreached itself?

Victoria re-wrapped the package in its folds of bright silk, her hands trembling so that she could barely hold it, and replacing it in its hiding place, closed the hat box and pushed it back into the cupboard. And as she did so she heard a faint sound outside the open window; a scrape and rustle that might have been a bird among the creepers. Or had someone been watching her? She started up, shaking with panic, and pushing the camp bed into place, ran from the room.

Em was walking slowly across the hall at the far end of the corridor, supporting herself on a stick and evidently on her way to the verandah and tea, but Victoria pretended not to have seen her and took refuge in her own room, banging the door behind her and locking it. She did not want to face Aunt Em's shrewd old eyes just yet.

She leant against the closed door, panting and shivering and fighting a panic desire to run out of the house and keep on running until she had put as much distance as possible between herself and *Flamingo*.

She must tell Drew. He would know what to do.

Or Mr Gilbert. No, not Mr Gilbert!—he was a policeman first and he would not be able to remember that he was also a friend. She could not do it. She was as bad as Em or Mabel, or any other woman, when it came to that.

It was at least a quarter of an hour later that she went out on the verandah and found tea and her aunt waiting for her.

Em did not look as though her afternoon's rest had benefited her, but her old eyes were as sharply observant as ever, and she dismissed Zacharia with an imperious wave of the hand, and said: 'What has happened, dear? You look as though you had seen a ghost.'

'Not a ghost,' said Victoria with a shiver in her voice. 'A poltergeist.'

'What on earth do you mean!'

'N-nothing,' said Victoria. 'I didn't mean—Aunt Em, I have to tell you something. I can't stay here any longer. I'd like to go as soon as possible. I know I'm being ungrateful, and—and—ungrateful, but I must go!'

Em said gently: 'Sit down, dear. I can see that something has happened to upset you. Here—have some tea. No, drink it up first... That's better. Now tell me what is the matter. Is it Eden?'

The cup in Victoria's hand shook so badly that the tea slopped into the saucer, and she put it down hurriedly and said breathlessly: 'Why do you say that?'

Em sighed a little heavily and shrugged her shoulders: 'I don't know. You were engaged to him once, and though I thought that was all over, I have not been so sure during the last few days. I know him very well, you see, and I am not unobservant—even though I may be a silly old woman! Has he asked you to marry him? Is it that?'

'Y—yes,' said Victoria. 'But it isn't that. And I couldn't marry him. *Ever!* Not even if he were the—last person on earth!'

She shuddered so violently that her teeth chattered and she could not go on.

Em's brows drew together in a grimace of annoyance and she said tartly: 'Really, I had credited Eden with more intelligence! I am not surprised that you should feel disgusted. It can hardly be pleasant to receive a proposal from a man whose wife has just been murdered. In the worst *possible* taste! He must have taken leave of his senses. But he has been under a great deal of strain, and you must make allowances, dear. He is not himself just now. I will send him away for a month or so. To Rumuruti perhaps; just as soon as this dreadful business has been cleared up. There is no reason at all why *you* should leave.'

Victoria said desperately: 'You don't understand! It isn't that. It's—it's something else. I can't explain! But this afternoon I found out something that has—has made me realize that I must either go away, or go to the police. Th—that's all!'

She pushed back her chair and stood up, trembling with the effort not to burst into tears, and would not meet Em's shocked gaze.

Em said on a gasp: '*Victoria!*'

'I'm sorry,' said Victoria, her voice high and strained. 'I shouldn't have said that. I didn't mean to. I won't say anything else. But I must go away. I must! I know it's cowardly of me, but I can't help it.'

Em's face was grey and drawn and bleak with anger, but she spoke in a strictly controlled voice, as though she were some efficient governess dealing with a naughty and hysterical child:

'I do not know what you are talking about, but I can see that you are in no fit state to make any rational decisions at the moment. I am afraid it is quite out of the question for you to leave for Nairobi immediately. Greg Gilbert would never permit it, and we cannot reach him at the moment to explain that you refuse to stay here. If you are of the same opinion tomorrow morning you can talk to him yourself, and perhaps you will be able to persuade him to let you leave. But you will have to resign yourself to staying under my roof for at least one more night.'

Victoria's heart sank. She had forgotten Mr Gilbert. She found that she was staring at her aunt in helpless dismay, and she sat down again slowly, feeling weak and boneless and very frightened.

'No,' said Victoria in a whisper, 'I can't go away, can I? I had forgotten that. I shall have to stay.'

'For the moment, anyway,' said Em coldly. And went away, walking very stiffly and upright.

She returned some ten or fifteen minutes later, looking grim and implacable and inconceivably old, and ordered Zacharia to send Thuku round with the Land-Rover. Victoria had not moved. She was still sitting huddled in one of the verandah chairs, staring into vacancy.

'I'm going out to shoot something for the dogs,'

said Em without condescending to look at her. 'I shall not be long. Zach tells me that Eden has gone up to see the new bore hole, so I will drive in that direction and tell him that you would prefer not to see him just now.'

She stumped off down the verandah as the Land-Rover drove up, and Victoria saw her climb in stiffly, hoisting her bulk into the driver's seat, and remembered Eden saying that Em invariably worked off her feelings in this manner when she was upset. Poor Aunt Em! However fast she drove, she would not be able to drive away from this!

The Land-Rover bucketed away at a dangerous pace and vanished in a whirling cloud of dust, and silence settled down on *Flamingo* like a grey cloud on a hilltop.

Em had taken the dogs with her, and Pusser, who had been lying on the wicker divan posed against the vivid background of the three harlequin-patterned cushions that Zacharia had arranged in a neat row, rose and stretched elaborately, and jumping down with a flump on to the matting, stalked away and vanished down the verandah steps into the garden.

The low sunlight painted the acacia trees a warm orange and the shadows began to stretch out long and blue across the rough Kikuyu grass of the lawns. Now was the time to telephone Drew, while the house was empty and there was no one to hear.

But Victoria had underestimated the difficulties of getting a number on a party line, and when at last she got the Stratton number Drew was out and the servant who answered the telephone spoke the minimum of English, so that after a brief but tangled conversation she was forced to abandon the attempt to make herself understood.

Returning to the verandah she was startled to find Zacharia there, patting the cushions into place, straightening chairs and emptying ash-trays. He must have been in the dining-room, and he gave Victoria the blank, disinterested glance of an elderly tortoise, and went away down the front steps and round the corner of the house.

Em returned just over half an hour later, but it was obvious that the exercise and exertion had not on this occasion produced a particularly mellowing effect upon her. She looked grim and exhausted and her clothes were stained and dirty and clotted with the dust of the ranges. She slapped it off in clouds, and having wiped her face with a handkerchief on which she obviously cleaned her hands after assisting to degut the gazelle that was being removed from the back of the Land-Rover, said shortly:

'Eden won't be back tonight. He's ridden over to Hector's and he'll put up there.'

She made no further mention of their previous conversation, but talked instead of the progress of the new bore hole and the unusual dryness of the season. It seemed that she had met Mabel and Lisa out on the ranges. They had driven out more for something to do than for any specific purpose, and Em reported that Lisa looked more her old self.

'She says that she has got some of the account books that Gilly had brought up to date, and she asked if I'd send you over for them, as she can show you which sections will have to be completed, and which ones only need to be checked. I'd appreciate your help with them, if you feel up to it; I'm afraid I don't.'

Victoria said gratefully: 'Of course I will. I'll go now. It will be nice to have something to do.'

'That's what I thought,' said Em. 'Work is a very useful thing in bad times: it has to go on, and so one goes on too. Don't stay too long. It gets dark very quickly once the sun is down. You might pick me some of those delphiniums if you're not too late. I've done nothing about the flowers for days. I haven't had the heart to. But I suppose one has got to start again sometime. You'll find a pair of secateurs somewhere on the bottom shelf of the bookcase in the office.'

Em's office was not noted for its tidiness, for she was in the habit of using it as a junk room, and Victoria discovered the secateurs among the welter of raffia and old seed catalogues; dislodging in the process a pyramid of dusty cardboard boxes that cascaded to the floor.

She was stacking these back again when one of them fell open, spilling out several dozen wooden slips of the type used for making seed beds, and, from beneath them, a heavier object that slid out with a dull thud.

It was a very ordinary object to find in such a place: a well-worn and somewhat old-fashioned clasp knife faced with horn. But Victoria, touching it with shrinking fingers, saw that the small blade had been broken off short, and that there were initials cut deep into the horn. K. D. B.

So Em knew! Or if she did not know, she had

suspected. She had palmed the knife that Eden had given her—his father's knife—because she had realized that Gilly Markham had not died from snakebite, and she had been afraid. And later, when she had realized her mistake, she could not explain why she should have hidden it, so had blandly insisted that she herself had taken that knife to Crater Lake. She would not have done that for anyone but Eden.

Victoria lifted it with an unsteady hand and put it back quickly into the box, covering it again with the wooden slips and thrusting the box at the back of the shelf and at the bottom of the pile.

She stood up, breathing quickly as though she had been running, and taking up the secateurs, left the office; closing the door very carefully behind her as though it were vital that she should make no noise that might remind Em of where she had been.

But Em would not have heard anything, for she was sitting at the piano and drowning her troubled thoughts in a flood of melody. The music filled the room and flowed out through the open windows into the quiet garden, and Victoria paused on the verandah to listen to it, and being no more than an average performer herself was not critical of her aunt's execution, as Gilly would have been. Em was playing a Bach fugue, and playing it, in her niece's opinion, remarkably well. Victoria listened, soothed and enchanted.

She did not know at what point she began to be aware that there was something missing from the verandah, or why she should have noticed it at all—or been worried by it. But some elusive fragment of memory nagged at her brain; a sixth sense that whispered words she could not quite hear and drew her attention to something that she could not see.

She looked about her uneasily, but nothing had changed. The shabby wicker chairs and table stood where they had always stood, and Pusser's food and milk were still untouched. Why should she think there was something different about it? Something missing?

She gave an impatient shrug of her shoulders and turned away, and it was not until she had reached the gate in the plumbago hedge that the answer dropped into her mind as though it had been a dry leaf falling from the acacia trees above her—and with so little impact that she could smile at it, thinking only that it was a trivial thing after all...

One of the three remaining verandah cushions had been missing. There had been only two brightly patterned squares on the long wicker divan against the wall, though there had been three earlier in the day.

18

The Markhams' bungalow appeared to be empty, and Victoria could hear no voices, though from somewhere in the silent house there came a faint, intermittent sound that resolved itself into the plaintive whining of a dog.

There was no bell, and as no one answered her tentative calls Victoria went through an open doorway and found herself in Lisa's drawing-room.

It was an essentially feminine room. Pink and white and be-ruffled, with the accent on ribbons and roses. But at the present moment it bore a forlorn aspect, for the flowers in the white vases were fading or dead, there was a film of dust on the piano and the occasional tables, and the ash-trays did not look as though they had been emptied for days.

A familiar object lay upon the sofa and provided an incongruous note of colour against the chintzy prettiness: a large cretonne knitting bag in excruciating shades of blue and orange—the property of Mabel Brandon. But there was no sign of its owner, or of Lisa, and after a hesitant interval Victoria opened one of the doors leading out of the drawing-room and found herself on the threshold of an untidy office. If the account books were anywhere they should be here, and she was looking doubtfully about her when she became conscious of being under surveillance, and turned swiftly.

Lisa had entered the drawing-room by the verandah door and was standing quite still, watching her.

For a moment Victoria did not recognize her, for she had never seen Lisa dressed in this fashion before. She was wearing slacks and a shirt of faded khaki, both of which looked as though they might have belonged to her late husband, and in place of her usual high-heeled sandals she wore a shabby pair of tennis shoes, which accounted for the fact that Victoria had not heard her approach.

The room was already growing dark, and as Lisa was standing with her back to the windows Victoria could not see her face very clearly; but there was an expression on it that even in the uncertain light was sufficiently disconcerting to make Victoria regret that she had not waited until the morning before coming over to fetch Gilly's account books.

Lisa was smiling—but only with her red, rigid mouth: above it her violet eyes were fixed in a look that was as purely animal as that of a cat who is watching a bird, or a mousehole.

There was a curious moment of silence that had

the effect of being loud with suppressed sound, and then Lisa laughed.

It was a gay sound, light and genuinely amused, and she moved forward and said: 'So you did come! I wondered if you would. Em sent you for the account books, I suppose? They're in there. On the table behind you.'

Victoria said confusedly, conscious that she was stammering badly: 'I-I'm sorry. About w-walking in like this. It was r-rude of me, b-but there didn't seem to be anyone about.'

Lisa walked past her into the office and picked up a pile of account books from one of the cluttered tables.

'I know. But the servants are all to pieces because of Greg and his boys, and I don't know where that little beast Wambui has got to. She's been in an awful state since her boy-friend was dug up. I shall have to sack her. Here you are—I suppose this is what you want? It'll do to go on with, anyway, *'Tis enough. 'Twill serve!'*

She laughed again, as though at some exquisite joke, and said in a surprised voice: 'You know, Gilly was always saying things like that. Bits of Shakespeare. It used to madden me. But it's odd how those silly remarks seem to fit in.'

She came back into the drawing-room and said: 'Would you like a drink? There's gin and sherry, and there should be some whisky if Hector and Ken haven't drunk it all.'

'N-no thank you,' said Victoria quickly. 'I must be getting back.'

'What's the hurry? It isn't dark yet.'

'It's not that, but Aunt Em's alone. Besides I said I'd cut some delphiniums. We haven't had any fresh flowers for days.'

'Neither have I,' said Lisa, looking vaguely round at the limp and faded stalks that lolled in the flower vases and made a faint, unpleasant smell in the room. 'The best delphiniums grow by the knoll. The tall pink ones——'

She embarked on a long and disjointed account of the difficulties of growing flowers in a dry year, and as she was standing between Victoria and the door it was not really possible to push past her and leave. And yet Victoria discovered that she wanted to get out of that room as badly as she had ever wanted to get away from *Flamingo:* as badly as she had ever wanted anything. But Lisa continued to talk in her light brittle voice, and to keep between her and the door...

'I do wish you'd have something to drink. I don't like drinking alone. Mabel will be sorry to have missed you. She thought you'd be along a bit later. She'll be back any minute now. She's taking Dinah for a walk.'

A faint whining sound disproved her words, but she did not seem to have heard it: 'It's so good of her. Mabel is the kindest person. She knows how I hate taking out Dinah when she's like this, because Em's dogs sometimes follow us. You aren't going, are you? I haven't explained about the account books yet.'

Victoria, who had forgotten that she was clasping them, cast them a startled glance, and Lisa said: 'Give them to me, and I'll show you.'

She took them and carried them over to the window seat, where she laid them out carefully and slowly as though she were deliberately wasting time, and after studying them for several minutes announced that the ones with green covers dealt with the sale of fodder and vegetables, the red ones with fruit—mostly oranges—and the black ones with cattle.

'Very simple and kindergarten, isn't it? Gilly's idea. I don't think you'll have any trouble.'

Victoria scooped them up hurriedly and said: 'No. I'm sure I won't. Thank you so much. I really must be getting back.'

Lisa glanced over her shoulder at the sky beyond the window and said: 'Yes. I think you should. Blue is a difficult colour to see in the dusk. The delphiniums, I mean.'

She laughed lightly and stood to one side, and Victoria said: 'Good night. And thank you.' And went quickly out of the room.

The sun had gone and there were bats flittering in an airy ballet among the trees as Victoria hurried down the dusty path that wound between feathery clumps of bamboo, pepper trees and jacaranda. She was out of sight of the bungalow and had begun to walk more slowly when a nightjar flew up with a harsh cry that startled her, and something rustled in the bushes as though an animal, perhaps an antelope, had slipped past her unseen.

She stopped and stood listening, but a vagrant breeze blew in from the lake and rustled the leaves and grasses, drowning all other sounds. And when it died away she could hear nothing but a distant crying of birds from the papyrus swamp, and the sound of Em's piano, sweet in the silence.

She began to hurry again, and turning a corner, reached the gate and found that she must have forgotten to latch it, for it stood open. She closed it carefully behind her and walked on quickly through a grove of acacias, listening to the music that drifted out across the garden from the open windows of Em's drawing-room.

Em had abandoned Bach and was playing something that was unfamiliar to Victoria. A strange, passionate, haunting piece of music that somehow fitted into the scene as though it were a tangible thing and an integral part of the Valley.

The Rift Valley Concerto! thought Victoria. It could not be anything else. Toroni must have loved the Rift—or hated it—to write like that.

She had almost forgotten the delphiniums, but the weight of the secateurs in her pocket reminded her of them, and she turned off the path and walked across the grass to the foot of the knoll, where they made a sea of blue and pink and purple.

She had begun to cut the flowers when another breath of wind blew across the garden, filling the green dusk with soft and stealthy rustlings, and she straightened up and stood alert and listening. Had it really been only the wind that had moved among the bushes?

The secateurs slid from her hand and were lost among the flowers, and she was aware that her heart was thumping painfully against her ribs. She had not realized that it was so late, or that the interval between sundown and darkness was so brief. Down in the papyrus swamp beyond the shamba birds were crying and calling. As though they had been alarmed by something. . .

Victoria stood quite still, held by the instinct that will make an animal freeze into immobility in the hope of being overlooked, rather than draw attention to itself by running. And as she stood there a familiar figure materialized out of the dusk, walking towards her, and her heart gave a great bound of relief.

She called out a little breathlessly: 'I'm sorry I'm so late. It was the flowers——' And bent to pick them up.

Her hands were full of them when something suddenly slid into her mind; icily and with a blinding impact. Something completely impossible.

The piano was still playing.

The flowers fell from her hands and she jerked upright, staring at the figure that stood facing her in the dusk: staring, paralysed, at a stranger, suddenly and horribly unfamiliar.

Her eyes widened in her white face and her mouth opened in a soundless scream—as Alice's had done. But Alice had not fought, or even flinched from the savage sweeping stroke of the sharpened panga.

Victoria saw it coming and flung herself to one side, and the blow missed its mark and grazed her right shoulder, shearing through the short linen sleeve.

She saw the blade flash in the dusk as it lifted again, and she was struggling and fighting, gripped to something that was soft and yielding and as suffocating as a feather bolster; her hands round a wrist that seemed made of iron, fending it off, and her ears full of the sound of grunting, panting breaths.

She made no attempt to cry out, for she needed her breath and her young strength to fight for her life. Her foot caught in a rough tangle of grass and she stumbled and fell to her knees, and saw the panga lift again. But it did not fall.

There was someone else there. A dark shape that appeared out of nowhere and sprang at her assailant with the silent savagery of a giant cat.

Victoria, crouched on the grass, heard a hoarse gasping cry, and saw the shapeless scarlet-clad figure crumple and fall sideways. And then the green sky and the purple dusk darkened and closed in on her, and she pitched forward on her face into merciful unconsciousness.

There was a light somewhere that was hurting her eyes, and she felt cold and very sick and aware of a burning pain in her right shoulder.

There were voices too, and someone was saying: 'She'll be all right. It's only a flesh wound.'

A hand touched her forehead and Victoria shuddered uncontrollably and opened her eyes to find that she was lying on her own bed and looking up into Drew Stratton's face.

She said in a gasping whisper: '*Drew!*— Oh, Drew!'

Drew said: 'It's all right, darling. It's all over. Drink this——'

He lifted her against his shoulder, and holding a glass to her mouth, forced her to swallow something that tasted exceedingly nasty. But when he would have laid her down again she turned and clung to him.

'Don't go. Please don't go.'

'I won't.' Drew's leisurely voice was quiet and level and completely reassuring. And all at once she knew that she was safe—for always.

Someone who had been standing just out of range of her vision went out of the room, closing the door, but she did not turn her head, and Drew did not move.

She could hear cars arriving and leaving, and the occasional shrilling of the telephone. The house was full of muffled voices and movement, and somewhere a woman was crying with a hysterical despairing persistency. But none of it had anything to do with her, and presently Drew lifted her head and kissed her, and time and death and violence ceased to have any meaning.

She said at last, with her head against his shoulder:

'It was Aunt Em.'

'I know, dear.'

'Why did she do it?'

'I'll tell you in the morning.'

Victoria said urgently: 'No! Tell me now. I couldn't sleep—not knowing.'

Drew smiled down at her. 'You won't be able to help yourself, darling. Not after that stuff you've just taken!'

'Then I shall dream about it, and that will be worse. Tell me now.'

But Drew only shook his head, and presently she fell asleep, and when she awoke the sun was high, and it was Mabel Brandon, red-eyed with weeping, who had brought her breakfast on a tray, and after putting a fresh bandage on her shoulder, helped her to dress.

But Mabel would not answer her questions. She had only said: 'She's dead. She died at three o'clock this morning. Eden was with her. One should not speak ill of the dead.' And she had gone away, blowing her nose vehemently and making no attempt to disguise her tears.

The drawing-room had been full of sunlight, and Drew had been standing by the window looking out across the garden. He turned and smiled at her, and Victoria said unsteadily:

'Mrs Brandon says she—she is dead.' Even now she could not bring herself to say that name, because to say it was to admit the impossible. 'Drew, what happened? I don't understand. I don't understand anything!'

Drew said: 'Greg knows more about it than I do. Ask him.' And Victoria turned quickly and saw for the first time that there was someone else in the room.

Greg Gilbert gave her a brief smile that did not reach his eyes and left his face as grim and drawn as it had been a moment before, and when he spoke it was to ask what appeared to be an entirely irrelevant question:

'Did you ever know why Eden broke off the engagement between you, and married Alice Laxton?'

'No,' said Victoria, considerably taken aback. 'I suppose he—What has it got to do with this?'

'More than you would think,' said Greg tiredly.

'He broke it off because your mother told him that there was insanity in the family.'

'*Insanity!* Do you mean that I——' Victoria's face was white.

'No. Not in yours. Your grandfather married twice. But both Lady Emily's mother and her grandfather died in lunatic asylums, and there was always some doubt about the manner in which Eden's father met his death.'

'But—but it was a car accident!'

'Yes. But an odd one. Odd enough for a rumour to get around that he might possibly have engineered it himself. There was no shadow of evidence that he was abnormal, or even highly strung. But your mother heard the rumours, and because she knew all about Em's family history she believed them. And in spite of everything that the doctors say about insanity not being hereditary, she was very much against your marrying Eden.'

'Yes,' said Victoria in a whisper. 'I remember.'

'In the end she told Eden, as the only way of stopping it. He was young and impressionable, and it came as an appalling shock to him. I gather he went off for a week by himself and drank himself silly, and decided on a heroic gesture. He wouldn't tell you, because you would insist on disregarding it, and he felt he must do something quite irrevocable—burn his boats before he could weaken. He had met Alice Laxton a few weeks before, and through a cousin of hers he knew her history. Alice had had a bad riding accident in her early teens, and she could never have children. That was the deciding factor. He married her in a haze of self-sacrifice, youthful heroics, desperation and alcohol—and pure selfishness! And woke up to the full stupidity of what he had done when it was too late.'

But Victoria had no interest and little sympathy to spare for Eden just then, and she brushed the information aside and demanded bluntly: 'Do you mean that Aunt Em was mad?'

Greg said: 'No; she was sane enough. But she loved *Flamingo* too much and made a god out of it, and she had meant to found a dynasty: a Kenya dynasty. When she realized that Alice could never have children it meant only one thing to her: that there would be no heir to *Flamingo*. She had a shrewd suspicion that Eden was still in love with you, and she thought you were the right kind of girl for Kenya—as Alice was not! I think the seeds of the idea must have been in her mind for a long time.'

Victoria said: 'But the—poltergeist. They were *her* things. The things she liked best. She *couldn't* have done that!'

'Oh, yes she could. Not the first time. That was the cat, who had chased a bird round the drawing-room. But it gave her an idea for an alibi—that and the rumour that "General Africa" was hiding somewhere in the Naivasha area—and she decided to use it as a smoke screen. I think too that it appealed to some twisted instinct in her. She seems to have looked upon it as a—a penance for what she intended to do. A sort of burnt offering upon the altar of *Flamingo*. There was too much of the fanatic in Em's make-up: and plenty of cunning too, for she knew that if the broken things were her own personal treasures she would be the last person to be suspected of destroying them. But it must have been a small martyrdom to do it.'

Victoria said: '*Things*, yes. But not her dog!'

'Ah! The dog was a different matter. It had been her favourite, and it had switched its allegiance to Alice. She couldn't forgive that.'

Victoria shivered and said in a whisper: 'You said once that the first killing was the hardest. Perhaps that was why she had to do it. To—to practise.'

'It wasn't her first killing. She'd killed her manager, Gus Abbott. We always thought that was an accident, but it seems we were wrong. Abbott lost his nerve, and when *Flamingo* was attacked he didn't want to stay and fight. He wanted to save himself, and he thought he could make a break for it and hide in the garden. But to run away, and from a gang of Mau Mau, was to Em an unforgivable sin, and she apparently shot him quite deliberately. I think that afterwards it gave her a sense of power. To have done that and got away with it. Perhaps it swung the balance, and made it possible for her to plan the murder of Eden's unsuitable wife. For she did plan it. She seized on that first accident, for which Pusser was responsible, and kept on with a series of faked ones; and at the psychological moment she sent for you. It had given her a good excuse for doing so.'

Victoria said: 'She sent for me because my mother had died!'

'No, she didn't. If it had been that, she would have sent for you six months earlier. She sent for you because her plans were working out, and she murdered Alice just as soon as you were due to leave England and could not turn back. If she'd done it earlier, you wouldn't have come, would you?'

'No,' said Victoria slowly.

'Because of Eden. Yes, she knew that. You thought it was safe to come because he was married. But by the time you arrived here he would be free, and she was banking on his marrying you.'

Victoria went over to the window seat and sat down on it, staring out at the green lawns and the placid lake, and presently she said without turning her head:

'There are so many things I don't understand. The piano. Gilly Markham. Were there two records of the concerto? I found one, you know. It was in the false bottom of a hat box in Eden's room. I—I thought it must mean that he was the poltergeist, and that he'd kept it to blackmail her with.'

'Did you? That's irony, if you like! Em didn't know that. She said you told her that you'd found something, and you must leave at once, or go to the police. She went straight to Eden's room and realized that you'd been at the cupboard, and knew what it was that you had found. She thought it meant that you knew everything. That was why you had to be killed. She told us a great deal before she died. I think she was afraid that we might suspect Eden, and she had to clear him.'

'Then there *were* two records!'

'No. Only one. She needed it to manufacture that alibi, and she couldn't bear to destroy it. She smashed another one instead. One long-playing record looks much like another when it's in bits, and no one bothered to piece it together to read the label. She had the whole thing worked out by then. She went off ostensibly to shoot a buck, but actually to ensure that she had a good excuse for getting bloodstained—which was a point that had escaped me. And when she came back she sent Alice over to the Markhams', put a house-coat over her stained clothes and started to play the piano. And when she'd got rid of Zacharia she put on the recording instead, removed the house-coat and went out to meet Alice...

'She killed Alice with a panga in order to bolster up the "General Africa" angle, and she came back to the house and dropped it, with a piece of twine round the handle, into the rainwater tank outside her window. Then she came back to her room, took off her stained clothes, put on the house-coat again, and went back to the drawing-room where she was found by Zacharia, still playing the piano, half an hour later. After that it was easy. She removed the record, took it back to its hiding place, stopped to pick up her stained clothes and see them put into the boiler—Majiri did most of the washing at night—and went out to search for Alice.'

Victoria said: 'But the cushion! Why should she have needed that?'

'She didn't. That was a mistake. Mine, as much as anyone's! That cushion threw me right off beam, and incidentally frightened the life out of Mabel! Apparently there had been six of those cushions sold at some charity bazaar, and Mabel had bought two; one of which had disappeared only about ten days ago. Ken says he took it on a picnic on the lake and lost it overboard, but Mabel began to add two and two together and make it eighteen.'

'Then why was it there?'

'Someone had left it on the verandah rail by the rainwater tank, and Em knocked it off and it fell against the panga and got badly stained. It couldn't be left there with the stain on it, so she ran back with it and threw it into the bushes. It was the best she could do, and as it turned out it provided her with an alibi that she had never even thought of—which is why she took another with her when she went out to meet you! She thought she'd covered everything, but she hadn't.'

Victoria said: 'You mean Kamau.'

'Kamau—and Gilly Markham.'

'*Gilly?* But he didn't see her! He only heard her playing. He said so.'

'No he didn't. We merely jumped to the conclusion that that was what he meant. But Gilly was doing a very stupid and dangerous thing. He was letting Em know that he knew the difference between her playing and Toroni's. Gilly knew quite well when Em put on the recording of the concerto. And he wanted that job at Rumuruti and thought he could blackmail her into giving it to him. He should have known better.'

Victoria said in a whisper: 'Then—then that was her too.'

'I'm afraid so. It was a fairly easy job I gather, and done in the way I had outlined—She carried a dead puff adder to the picnic inside her cushion. But Mabel threw a spanner into the works by hiding the clasp knife, and Hector by palming the iodine bottle.'

'But *why?*' demanded Victoria. 'Why should they have done that?'

'Because they both knew that Gilly hadn't died from snake-bite, and that Ken had been hanging about *Flamingo* on the evening that Alice was murdered, hoping to see her, and that Gilly knew it. They also knew that Ken had quite a collection of poisoned arrows—they are a dam' sight too easy to come by in this country! And the knife was Ken's. Hector had borrowed it earlier in the day. Mabel threw it into the lake, and Hector apparently did the same thing with the iodine bottle because it had come out of Mabel's pocket. They both seem to have acted on a silly spur-of-the-moment panic.'

'But it wasn't Ken's knife!' said Victoria. 'It was Eden's. Or rather, his father's. It's here. In the office. I found it.'

Greg did not show much interest. He said: 'Did you? Eden said it was somewhere around, but he couldn't remember what he'd done with it. It had been lost; which was why Em said she'd taken it to the picnic, and described it in detail. She thought it wouldn't turn up again, and she'd realized by then that no one thought Gilly's death was an accident, so that laying claim to it made it look as though she were shielding someone. It was quite a good line in double bluff, when you come to think of it. Em was a good poker player.'

'I suppose she killed Kamau too,' said Victoria, looking very white and sick. 'She went out shooting that evening too, after Mrs Markham had been over.

Like—like she did that other time; and last night. Did she kill him?'

'Yes. And it was poetic justice, as it happened. Em thought she knew a lot; but she didn't know that she had killed the man who half the security forces in the country have been hunting for years. Kamau was "General Africa".'

'Good Lord!' said Drew, startled. 'Are you sure of that, Greg? How on earth do you know?'

'Wambui told us,' said Greg. 'She knew. And so did old Zacharia. In fact you'll probably find that there's hardly a Kikuyu from here to Nairobi who didn't know it, but they kept their mouths shut. They were frightened stiff of that man. Specially after he'd killed his only real rival, "Brigadier" Gitahi, and actually collected the Government reward for doing so!'

Greg looked from Victoria to Drew and back again, and said 'You don't know how lucky you are, Miss Caryll. If it hadn't been for Wambui, you'd probably have gone the same way as Alice. It was Wambui who knifed your aunt. She'd been laying for her. She said Kamau had told her that it was the "Memsahib Mkubwa" who had killed the small memsahib, and she was sure that she had also killed Kamau; and now he was avenged. I don't know what the hell we're going to do about that one. Technically, she ought to hang for murder; but actually she saved your life. We didn't hear until pretty late that you had tried to ring Drew, and we wouldn't have got there in time.'

'And—and if you hadn't, you would have thought it was someone else,' said Victoria in an almost inaudible voice. 'Eden, or Mrs Markham, or one of the Brandons. Or an African.'

Greg shook his head. 'Not this time. The pattern was becoming too plain and she wouldn't have got away with it again. Also I think Mrs Markham had tumbled to it at last. It seems that Em had told her that she was going to send you over to get some account books that were of no immediate interest. And Em had asked Alice to pick some flowers too: the knoll was out of sight of the house. I think Lisa guessed.'

Victoria nodded, remembering that curious interview in the Markhams' drawing-room and how it had seemed to her that Lisa was deliberately delaying her—until it got darker. Lisa who had loved Eden, and been driven frantic by jealousy.

A car drew up outside the house and they could hear voices on the verandah. Greg Gilbert looked at his watch and said: 'That will be for me. I must go.'

He turned to Victoria and said: 'I'm afraid you're going to find that there are a bad two or three days ahead of you, and a lot of police procedure to be got through before you can put all this behind you and try and forget it. But I've promised Drew that I'll leave you alone until tomorrow. Goodbye.'

He went out of the room, closing the door behind him, and Victoria was silent for a long time, twisting her hands in her lap and staring before her.

She said at last: 'You thought it might be her, didn't you.'

Drew did not answer for a moment or two, and she turned to look up at him.

'I—wondered,' said Drew slowly.

'Why?'

'I don't know. A lot of trivial things. But they added up. The first time was when Kamau had disappeared. Even Greg thought that he had just made a bolt for the Reserve, but when Em spoke of him she used the past tense. As though he were dead.'

'Was that all?'

'No. She couldn't stop talking about the things she had done. Remember the times she accused herself of killing Alice—and Gilly? She put it in such a way that we didn't take it seriously. But it was interesting. And then suddenly she said something that was more than merely interesting, and I began to wonder again. She quoted something from Macbeth; do you remember?'

'Yes,' said Victoria. 'Something about if she had died before, she would have lived long enough. I didn't know it was from Macbeth.'

'Had I but died an hour before this chance, I had liv'd a blessed time', quoted Drew. 'Macbeth says that, when having murdered Duncan, the murder is discovered. I was interested in the workings of Em's mind; and I didn't like it. I was afraid for you then, and I began to consider seriously the possibility of Em being the murderer. I went to see Greg, which was why I was out when you telephoned. I was at his office until about six, and when I rang my house to say that I'd be back late I was told that the new memsahib from *Flamingo* had wanted to speak to me. I knew it must be you, and that you wouldn't have done that unless you had been frightened.'

Victoria nodded without speaking, and turned to look out of the window again; and presently Drew asked a question that he had asked her once before in that room: 'What are you thinking about?'

'Eden,' said Victoria, as she had said then. 'Drew, you don't mind about Eden, do you?'

'Do I have to?' asked Drew.

'No,' said Victoria, 'Not any more.'

She did not turn her head, but she groped for his hand, and finding it, held it to her cheek; and he felt the wetness of it and knew that she was crying: for Eden and Alice—and Em.

Outside on the drive a car started up and drove away with an impatient blare on the horn. Greg and the police had gone, and the house was quiet again. But there was no longer any awareness in its silence. The tension and the trouble that had filled it had departed from it at last. It had ceased to be a Graven Image demanding sacrifices, for its High Priestess was dead, and it was only a pleasant rambling house whose windows looked out across green gardens to the wide beauty of Lake Naivasha and all the glory of the Rift Valley.

If DEATH IN KENYA has whetted your appetite for more mystery and romance, M. M. Kaye-style, pick up DEATH IN ZANZIBAR, also available in paperback from St. Martin's Press:

"*Death in Zanzibar* is a thoroughly engrossing novel. It has the rich and dramatic story of romance and conflict which we have come to expect of M. M. Kaye, plus a diverting mystery which has a logical but very surprising climax. This should be a really double-double-plus, and indeed it is. My congratulations to the publisher, the author and to her millions of devoted readers."

—Mignon G. Eberhart

"M. M. Kaye is a master at providing suspense . . . *Death in Zanzibar* is highly recommended."

—U.P.I.